Love Me to D...

The luminous dial of the nightstand clock read 1.42.
Slipping into her robe, she went out. She could hear him
tinkering with something in the study. She made her way
through the darkness to the open door, the wedge of light
cast by the desk lamp. Reaching for the door, she looked
in, gasped.

Spread on the desk in front of him were the parts of a
pistol . . .

STRANGER IN MY BED

**by the author of *Visiting Hours*
and *Next of Kin***

Berkley Books by Anne Coleman

VISITING HOURS
NEXT OF KIN
STRANGER IN MY BED

STRANGER
IN MY
BED

ANNE COLEMAN

BERKLEY BOOKS, NEW YORK

STRANGER IN MY BED

A Berkley Book/published by arrangement with
the author

PRINTING HISTORY
Berkley edition/November 1993

ISBN: 0-425-13979-4

BERKLEY®
Berkley Books are published by
The Berkley Publishing Group, 200 Madison Avenue,
New York, New York 10016.
BERKLEY and the "B" design are trademarks of
Berkley Publishing Corporation.

PRINTED IN THE UNITED STATES OF AMERICA

10 9 8 7 6 5 4 3 2 1

Oh, how many torments live in the small circle of a wedding ring?

—COLLEY CIBBER,
The Double Gallant, Act I, Sc. ii

STRANGER
IN MY
BED

⁓ ONE ⁓

The door buzzer droned just as Derrick lit the last candle. The table was set, the roast and vegetables done, Lyssa was in the kitchen preparing the salad, having just finished uncorking and decanting the Bordeaux.

"I'll get it," he said.

In the kitchen Lyssa whipped off her apron, fussed with her hair. Derrick opened the door to Reggie Carlyle, his boss, and Reggie's new wife, Doreen: blond, full-figured, starry-eyed. And statuesque, towering a foot over Lyssa and almost as much over Reggie. Derrick greeted them warmly as Reggie thrust a bottle of Dom Pérignon at him. In from the kitchen Lyssa had floated, pausing en route to the foyer to turn up the volume on Aaron Copland's *Appalachian Spring,* played by the New York Philharmonic conducted by Leonard Bernstein, and one of Derrick's favorite pieces. Reggie came waddling up to her grinning under his massive beetle brows, his arms outstretched; they hugged.

"You look radiant," he said.

"You got a bee-yoo-ti-ful apartment," cooed Doreen.

Lyssa liked Doreen; she found her sweet, sincere, colorful, funny without realizing it. The stereotypical wide-eyed, dumb blonde. Her intellect had to be of scant concern to her new husband; her bust had to be at least a 48-D.

They paired off, and Lyssa conducted the tour. Doreen loved the scrolled teak sofa table, the camelback sofas, Lyssa's modest collection of antique glass. And seemed awed by the splendid view of the city by night, with the airport's tower lights flickering in the distance. She bubbled over Lyssa's pride: two Isfahan carpets, inherited from Grandmother Graham.

"Bee-yoo-ti-ful! The symbols all have a meaning, you know. You see the palm trees? They mean the fulfillment of secret wishes, they could be a blessing, too. The weeping willow's no good, it means sorrow and death. You're lucky, no weeping willows."

To Lyssa's amazement Doreen knew all about Iranian carpets: how the colors were made, how they were applied, where the designs came from, how the weavers took their patterns from the nature surrounding them.

"You see these chrysanthemums? They stand for happiness and fertility. Lotuses, too, but you don't have any lotuses. You got iris, though, only the best carpets have irises. They stand for religious liberty. Did you know that?"

Lyssa laughed. "I don't know anything, except that cleaning them is supposed to be a fine art in itself. I don't dare trust them to a cleaner."

"Don't you ever. Clean them yourself. Take them out in the country in midwinter and scrub them with snow that's just come down fresh. They come out bee-yoo-ti-ful. I know lots about them, my daddy imported them from Iran. We used to have tons in our house in Auburn Heights, outside Detroit."

"You come from Auburn Heights?"

"A hundred years ago."

"I went to high school there."

"I missed high school. I mean I went in L.A., I been living there since I was twelve."

Derrick carved the roast with affected ceremony. It had emerged from the oven medium rare, as both he and Lyssa preferred it. As he carved he extolled Lyssa's cooking ability.

"I try," she said, "but my talents—"

"They're not limited," Derrick cut in. "I keep telling her."

"I was going to say primitive."

Appalachian Spring came to its spirited ending, and *Rodeo* began. Reggie seemed to enjoy Copland, bobbing his great, round, sparsely thatched head between forkfuls of meat and vegetables. Derrick refilled his wineglass.

"Excellent Bordeaux," said Reggie. "Like it, honeybee?"

"I like anything with a kick," she said, grinning, "even beer. You're not drinking, Derrick."

"Derrick doesn't drink," said Reggie. "He's Cambridge Equipment's house teetotaler."

Derrick frowned. "What a pathetic word. Couldn't you make that abstainer?"

Reggie laughed. "How about water-wagon driver?"

"Leave him alone," said Lyssa.

Reggie raised his glass. "A toast to a man with willpower. You've never said, Derrick. How come you don't drink?"

"Long story."

"Which you'd rather not get into. I can accept that. One last question—did you ever?"

"It's none of your beeswax," said Doreen.

The subject was dropped. Lyssa saw gratitude in Derrick's expression as he glanced at Doreen. He was no prude about drinking, didn't criticize others for doing so, and didn't beat the drum for abstention. His first wife had been killed by a drunken driver; and yet it wasn't the other man's condition that changed his mind about drinking but his own at the time. What he perceived as his own. He and his wife had come from a party where both had a couple of drinks—only a couple. He wasn't drunk, wasn't "feeling good" when he got behind the wheel, but from that night on he told himself that had he not had any liquor in him, not so much as a sniff of brandy, his reflexes would have been a hundred percent instead of "a fraction less." And he would have avoided the accident altogether.

Lyssa and he had discussed it when they first started going together. She recalled telling him at the time that she could understand how he felt about the circumstances surrounding his wife's death. She could respect him for feeling so, but she couldn't agree with his thinking. He had had two glasses of rye over a four-hour period prior to leaving the party. A one-hour wait after imbibing two drinks would have guaranteed his complete sobriety while driving; not one but three hours had elapsed after his final drink, which had to have rendered him as sober as anyone could get. She suggested that his conscience was out of line, dealing unfairly with him, and that he should ignore it. He told her he could not. She could not persuade him to change his thinking. She gave up trying.

"Where are you off to next?" Reggie asked him.

"Seattle. This coming Monday." Reggie winced. "It's not that bad," Derrick went on, "it's April, spring. . . ."

"In the state of Washington it's winter ten months of the year," said Reggie, shivering, smirking. "Make him bring a scarf, Lyssa."

"It's not cold," said Derrick. "It just rains three hundred and seventy days a year."

"There's only three hundred sixty-five days in a year," said Doreen.

"It's a joke, honeybee," said Reggie.

"A bad one," added Lyssa.

Dinner was successful, in spite of Lyssa's reservations regarding the quality of the asparagus. Doreen wanted to sit on the terrace and enjoy the "splendid-become-spectacular" view of the city. Lyssa got sweaters for the two of them. She and the Carlyles enjoyed after-dinner drinks. The four of them got into two different conversations, with each occasionally sticking an oar into the other conversation. Lyssa and Doreen talked about clothes;

Reggie and Derrick talked business, as usual. Lyssa studied Reggie out of the corner of her eye as he pontificated about the company: Cambridge Medical and Surgical Equipment. Cambridge was considering acquiring a company that manufactured laser-surgical equipment. Reggie was interested in Derrick's opinion regarding certain aspects of the acquisition. But it was obvious to Lyssa, merely studying Reggie's expression as Derrick commented, that his mind was already made up. He wanted New Century Laser so badly, every time the name rolled off his tongue he practically drooled. It was no hostile takover; there was no public stock to be snapped up. All that was needed was a five-million-dollar loan.

"A lot of money," murmured Derrick. "A lot of debt."

"We've done a study, we can wipe it out in less than five years. We've got to go for it when chances like this happen along. Debt is the heart and soul of all expansion, you know that. They're dying to sell. If one of our competitors takes 'em over, two years down the line we could be eating their dust. Holding our own in the marketplace is not enough, Derrick, we've got to stay one step ahead."

Yes, Reggie's mind was definitely made up, nothing Derrick could say would change it, she decided. Why people who'd already decided what they intended doing asked others their opinions was beyond her. Practically everyone she knew was guilty of doing so. And half prefaced their request for the other's view with "you know how I value your opinion."

Still, she was fond of Reggie. He was a trifle crude, loud, tirelessly garrulous, but goodhearted, good-natured; he thought the world of Derrick and treated him regally. Had he not had a grown son by his first marriage, Derrick well might be Cambridge's heir apparent.

The one thing she didn't like about Reggie was the way he'd ditched his first wife. And "ditch" was the word. Take this money, we're no longer married—after nearly thirty-five years. Carol Carlyle: a cold fish, four

years older than Reggie's fifty-six, who confused snob-
bery with gentility and glitz with style, but nevertheless
didn't deserve dumping, and one day before her sixtieth
birthday. Reggie had dispatched her with a two-million-
dollar settlement; she'd wound up in Acapulco with a
twenty-eight-year-old live-in companion. Lyssa had no
idea what sort of relationship husband and wife had had,
but however wretched it may have been, it lasted a long
time and produced a son now thirty-two.

"You got some bee-yoo-ti-ful view," sang Doreen. "We
got nothing but trees; estates on all four sides. So tell me
some more about your business. I'm dying to see what
you've got. I bet your stuff is bee-yoo-ti-ful."

"We just got in four silk charmeuse robes by Natori
that you'd die for. Sexy as the devil."

Doreen gaped; the light blue eyes doubled in size.
"What color! What color!"

"Silver, with a lavender cast."

"Ooooooo. Reggie, you hear what they got in Lyssa's
store? What's the name again?"

"L'Image."

"L'Image. Reggie, remember the name for me."

"Honeybee, if you don't mind, we're talking business."

"Us, too. L'Image. Where, where?"

"Huron Street, just around the corner from Ackroyd
Shoes."

"I know Ackroyd Shoes, I got these Bruno Maglis there.
Never mind, Reggie, I know where the store is."

"What store?"

"Lyssa's. L'Image."

"Good, good."

The Carlyles left at 11:45, a respectable hour for a
Wednesday night. Reggie Carlyle was a man who could
stretch a good-bye into fifteen minutes at the door; Doreen
helped ably. Lyssa didn't mind; she enjoyed them both
and the dishes could wait till morning. Derrick got their
elevator for them. He finally shut the door behind him,

leaning against it, loosening his tie, grinning wearily.

"Are you as bushed as I am? He always does this to me. Pushes me into a corner and pumps me about New Century Laser. This has been going on for six weeks."

"Will Cambridge acquire it?"

"I don't know. Neither does he, apparently; all he does is talk about it. I mean if you're really, honestly committed to something, you don't keep talking about it, do you? So now you've really gotten to know the second Mrs. Carlyle, what do you think?"

"She's darling."

"She's built like a—"

"Never mind. She's sweet, Derrick. Only you'd better be prepared. I got the impression she's going to come barreling in the door and buy up ten thousand dollars' worth of stuff."

"*I* be prepared?"

"For Reggie to complain."

"You think he cares about money? He's got eight skillion dollars." She had started cleaning the table. "Let that be—I'll help in the morning. I think I'll go in late tomorrow. I need catching up on my zees."

"Lucky you. I open the store tomorrow. Agnes won't be in until Friday. She's out of town visiting her mother."

She stepped into the shower with him. He pulled her close. She kissed him.

"I love you," she whispered.

"I adore you."

His hands slid up her back to her neck and he kissed her passionately. She reveled in him, so deeply in love was she, so content, happy, there were times she could not believe her good fortune. Life was not just good to her—life treated her beautifully, magnificently. She had it all; she thought fleetingly about Carol Carlyle. Reggie's first wife had the money but also the memories, the good and bad and the suffering that came with the dissolution of her marriage. A little late for a second start. Lyssa could kick

Reggie, in spite of her fondness for him. Doreen she had no beef against; she was no temptress, she hadn't lured Reggie into bed; he'd jumped.

The water plashing on them loosened the slight knotting in her shoulders and the back of her neck. He was humming: "*Dancing in the Dark*." They began to dance. She could feel his beginning erection. She broke from him, lathered him, lathered herself, washed off the day, fled the stall. They dried each other hurriedly, haphazardly, leaped into bed, leaving the water running in their haste. And jarring the bed so against one of the nightstands that it nearly upset the lamp, knocking over the clock.

He kissed her and kissed her and kissed her: wildly, tempestuously, nonstop, traveling along her face and neck and upper body, her every place, her most intimate recesses. The fire raged, melting her, dissolving her. And he was atop her, her hand reaching down to seize and guide his throbbing erection.

And her mind and heart filled with music.

~~~~ TWO ~~~~

Doreen came into L'Image wearing a red pleated skirt and matching beret, with a thigh-length black sweater roped with gold chains, and Impo flats. Along with wild-looking Tura glasses and gold, gold, gold: earrings, necklace, rings. It was late afternoon, there were few customers in the store, only three actually; customers and clerks gaped in unison. Lyssa greeted her. Doreen burst into babble.

"I told you I'd darken your door. Isn't this lovely? How

could I ever walk by and not pop in? Bee-yoo-ti-ful! I love that scallop-collared suit in the window and the short lace dress, like a slip. Calvin Klein? I bet it costs a fortune."

"Not that bad, seventeen hundred."

"No kidding? That's cheap."

The figure $10,000 swam into recognizability before Lyssa's mind's eye. Reggie and Doreen had only been married about three weeks; Derrick and she had attended the wedding, a small, quite private affair held in the groom's house. They'd been introduced to Doreen, the two of them had chatted briefly, warmed to each other, but hadn't had much time to get acquainted. Last night had taken care of that. Doreen wanted to see the Calvin Klein dress. Lyssa thought her a trifle too busty for it, even though she had the necessary legs. It was delicate; Doreen was not.

"Try it on. . . ."

While she was in the dressing room two of the clerks, Ellie Hagen and Jenny Mosconi, came practically running up to Lyssa.

"Who . . ." began Ellie. She was a pretty redhead almost as gaunt as Derrick, very tall, well over six feet in flats.

Lyssa sketched Doreen briefly. Jenny, who was about half Ellie's height, was preparing to erupt with questions when Doreen reappeared. The dress was beautiful. She was also, but she looked ridiculous in it. Not enough dress for her Amazonian proportions. Actually she looked like a grown woman in a twelve-year-old's party dress.

"It's my size, I think," she said, frowning in disappointment. "And it fits, I guess, but I look—"

"It's beautiful." said Lyssa. "But not for you, I don't think. If you're interested in evening wear, I do think I've got something."

She led her to a Gianfranco Ferre suit, with a double-breasted vest and wide-cupped trousers in silk and cotton.

"I love it, I love it, I love it!"

"It's terrific for spring. It needs gold accessories and coppery hues in makeup."

"That's okay, that's fine."

"And it does dip pretty low in the front."

"Pretty low? It's all the way down to my naval. Reggie'll love it."

She tried it on, fell in love with it, bought it for $3,800. She also bought a Jill Sander khaki suit—jacket and pants, worn without a shirt—for a little over two thousand dollars. Between the two purchases, they got to talking about last night.

"I told Reggie after not to talk about drinking to Derrick, but you know Reggie. Better than I do." The subject raised was just as speedily dropped. "You knew Carol, didn't you?" Doreen went on.

"Pretty well. I guess as well as any of the company wives. She wasn't easy to get to know. Of course, she had her own circle of friends."

"And you're a lot younger." She lowered her voice. "I have to tell you, Lee . . ."

And just like that Lyssa had a new name.

" . . . I felt, you know, kind of funny marrying a man who'd . . . you know . . . his wife. It came right out of the blue. He asked me to meet him for cocktails one afternoon about a month ago. He told me she was getting a quickie Mexican divorce, but because he wanted her to, you know? And almost without taking a breath, he asked me to marry him. I'd never been married and I didn't see it coming. I liked him. A lot. He was good to me and a real gentleman. A girl likes a man to hold the door for her and help her with her coat. I do, I'm crazy about the little things. And he's very sweet."

"He is."

"And gentle, if you know what I mean. So I said yes, and here I am, Mrs. Reggie Carlyle. Only I do still feel funny about her. I took him away from her."

"I don't think so."

"You don't?" Her eyes lit up; relief poured over her.

"Reggie Carlyle's got a mind of his own. He fell in love with you, he wanted to marry you. Look at it this way. If you hadn't come along, it would have been somebody else. Don't misunderstand, don't take that the wrong way."

"No, no, keep talking."

"I think—and it's just my opinion—that his and Carol's marriage just ran out of gas."

"That's what he said! That's what he said!"

"And who knows, he probably would have left her even if there was no one else."

"You really think? Gee, I never thought of that. But it makes sense and makes me feel a lot better. I love him, Lee."

Doreen suddenly seemed to want her approval; Lyssa didn't see it as necessary, even thought it was irrelevant. Their marriage was none of her business. She got her off the subject and back onto clothes. Doreen got off clothes and onto Derrick.

"He's handsome. . . ." She batted her eyes, grinning impishly.

"His nose is too big, his chin too small."

"Oh, go away, he's very good-looking. He has the most soulful eyes. I said to Reggie at the wedding, 'That Derrick Morgan has the most soulful eyes.' I did, ask him. Hey, let's go out and have a cup of coffee."

"Let's go back in the office and have one."

The store office was about four times the size of a phone booth. Lyssa drew coffee from the machine. She paused.

"Would you rather have tea?"

"No, I'm a coffee person, but you can have it if you like."

Lyssa grinned. "I think I will."

She sat at her desk sipping, eyeing Doreen over the rim of her cup. She truly was delightful and, even better, loved designer clothes. Would that Reggie would be as impressed as she.

"Can I ask something personal?" asked Doreen. "Does Derrick ever talk about the business to you?"

"Almost never."

"Reggie, too. They talk when they get together, but not to us. It's funny, every man I ever went with you couldn't stop talking about what they did. Not Reggie."

"Maybe they're both just sympathetic, sensitive to their wife's position. What do we know about medical and surgical equipment."

"What do we want to know, right? Derrick's a hotshot salesman, right? I mean the biggest one Reggie's got. And it's all out of town."

"Yes, he's all over the map. They outfit operating rooms, everything from operating tables and overhead lights to sponge stands and waste buckets. All the machines: the anesthesiologist's, the suction machine, heart monitor . . . Now, from what I heard last night, they're getting into laser-surgery stuff. I gather it's the coming thing."

"Reggie doesn't tell me boo. I figure he thinks I'm too dumb to understand, or he'd bore me stiff—I mean about the business end of it. But I'd be real interested in the people. They've only got like thirty or forty employees, it must be like a family. And I bet they quarrel sometimes, like a family. And there's got to be office gossip." She pouted. "I wish Mr. Clam would open up."

"Maybe we're better off not knowing what goes on from nine to five."

"The business is only four years old. You know, that's another thing."

"What?"

"Carol. Her parents left her loaded. She put up a lot of the money that got Cambridge started. Did you know that?"

"Derrick might have mentioned it."

"Reggie thinks the world of Derrick. Over and over he tells me he's his right arm. And him with a grown son of his own. You ever meet Brian?"

"Years ago."

"He didn't come to the wedding. Oh, I can understand why not, understand why he's ice-cold to me, too. I can't do much about that. But he's a real snob, like his mother. I shouldn't say that, but it's so. Not Reggie—he hasn't got a snobby bone in his body, bless his heart. Carol made Brian what he is, spoiled him rotten, so Reggie says. He sure does act spoiled. The other day he called up looking for Reggie. I answered the phone, he says, 'Is Father there?' Not 'my' father—Father."

"It could have been worse, he could have said Pater."

Doreen reacted blank-eyed.

"I think it's Latin. Anyway, go on."

"I said he was in the office. This was this past Saturday. Reggie always goes in for a couple hours on Saturday to catch up on stuff that gets ahead of him during the week, you know? Brian says to me really cold, like ice, 'I already called the office,' like I'm lying to him, you know? I said that's where he is. He says 'mmmmm,' just 'mmmmm,' and guess what? Hangs up. How can anybody so snobby have such bad manners?"

"He resents your displacing his mother."

"Oh no, he hates Carol. Reggie told me. Can't stand her. He went on a roaring drunk the night she left town. You know, celebrating."

"However he feels about her, he's still not automatically going to accept you."

"Funny you should say that, because deep down I think he'd like to. At least like to hop in bed with me. You should have seen him the day after the wedding. I was upstairs, he'd come to the house to put the bite on Reggie, what else? Reggie was on the phone. I came out of the master bath and there was Brian with his hand on his you know what. I had to push him aside and run by him. I was so shocked, it was sickening. I was so tempted to spill the beans, but I didn't."

"You were smart not to."

"Reggie would have broken his jaw."

"No . . ."

"He would, too. He's the easiest-going man in the world, he hardly ever loses his temper, but when he does, look out. I've seen him lose it a couple times. Once, the afternoon bartender at the Cherokee Club said something off-color. Reggie reached over, grabbed him by the shirt, and told him. 'Apologize, pigface, or I'll fucking beat you to death!' That's what he said. I could feel my face getting all red. He's a little overweight and he's no kid, but he can still handle himself. You talk about a knight protecting his lady fair, it was bee-yoo-ti-ful. That's something else, nobody's ever made me feel like a real lady the way Reggie does. He's got me up on a pedestal. I love it!

"Did I tell you Brian left town for good? Quit the company, and good-bye. Maybe Reggie gave him a bundle to leave, you think? No, a father wouldn't do that to his only son. No, I guess with me in the picture Brian just couldn't see hanging around. Good riddance."

She sailed out the door singing, swinging her purchases. Jenny and Ellie came over.

"What a character," said Jenny in a tone bordering on awe.

"She's great," said Lyssa quietly. "I love her."

And did Reggie? she wondered. Or was he in love with the idea of showing her on his arm, particularly in public in front of men his own age, men with wives like Carol?

That was nasty, uncalled for. It well might be he'd been waiting for her his whole life and really did have her up on a pedestal. She hoped it was rock solid, firmly anchored, permanent. As for herself, she would never have been able to trust a divorced man. They came to you with experience in divorce.

~~~~~ THREE ~~~~~

Derrick's flight to Seattle Monday morning was insidiously early, by Lyssa's standards, by his own: 7:38. She packed for him Sunday night.

"I am not a morning person," he declared.

"You think I am?"

As always, she made a list of things he'd be taking; pretty much the same list for every trip, the only variations in clothing having to do with the weather of his destination city. Reggie's suggestion, though uttered in jest, was neverthless sound: she packed two scarves, one his polka-dot red-on-blue silk scarf. She also restored the winter lining to his raincoat, which he'd taken out the last week in March. He was in the bathroom collecting his razor, toothbrush, and other toilet articles.

"Don't forget your epinephrine, the Bronchodane."

"Got it, got it."

Said with a tinge of resentment. He had been bedeviled by extrinsic asthma since he was a teenager. In the four years they'd been married she could recall two what might be termed dangerous attacks. He was allergic to pollen, to mold spores and other airborne invaders of the eyes and bronchial tubes. The first of the two prolonged attacks had taken place in southern Spain when they were on a twelve-day tour of that country's provinces. It had lasted nearly four hours and frightened her terribly. Luckily a doctor was found and adrenaline injected. Early on, Derrick had been warned that prolonged or frequent attacks could become dangerous if he was weakened by fatigue or inadequate nutrition, if his oxygen consumption was too low, or if emphysema developed. Exposure to sudden changes in temperature or humidity, overexertion, emotional stress, powerful odors, smoke—too many things could trigger an attack. Emphysema was her chief concern. He had never smoked, but that in itself was no guarantee of exemption from the disease. Her mother, a heavy smoker, had died in her fifties of emphysema; Lyssa was determined that Derrick would not fall prey to it. He respected his condition and took good care of his health, but was careless and forgetful about little things. She always packed for him; when he packed for himself, he would open his bag in his hotel and discover things like one sock, toothpaste and no brush, his electric razor cord and charging stand left behind.

She insisted he pack an umbrella. He demurred.

"My God, Lys, you make me feel like a grammar-schooler. You know it's possible it won't rain a drop the whole six days."

"That isn't what you told Doreen Saturday night."

"I was kidding."

"It could rain constantly. The last thing you need is a head cold. I wish you didn't have to go—I mean to Seattle, of all places."

"They're breaking ground for a new general facility. Four operating rooms."

"No waiting—"

"I'm being serious. Seattle is important. We're talking about a lot of money, a lot in commissions. As things stand, I figure the worst we can do is a split with Kenworthy or one of the other big outfits on the whole package."

She stood at the foot of the bed snugging a pair of shoes in their bag into a corner of his suitcase. She paused and looked up as he came out of the bathroom with his toilet-article bag. It was the first time she could recall his going into detail about his work out of town. It was almost as if he was taking her into his confidence. She never had understood the reason for all the mystery about the job. It wasn't exactly top-secret stuff, equipping operating rooms.

"Let me get this straight," she said. "George what's-his-name—"

"Chakirides."

"—made the contact with the city officials, he lays the groundwork, you come in, fill in the details, close the deal."

"Something like that."

"Something?"

He suddenly didn't want to discuss it further. She didn't press him. She'd tried before, a few times; his response was always the same: "Nothing extraordinary, it's just a selling job. It could be widgets or Boeing seven-fifty-sevens, it just happens to be medical and surgical equipment."

That was that. Once she had asked to go with him; he had stiffened before her eyes, then caught himself and visibly relaxed. And launched into a lengthy litany of all the reasons why she'd hate traipsing along: he was tied up in meetings from morning till night, usually with the dullest people imaginable. Who can be duller than high-level city officials and state employees and hospital directors and administrators? His main reason for declining her offer to go with him was that they wouldn't be able to do anything together, even enjoy dinner. He described it as ten days' work compressed into three or four, no time off, no time to relax, no time to breathe.

Besides, she really couldn't steal time from the store, it wouldn't be fair to Agnes.

"Let's see your Bronchodane."

He groaned and muttered, unzipped the little bag, and produced his medication.

"You don't trust me," he said, putting on a sullen expression.

"You I trust, implicitly. Your concentration is some-thing else. It's about as dependable as the weather. I've packed your folding umbrella."

"How about my hip boots and sou'wester?"

He laughed, kissed her, swung her about, around the bed out of the way of the suitcase, plumped her down on the bed. She kissed him tenderly.

"Take care of Mommy's little boy," she murmured. "Get plenty of sleep."

"Don't get overtired. Stay out of smoke-filled rooms. Get plenty of fresh air. Eat right. I know, I know."

"To know is to do."

"God, you're getting more and more like my mother every day."

"You need a mother; when you travel you do. How are you getting to the airport in the morning?"

"Company car, what else?"

"That early?"

"The limos roll around the clock, Mommy. The driver'll be downstairs at six sharp. I'll bet you. You stand on the terrace and look down at one minute of and you'll see him pull up. Wanna bet?"

"I'll take your word for it. You'll be back Sunday."

"I'm going to try for Saturday night—early so we can go out."

"You'll be exhausted."

"I'll be fine. I'll need a Saturday night out. I'll call you Friday, not that I won't call before. But it won't be till then that I'll know one way or the other. I'll do my damnedest to wrap it up and sneak out of there early. Now . . ." He started to remove her clothes.

"Don't, not yet. I'm not done packing."

"It can wait, this can't."

"Animal!"

"Cold fish!"

"Who you calling cold fish?"

On her back, digging her heels into the covers and

wheeling about, she pushed the opened suitcase on the floor. Surprisingly it landed flat, spilling none of its contents. She pulled him down on top of her, undid his belt, and started on his trousers. And stopped.

"Not on the bedspread."

"Okay, okay . . ."

They made love with the covers thrown back: glorious, delicious, soul-stirring love. It was eleven when they finally lay back, too exhausted to continue. She picked up the clock.

"My God, you have to get up at five!"

"It's okay, six hours is enough."

"You need eight."

"I'll sleep on the plane."

"You never do."

"Set it for five. Better yet, quarter after."

"What difference will fifteen minutes make?"

"Give it to me, I'll set it."

"I'll finish your packing."

"It's okay, I've got enough stuff."

She scoffed. Naked, she finished packing. He sat up in bed staring at her.

"You're beautiful."

"Where's your Filofax?"

"In the study. I'll get it in the morning."

"Get it now, pack it now."

"You're a tough cookie, Mommy."

"And you're soft."

"I resent that."

"I wasn't talking about *that* and you know it. Get the Filofax."

Six minutes to six. He was ready. She stood on the terrace, protected from the downpour by the terrace above. She was in robe and mules, her coffee set on the little table. Umbrellas, black and in all colors, floated up and down the sidewalks below like flowers in a stream. The light changed, and a gray stretch limo rounded the corner and pulled up in front of the building.

"He's here." She joined Derrick in the foyer. "Got everything?"

"Everything."

"You're sure."

"Of course not, when am I ever sure I've 'got everything'? Isn't that what I have you for?"

He smirked, kissed her tenderly, opened the door.

"Got your ticket and boarding pass?"

He patted his pocket. "Got 'em, Mommy."

The elevator came immediately. They kissed.

"If the food on the plane is no good, don't eat it. But don't starve. Got your Bronchodane?"

He made a guttural sound of mock despair, boarded the elevator, grinned, waved, and was gone. She stood for a few seconds with the flat of her hand against the closed doors. Then went back to the terrace and stood sipping her coffee and looking straight down. A whole new display of flowers floated below. His driver came to meet him holding an umbrella for him, opening the door. Off they went. She went back to the hall door looking for the morning paper, but it was too early for the delivery. She was curious as to today's weather in Seattle.

It was no doubt raining.

FOUR

Agnes Pelletier was not a happy camper; her mother's complaining invariably drained her. Dry. From every three-day visit she returned looking as if she'd been gone six months, and always exhausted. She was ten years older than Lyssa's thirty-three. At the moment she looked twenty years older. Her bleached blond hair, customarily beautifully, perfectly styled, looked somewhat disheveled, as if she'd taken one look at it in the mirror that morning and given up on it before starting. Bags hung under her slightly bloodshot green eyes; she looked like she was on the verge of yawning.

"How's mother?" Lyssa asked.

"You're funny. What mother? I have a mother? Hey, out of sight, out of mind, right?"

"I'm sorry."

"I apologize, dear heart, Mother dear is aces. Nobody in truly poor health can be that abusive. Abusing people takes energy, stamina. She's loaded. What am I saying, 'people'? I'm her only target. She saves it all up for me. I bet you she writes down every barb, every cut, works up a whole new list between my visits. And when I walk in the door, she lets fly. The slings and arrows of outrageous fortune are nothing compared with her arsenal. God, I wish I had a sister, I wish I had four. Divide the pain, share it, you know?"

"What does she say?"

"What doesn't she? Why am I still single? No, she doesn't put it that way, she asks how come I can't find a decent man. What's the problem? Are your standards too high? Or too low? Do you have any? That's her genius, Lys, one question, the opener, leads to sixteen more. They come at you in volleys, I swear."

Lyssa laughed.

"You think it's funny? You take over, you visit her, twice, even once, you'll come away wanting to kill yourself."

"Oh, for God's sake, Aggie, she's your mother, she can't be that bad. She's only on your case because she cares about you."

"No no no no no, that's what you think. What every outsider thinks when mother and daughter go after each other with knives every minute they're together. Not true, dear heart, prevailing myth. Picking on me isn't in my best interests, it's in hers. It's the electricity that keeps the old bag's motor purring. She enjoys it, she loves it, she lives for my visits. Look what's coming up the walk, my prime target!"

"You can't tell me all you do is fight."

"No, there are respites. We're only human, we run out of energy, we have to recharge our batteries between battles. Wars aren't fought continuously. That's what it is, you know, war."

"You just rub each other the wrong way."

"That, dear heart, is the understatement of the decade. We are mongoose and snake, fire and forest; I'm the trees. You're looking at the western hemisphere's foremost whipping girl. Oh, I retaliate, defend myself. For all the good it does me."

"How old is she?"

"I know what you're thinking. Not old enough. And healthy? Christ Almighty, she's in better shape than Jane Fonda. I swear, I don't stand a chance."

"Maybe you shouldn't go visit her, maybe it's that simple."

"Oh sure, what happens then? She visits me. Understand something, Lys, this is a woman capable of starting an argument over how I unfold my napkin and place it on my lap at lunch. You know how poets can find beauty in anything? Irma can find something to criticize in anything. Has anyone every criticized you for how you breathe? How you walk?"

Two customers came in, rescuing them both from the conversation. Agnes approached them. Lyssa retired to the back to check a shipment that had just come in. Ferragamo bags. She was checking them against the manifest when Agnes came back.

"Somebody here to see you."

"Customer?"

"A man."

"Stranger?"

"I never saw him before. He's outside by the cash register."

Immediately Lyssa thought of Derrick en route to Seattle. Good God in heaven, had the plane crashed? She swallowed, she could feel the color drain from her cheeks. Agnes noticed.

"Hey, take it easy, are you expecting anybody?"

"No."

"He's waiting. Take him in the office before he drools all over the lingerie. Right, he's not exactly a male model. I'll finish checking out these bags. Boy, aren't they gorgeous? I wish I could afford six."

Lyssa went outside, wondering why her heart was suddenly pounding. If there was a crash, they didn't telephone if they could tell you in person. At least someone had once told her that. The visitor was still standing by the cash register near the door, looking decidedly uncomfortable, trying to avoid looking at the lingerie display. He was in his fifties or early sixties, with a potbelly, and an off-the-rack suit that looked to be just starting to get shiny at the elbows. He wore a brown tie with a black shirt; she thought of the Mafia in the movies, but they wore white on white or black on white, she couldn't remember. He didn't look at all Mafia, he looked uncontrollably Irish. Round, red face, whiskey cheeks, little gleaming eyes buried in their sockets. He looked as if when he opened his mouth, a brogue would come spilling out. It turned out a good guess, although he had no brogue.

"Mrs. Morgan? My name is Joe Walsh. Is there someplace we could talk in private?"

"What do you want, Mr. Walsh? What is this?"

"I can explain. I will, but I think it's best in . . . in private."

He was warm, almost apologetic. He seemed sincere and very anxious to talk. He also seemed harmless. His breath reeked of mouthwash, no doubt masking his hangover breath, although he didn't look hung over. She took him into the office. They sat with the little desk between them. He dug inside his jacket and produced a badge.

"Police?"

"Detective."

His accent was slightly southern.

"Metropolitan Atlanta Police. I have to be up front with you, ma'am, I'm retired. Last year. I'm strictly on my own. There's no law that says you have to answer any questions, if you don't want. Only it could be in your interests to cooperate."

"Cooperate in what? What do you want?"

"I'm getting to it. Mind if I smoke?"

"Very much."

"Right."

"Does this have to do with my husband?"

"Yes."

Her heart quickened. "Has something happened?"

"No, not that I know of. This is an old beef."

" 'Beef'?"

He looked suddenly uncomfortable. "You mind if I chew a stick of gum?"

"Go ahead. Just get on with it."

He proffered the pack, she declined. He crammed two sticks in his mouth.

"Your husband lived in Beulah Heights, just outside Atlanta five years ago, right?"

"Yes . . ."

He had gotten out a disreputable-looking dog-earred notebook. He flipped pages, found his place.

"He was married. To Elizabeth Warrener, is that right?"

"Yes, she was killed in a car accident."

"That's what he told you."

"That's what happened."

"Mmmmm."

"What does that mean?" Already, this quickly, he was wearing down her patience, the little she had to start with.

"That accident was the night of December seventeenth, 1988. That was a Saturday night. He and his wife were driving home from a party, they stopped at a stop sign, and a drunk came barreling out of a side road, smashed into them, killed her, drove off. Mr. Morgan was disoriented, didn't catch the plate number, the killer got away clean."

"That's true."

"So he claims."

"Now see here, Officer—"

"Detective. Walsh. Joe Walsh."

"You think he made it all up? Is that what you're trying to say?"

"No no no, it's just that there's certain things I . . . wonder about. I . . . I was hoping you could help me. Let me explain."

"I wish you would." She glanced at her watch.

"I promise I won't take much more of your time. I appreciate you giving me this much. Like I said, I'm retired now and this is an old case, buried in the files, and I got nothing to do with my time and so I dug it out and got to thinking back and I remembered there was something bothered me about it."

"Would you mind being specific?"

"That's my problem, I can't put my finger on it. Only when you've been a detective as long as I have, you develop certain instincts, like . . . like a woman's intuition. A little warning voice that tells you something's wrong. Believe me, I'm not throwing out allegations here."

"You could have fooled me. What do you call implying he's a liar?"

"I didn't imply that. I don't call anybody a liar, there could be a lawyer under your desk." He grinned. She scowled, staring stonily, a look that said, "Get on with it and get out." He went on. "What have we got? A hit-and-run. It happened on Boulevard Road, just south of Route twenty. His wife was taken to Mercy Hospital and pronounced dead."

"And?"

He paused in his chewing. The expression that came onto his face suggested that he intended to go all out. Spill the beans? What beans?

"Say what you have to and please leave, okay?"

"Right. I investigated, did I tell you that? The case was all mine. The trouble is, I didn't get to it till after she died. By then the accident site had been pretty much cleaned up. We had pictures, of course, and the cops' report. The first two on the scene. I talked to your husband at the hospital. He was pretty shaken up, of course. He described the accident to a tee, every detail. Thinking back on it, he must have told that story ten times and never missed one detail. Every step in the right order. They were at the party, they left, they were sober, she was fine—"

"Why shouldn't she be?"

"Both were. Fifteen minutes later they stop at a stop sign, the drunk comes barreling out, broadsides the front door on the passenger side, kills her. And tosses a bottle into the bushes, which the cops found. No fingerprints. He could have been wearing gloves; it was December, cold enough. Anyway, he goes barreling off, weaving, typical drunk driver. He hit them, she hit her head, died on the way to the hospital. That's your husband's story. Vehicular homicide cut-and-dried, no autopsy."

"Why should there be?"

"There shouldn't, no need. He didn't want one, there wasn't any. But it just doesn't go down, refuses to. My problem is I don't think that car killed her. I'm not saying it couldn't have, but I don't think it did."

"You're not making sense."

"I think it was a setup. I think she was drugged at the party. He helped her into the car. A few minutes later she passed out, sitting there slumped, without her seat belt fastened. Oh, it was fastened when the cops found her, but . . . Anyway, he, Mr. Morgan, stopped by the side road, the 'drunk' driver comes shooting out—"

She slapped the desk, shooting to her feet. "That's enough! It's crazy. *You* must be!"

"Please, I'm only trying to tell you like it was."

"Like you want it to be! With so much free time on your hands, how many cases have you dug back into? Ten? Twenty?"

"Just this one, I swear. Mrs. Morgan—"

"This conversation is over. I refuse to sit here and listen to you, a perfect stranger, drag my husband through the mud. He went through hell when she was killed. He still hasn't gotten over it, not completely. He never will. You don't know the first thing about him. He's honest, hardworking, decent. He loved his wife, he had no reason in the world to kill her. Have her killed, whatever . . ."

"He collected four hundred thousand in insurance."

She froze. "He did like hell!"

"Four hundred thousand dollars tax free. You don't believe me, ask him."

"I don't believe you and I can't be bothered asking him. I think you better leave."

Up came his hands defensively, his expression defeated. "Okay, whatever you say. Like I said before, there's no law says you even have to talk to—"

"I heard you the first time. Just go and don't come back. It won't do you any good."

"I'm sorry, Mrs. Morgan, I know this must hit you like a ton of bricks, but I'm only doing my job."

"You don't have a job, remember? Good day, Mr. Walsh."

He left shrugging and shaking his head. She stood watching him until he was on the sidewalk and shuffling up to the corner and out of sight. Agnes and Jenny came up to her.

"What was that all about?" Jenny asked.

"Nothing."

"You're trembling," said Agnes.

"I'm not. I'm fine, let's just drop it. Did you finish with those bags or shall I?"

Agnes was not interested in the Ferragamo-bag shipment. She wanted to pursue the conversation; Jenny, too. Mercifully, their timing perfect, three gorgeously dressed women came in.

~~~~ FIVE ~~~~

She paced the terrace. Pouring herself a Scotch and water, she had yet to taste it. It was 6:30, still twilight, but the city below was brightly lit. The rain had left the air damp and with the suggestion of a chill. She had draped a sweater over her shoulders.

Walsh. Why had he approached her? If he thought he had something, why not sit down with Derrick? Why detour around him? Actually, why talk to either of them?

Of course, Derrick was out of town; maybe he'd tried to contact him at the company and, when he could not, decided to speak to her, hoping to keep his trip from being a complete wild-goose chase. She hadn't asked if he'd tried to talk to Derrick, he hadn't said.

He, Walsh, obviously didn't have anything concrete, only his suspicions. Or could it be more than suspicion? He was, after all, a professional; detectives didn't go around badgering people associated with suspects without something of substance to motivate them. What did he have that he hadn't revealed? Was it just the insurance money? It couldn't be that. Insurance companies conducted their own investigations into homicides, into everything, separate and apart from the police; they wouldn't have paid Derrick a dime if there was the slightest suspicion surrounding her death. Ask him, Walsh had said, ask him if he didn't come into $400,000. So what if he did? She could hardly ask him, it was no business of hers, it all happened before they'd even met.

And yet Walsh had trekked all the way from Atlanta to Bellingham, Michigan to question her, no doubt hoping she'd let slip something that might bolster his case. What case? What exactly did he have? Thinking the worst, the absolute blackest, most farfetched scenario—if Derrick actually had wanted to murder her, he'd hardly concoct such a bizarre plot. It was much too cumbersome and involved; too many possibilities of things going awry. And to be totally dependent on an outsider . . . to bring someone in to do his killing for him and have to pay him would be stupid. The man could blackmail him the rest of his life.

"What's the matter with you!" she said aloud.

Walsh had her thinking like he did. How could she even imagine such a thing? It was ridiculous; worse, it was outrageously unfair. Dead wrong. He wasn't just barking up the wrong tree, he was in the wrong woods. Why the devil didn't he divulge what he had that had sent him nearly a thousand miles from Atlanta to Bellingham? If he had something to go on and he must, wasn't she entitled to know? For her protection?

"There you go again!"

The phone startled her so, she jumped.

"Damn!"

She ran to snatch it up. "Derrick?"

"Lee? It's me, Doreen. You okay?"

"Sure, sure, how are you?"

"You sound upset. Of course, you're expecting Derrick to call; want me to hang up?"

"No, that's okay, he usually doesn't call till late."

"The reason I'm calling is Reggie's got a big board meeting or something tonight and I'm home alone and I was wondering . . . did you eat yet?"

"No . . ."

"Good. How about we meet downtown and have a bite and girl talk?"

"I'd love to."

"My treat."

"Dutch."

"Whatever. Any place you like special? How about Bassini's on Front Street?"

"I don't think I know it."

"It's northern Italian. They do a terrific veal Sorrentino with eggplant, prosciutto ham, and mozzarella. I have big-number cholesterol, but I can't stay away from mozzarella cheese, especially theirs. What do you think?"

"It sounds great. Why don't I pick you up at about ten of eight?"

"I'll pick you up. I want you to see my new Mercedes."

"What is it?"

"The coupe, number five hundred something, I think. Anyway, it cost a fortune. And it's bee-yoo-ti-ful. And you can smell the leather like crazy. What time is it?"

Lyssa glanced at the basket-top English bracket clock on the fireplace mantel. It was getting on to 6:40. Doreen agreed to pick her up at 7:50. Lyssa hung up charged, eager for the sight and company of her best customer in three weeks. Doreen was a breath of fresh air, which, at the moment, was far more important than a well-heeled patron. She seemed eternally up; to be sure, being married to Reggie's millions offered scant opportunity to get down . . . about anything.

She stood staring down at the cradled phone. Derrick would call around eleven, she'd say nothing about Walsh's visit. Wait; that she couldn't do, she had no right to keep it from him. Still, it wasn't something to bring up over the phone, it could wait till he got home. Walsh wouldn't be back; she'd sent him away empty-handed. Only, would he eventually want to talk to Derrick? It had to get around to that. Maybe her best course would be to forget the whole thing, at least till Derrick got back. What a dismal day, what a break: five years and suddenly old ghosts coming back to haunt them.

"There you go again—again!"

Doreen's new car was a dream: the 560 coupe. Ivory with black trim; it purred. The top down, she sat at the wheel looking like a child with a new and what was to become favorite toy, shifting the wheel back and forth in pretend driving as Lyssa approached, sweeping one hand, indicating the interior, honking—to the amusement of Otto, the doorman. He held the passenger door for Lyssa.

"A Cherman car, *nicht?* Merzedes. They know how to make cars in Chermany. Zo handsome . . ."

"You like it?" Doreen asked. "How much you give me for it?"

He laughed, they laughed and drove away. Front Street wasn't the most impressive street in town. Lyssa had pictured Bassini's restaurant as a family dive, with place mats of Italy and its chief tourist attractions in place of a tablecloth, cheap and garish appointments, a low ceiling, and menus enclosed in plastic and slightly splattered with the day's blue-plate special. She was to be pleasantly surprised. The waiters were uniformed in maroon jackets and black bow ties, the music wafting from unseen speakers was an unidentifiable trio playing ultramodern jazz, with taste and discipline. The table-cloths hung almost to the sumptuously carpeted floor and the menus were heavy, extraordinarily expensive looking, gold-tasseled, and offered no entrées under twenty-seven dollars. Bassini's had ambience, charm, and class. And Mrs. Carlyle was practically kowtowed to when they walked in. Every table appeared taken, but somehow Anthony, the maître d', found them one in a quiet corner. He lit their candle and snapped his fingers and a waiter fairly leaped to the table to serve them. Lyssa ordered Chardonnay, Doreen chose a light beer.

"I'm just in a beer mood, you know? You ever get in a particular drink mood? I do all the time. I make it sound like I'm a drunk, but I don't drink that much. Almost never at home, except beer and wine at dinner. I had an uncle, my mother's brother, who was an alky, and he sort of soured everybody in the family. I mean you could see from Uncle Carleton what you could turn into if you overdid it. It was scary. I never even took a drink till I was sixteen. You see anything you like on the menu?"

"Everything."

"The veal Sorrentino is great. And that veal chop with wild mushroom ragout is very good, too."

She pronounced ragout "rag out." Lyssa had no great urge to correct her. She ordered the veal Sorrentino and the house salad with vinegar and oil. Doreen had a hard time deciding, eventually taking Anthony's suggestion of the salmon with Pinot Grigio caper sauce.

"Something the matter, Lee?" she asked when Anthony and the waiter retreated.

"Hard day at the office."

"I know, you mean at the store. So this is good for you to get out and relax. Running that place must be hard work, so many little things to see to. You've got bee-yoo-ti-ful stuff, I mean it. I've seen a lot of shops in this town, and yours is right up there. What's the name again?"

"L'Image."

"L'Image. French, right? Very classy. How long you been in business?"

"Almost six years now."

"That long? Is business good?"

"Always. Women with money love to spend it. Clothes and jewelry run number one and two, I'd say."

"Clothes, jewelry, cars, shoes. Shoes women spend tons of money on. If you got it, you spend it on everything. Last time I counted, I think—let me see—I think it was sixty-three pairs of shoes. Of course, I don't wear them all; I get them home and try them on again and sometimes they've lost it. What it was that turned me on to buying them. I should take them right back, but I hate to do that to the clerk. I guess with sixty-three pair I maybe wear thirty. Maybe more, thirty-two. Maybe thirty-three."

She was having a hard time deciding. I should only have her problems, thought Lyssa. And yet, what problems did she herself have? Nothing with the store, not at the moment, nothing with Derrick, with their marriage. Detective Walsh. Was he a problem? Would he develop into one? He'd certainly succeeded in getting her sufficiently exercised to qualify himself as one.

Was he really worth even a small fraction of the concern she'd devoted to him since he walked out of the store? Out of her life? Probably not. Definitely not. Only why couldn't she rid her thoughts of him? Maybe it was him, his demeanor, his personality; the way he'd let it all out, almost apologetically, and with all the consideration he could muster in respect to her feelings. If only he told her what he had that was concrete. Thinking back on their conversation, all he'd really done was pick around the edge of the thing. What had made him say he thought Elizabeth had been drugged before leaving the party? Was he implying that Derrick drugged her, in effect preparing her for what was to come? That in itself was all that was needed to incriminate him, at least to Walsh's way of thinking. Which was generally the way it worked. If there was a hole in somebody's story or you even thought there was, it invariably set you digging deeper.

Only why hadn't he done his digging back then? Why close the file and go on to the next case? Why these "second thoughts" all of a sudden? Or were they? He'd said that he wasn't satisfied with the outcome of the thing at the time; still, his superiors must have been, and the insurance company. But not Detective Joseph Walsh. *It just doesn't go down,* was the way he'd put it, *it refuses to.* She could hear his voice repeating that.

"Lee?"

"Yes?"

"You're a million miles away. Something's wrong, isn't it? Only you don't want to talk about it. It's none of my beeswax."

"I'm afraid it is personal."

"With Derrick; I understand. Keep it to yourself, only don't let it bug you, so it spoils your dinner, right?"

"Right."

Their glasses were nearly empty; the waiter materialized behind Doreen. Lyssa ordered a Bloody Mary.

"Your uncle Carleton story scared me a little," she confessed, and laughed.

"Uncle Carleton didn't drink wine and Bloody Marys. He drank gin straight out of the bottle; two fifths a day. Even more on weekends. He sold cars, very successful. A bachelor. I think he had a problem. I think he was a homosexual, but I could never understand. There's lots of homos that don't drink a drop. Sometimes Reggie drinks too much. Not that he's a drunk or anything, nothing close to Uncle Carleton. But he comes home late from meetings and he's feeling no pain. He's not loud or mean or anything—he's just a little wobbly, and I have to put him to bed. He sings a lot. It's funny, he never gets that way with me or at a party or anything. You saw how much he drank last Wednesday. He drove home, he wasn't even slightly tipsy and there was no dancing or anything, so he could sweat it out of his system; he just didn't have that much.

"It's only when he comes home from his business meetings, the late-night meetings, that he's . . . you know. And not all the time. I figure maybe once every six weeks, even eight weeks. Once every seven weeks. Sometimes twice in seven weeks, but then not for seven more, so it comes out the same average. Listen to me, I'm boring you stiff; boring myself. I'm sorry. How do you like your veal?"

"Marvelous."

"Isn't it good food, though? I wish I could cook. I can't cook or sew or do anything domestic. I never had to. The guys I went with never wanted me to do anything around the house. Stuff like that, I mean. I'm lucky we've got a butler and a maid who can cook."

She talked about the company and the demands the job put on Reggie, demands he willingly accepted. Not surprising, considering his salary. One thing about him annoyed her—the way he had "carried" his son, before Brian left town.

"He never bellyaches about anything except Brian. I don't know what he did, but whatever it was, he didn't work very hard at it. Reggie kept saying somebody always had to clean up after him, like he was a little kid and spilled his cereal. He couldn't stand Brian taking advantage of his being the top man. The worst thing about it, he used to say, was that Brian had no—you'll excuse the expression—balls. And he wasn't really interested in working, at least not for Reggie. Good riddance.

"How can you take your pay if you know you haven't earned it? I mean every job I ever had, I worked hard: salesclerk, drugstore clerk, costume-jewelry-counter clerk, manicurist. I went to hairstyling school when I was eighteen; I didn't graduate because I met this guy and you know . . . But I sure learned a lot about hairstyling. I love the way you flip yours up the sides, it's perfect for your face."

"It's easy."

"Working girls should have easy hairdos, on account they don't have the time. Oops, I don't mean *working girls* working girls, I mean career women, like you." A wistful expression came onto her face. "I wish I had a job, only Reggie doesn't want me working. Almost every guy I ever went with didn't. Some even made me quit what I was doing. Most guys just want you home in your apartment waiting for them when they feel like coming home. You can get sick of TV and the supermarket papers print the same old stuff, always about Elvis and flying saucers and JFK's ghost and weird people. Do you believe there's flying saucers? I do. I had a girlfriend once who had an out-of-body experience. You know what that is?"

"Where you think you leave your body and fly around?"

"Oh, but you really do. She did, lots. I'd love to try it, but you have to have the power, and it's rare. Like people who've been taken on board flying saucers. That happens, but it's rare. You miss Derrick, don't you?"

"I always do. He's going to try to finish up and get back by Saturday."

"That'd be nice. It's no fun sleeping in an empty bed. I'd be scared to. You're lucky you're on the eleventh floor, you don't have to worry about anybody breaking in. I sure get uptight when Reggie stays out late, like at one of his meetings. Burglars love to pick on big houses."

"You're not alone, you have the servants."

"They're in their own quarters, miles away from our bedroom."

"Don't you have an alarm system?"

Doreen glanced down at her half-eaten entrée. "I don't put it on. Reggie showed me how, but it's very complicated. Hey, what say we have dessert and go for a ride? I know a great place, Charlie's Web, out off Route twenty-three. There's an acid-rock band that'll kill you."

"I'd like to, but I really should head home, Derrick'll be calling and—"

"It's been a rough day and you need your sleep, I understand. Maybe some other time."

"Definitely some other time."

"We have time for dessert and coffee, though, haven't we?"

"Of course."

Doreen covered her hand affectionately. "Don't worry about him. He's not that kind. Believe me, I can always tell."

"What kind?"

"He doesn't fool around."

Lyssa laughed. "That's the last thing I worry about with Derrick."

"Lucky you, it's the first thing I worry about with every man that comes into my life."

"Not Reggie . . ."

Doreen shrugged, assuming her most wistful expression.

"You know something, all the money you could ever spend, the biggest house, the best of everything, all of them are nothing compared with having a man who wants only you. Nobody else in the whole world but you. That's the perfect life. And you've got it."

"I think so."

"Hang on to it."

She leaned forward, lowering her voice to a conspiratorial whisper. "Talking about Reggie, something funny happened last night. Not funny, more scary. I've got to tell somebody or I'll burst. I think something's going on, Lee, I mean with the business."

"What?"

"About eleven last night the phone rang. Reggie was in his study with the door open. He always does work in there Sunday nights, sort of planning the week to come, all his meetings and everything. Anyway, I was next door arranging flowers, taking out the dead ones, you know. I heard him pick up. Right away he got uptight. I did a bad thing, I couldn't help myself. I sneaked up and listened beside the doorjamb. I don't know who it was called, but it was business, something about the feds and taxes."

"The IRS."

"Right. Reggie kept repeating a name: Cochrane."

"Cochrane, Cochrane . . . isn't he the chief accountant at Cambridge?"

"He was. He left last January. Or got fired. Something's going on, something heavy. When Reggie got off, he was boiling. He came storming out before I could move hardly. I made believe I was just coming up to the door instead of already being there. God forbid he catch me eavesdropping on business. He was burning. He says what the ef you doing, listening in? I said I wasn't, I just . . . got here. I was fixing the flowers. Who was it? None of your effing business, he says. Lee, I've seen him lose his temper, but never like that, nothing close. If I was a cat, he would have kicked me through the window."

"It was the company he was discussing with whoever it was, not his personal taxes?"

"Was it Cambridge, definitely? What do you think it means?"

"Maybe the company's in trouble with the IRS."

"What sort of trouble?"

"Tax trouble, dear, what else? Sometimes accountants and bookkeepers leave companies with monumental grudges and run straight to the IRS. Sometimes they even copy the books."

"Can they do that?"

"If you blow the whistle on somebody who owes a lot in taxes, the IRS gives you a percentage of what they collect. There are people who've made lots of easy money that way."

"He didn't tell me what it was about and I wasn't about to ask, no way. We went to bed, he was still boiling. But next morning he was his old self again, warm, sweet. And not a word about the call. But something's going on. Please, don't tell Derrick. If it ever got back to Reggie, he'd kill me. Please don't say anything, promise?"

"I promise."

Sincerely but reluctantly. If Cambridge was in tax trouble, it had to affect Derrick; he had almost as much at stake as Reggie and the other officers. He was entitled to know. But the worried look in Doreen's eyes confirmed that he wouldn't be hearing it from his wife.

～～ SIX ～～

Derrick got home around four Saturday afternoon. He looked pushed through a wringer. He dropped his bag, kissed her, and fled to the shower. Lyssa sat on the toilet seat talking to him as he washed away his weariness.

"You were dead right about the rain—incredible. I never knew the U.S. had monsoons."

"Did you sell them?"

"Everything. It was unbelievable, I couldn't miss. I swear their tongues were hanging out when I got there.

They'd seen all the catalogs, of course, and had a million questions."

"But you had all the answers."

"All the right ones. Reggie's right, you know, about acquiring that surgical-laser outfit. Laser surgery's getting bigger fast. What's been happening around here? How's business?"

"Good, fine."

She stood holding the bath sheet, wrapping it around him as he stepped out.

"Where do you want to go for dinner?" he asked.

"You're too tired."

"I'm not, where?"

She told him about Bassini's and about meeting Doreen for dinner. Like her, he hadn't even heard of the place. She raved about it; the only problem was he wasn't crazy about Italian cuisine. They decided on Le Papillon, which both liked; he loved their Chateaubriand. She went to call and make a reservation. He came into the bedroom as she was hanging up the phone. She got out his robe for him.

"What'd you do all week besides slave at the shop?" he asked.

"Sweetheart, we have to talk."

His grin vanished; it was as if a shadow fell over his face.

"Serious?"

"A man came to see me last Monday. Joe Walsh, he came all the way up from Atlanta."

Adding where Walsh had come from had no effect; his name had struck like a hammer blow.

"What the hell does he want? What did he say? It doesn't matter. He's an old man, Lys, probably getting a little dotty. He has to be retired by now. He was in charge of the investigation into Elizabeth's death."

"So he told me."

"Well, what did he want!"

"Calm down and I'll tell you. He's . . . not satisfied that her death was accidental."

"He's crazy."

"He didn't act like he was."

"The son of a bitch can't let go of it. Five years and he still can't. What did he say? What did he say?"

"If you'll stop interrupting—"

"What!"

"He seems to suspect—"

"What do you mean 'seems'? Don't try to soften it, tell me what the son of a bitch said. He doesn't think it was accidental, right? He thinks it was all planned. I arranged it so I could collect her insurance."

"Four hundred thousand dollars. You never told me."

"Why should I?"

"It's none of my business, you're right."

"Goddamn doddering old fool, he's got nothing better to do than dig into old files, closed cases. Did he happen to mention that in his report he stated it was, quote, 'clearly and unquestionably an accident'? His exact words. Drillon, the chief of detectives, accepted it, so did the insurance company. And they conducted their own investigation. They paid off without a murmur. Case closed. You know, there ought to be a law, some sort of protection, against pea-brained asses digging into old files."

"Closed files."

He stared. "Are you calling me a liar?"

The question surprised her, threw her slightly off balance. "I'm not calling you anything, I haven't the slightest idea what this is all about."

"Oh, come now, you're not deaf, you heard him. He told you everything—his version. I wonder if he showed up at the office asking for me before he went to see you. No, he wouldn't dare, I'd have tossed him out on his ass. He knows that. Somehow he must have found out I was out of town. And made a beeline for you, hoping he could wheedle information out of you."

"What could I possibly tell him?"

"Who knows? Who knows how the son of a bitch's mind works?"

"Will you stop shouting?"

"He was on a goddamned fishing expedition."

"I realized that ten seconds after he started talking."

He was pacing, he was furious. He astonished her. He spun around.

"What did you tell him?"

"What in the world could I? What do I know about any of it?"

"He obviously thinks I told you about it, he hoped I did. Where is he now?"

"How should I know? Gone back to Atlanta, I assume. He didn't let me in on his travel plans, okay?"

He stood gaping at her. "I'm sorry, none of this is your fault; here I am sounding off at you like all of it is. It's just . . . upsetting. I hate it when my thoughts go back to then. Everybody's got black memories, and that's my blackest. But having some son of a bitch come to town and throw it at *you* is intolerable. He's lucky he didn't approach me, I wouldn't have thrown him out, I probably would have knocked his head off, the son of a bitch!"

"He's probably gone back."

"I doubt it. He's got nothing but time and a fat pension. Oh, he won't come to see me, at least not right away. He'll want to see you again."

"Why should he bother? He knows now I don't know anything about it. Why come back?"

"You don't know him, he's not exactly brilliant, he's a plodder, but he's like a damned bulldog. He's got his teeth back into it and won't let go, you watch. He's strictly on his own, he's got to be. That's the one thing that worries me—he's got nobody to answer to. Well, I'll be damned if I'll let him get away with hounding me, harassing me. . . ."

"He's not."

"I'd like to know what you call it!"

"Derrick, don't shout. Look, here's an idea. Why not call his superior, tell him what's going on . . . ?"

"Forget it, Drillon has no authority over him, not anymore. I know—ask him to talk to him, off the record. Believe me, even if he agreed to, it'd go in one ear and out the other."

"He's really got you worried, doesn't he?"

"What's that supposed to mean?"

She raised her voice. "It means he's got you worried. Or you wouldn't be getting so exercised."

"Exercised, my ass, I'm goddamned mad! How would you like it if somebody turned up and reopened one of your old wounds?"

"Are we going to carry on about it for the next six hours? Through dinner?"

"No. Look, do this. If he comes back, don't talk to him. Just tell him to leave you alone. Tell him in no uncertain terms."

"I'd already planned to."

His smile came back, he appeared to relax. "Good." He held her and kissed her. "And if you like, we'll sit down and I'll tell you the whole story. Exactly as it happened, not his twisted version."

"You don't have to. It's in the past, let's leave it there."

"Good thinking. I'm going to lie down a couple hours, okay? If anybody phones, don't wake me."

She tucked him in and stood over him, watching him fall asleep. He did so in seconds. What a gift . . . She fussed with the covers, kissed him lightly on the forehead, and went out. Standing on the terrace watching the sun descend over the airport, turning from copper to vivid crimson, she thought about Walsh: his red face, his baggy suit, his apologetic air, shuffling walk. It made no sense whatsoever for him to come back. He'd struck out with her, why try a second time? The discussion with Derrick was over, *she* wouldn't resume it. Nor would he.

He'd been furious. Was he really, or was it a mask for his fear?

"Fear? What does he have to be afraid of?"

~~~~ SEVEN ~~~~

She got to the store ten minutes late Monday morning. For good reason, Derrick wanted to stay an extra hour in bed. He seemed to be deservedly reveling in his triumph in Seattle, and something of a flair for the theatrical urged him to show up at work a little late, thereby keeping Reggie and everyone else on tenterhooks, awaiting his report.

Agnes met her at the door. "You've got a visitor. He's in the office."

"Not . . ."

"I'm afraid so, dear heart. He was draped against the front door when Jenny and I opened up. He looks like a detective. Is he? Are you going to tell me what this is all about?"

"I'm beginning to wish I knew myself. Damn, I'm really not in the mood. Maybe you'd better send one of the girls out to find a policeman."

"Lyssa, what's going on? You know you'll tell me sooner or later, you might as well make it right now."

"I'll tell you after I get rid of him, I promise."

They stepped apart to let a customer enter. "You'd better," said Agnes.

"On second thought, never mind the police. I can handle him."

She went through to the office. Ellie and Jenny stared her all the way to the rear door. He was sitting in the visitor's chair with his hat on his lap, looking like an elderly job applicant. He was chewing gum, but there was a cigarette stub in the ashtray and the place smelled of smoke. He stood up, she could hear his joints cracking.

"Morning, Mrs. Morgan, please forgive me for barging in again, but there's noplace else to wait, isn't that so?"

"Mr. Walsh, I don't want to be rude, but I honestly don't think we have anything further to talk about."

"That's right, but there are a couple loose ends I figured might interest you."

"I really don't see how they could, I've no part in any of it."

"That's true. I just, well, would you mind telling me how your husband reacted when you told him we'd gotten together? I know he's back in town, due back Saturday, wasn't he? So, was he upset?"

"Would it surprise you to hear I didn't even mention it to him?" she asked coldly.

He was eyeing her steadily; he looked to be assessing her. Evaluating her honesty? Could he believe what she told him?

"You'd rather not say, I understand."

"If that's all . . ."

"That's it." He started for the door. "Have a nice day." He took one step out, paused, and turned around. "One last thing you might find interesting. Might interest him." He came back in and leaned against the jamb. "Since last we spoke, I've been doing a lot of thinking. You know how sometimes when you're wrestling with a problem, it's a good idea to drop it, step back, and look at it from a whole different angle?"

"Mr. Walsh . . ."

"I'm going, I'm going, just let me finish. That's what I did, and wouldn't you know it, I got a flash. I said to myself maybe I'm going about this all wrong, maybe it's not your husband I should be thinking about, but that other fellow. The driver. You notice I don't say drunk driver because I'll give you a hundred to one he was cold sober. Tossing that empty whiskey bottle out was the clincher. It was supposed to be a dead giveaway he was drunk, that and the way your husband says he drove away, weaving up the road. But if you really are driving drunk, you don't advertise it by throwing a bottle out.

"No, he's the one I should be looking for. Your husband didn't catch his plate number, which in itself is kind of strange, wouldn't you say? If somebody smashed into me and drove away, the first thing I'd look for would be their license plate. Anyway, I'm going home and check on that car of his. I don't know the plate, I don't even know the make, but there had to be damage to his car. Which means he either had to ditch it or get it repaired. This is really something I should have done five years ago, check all the auto-repair shops. But, of course, I had no reason to suspect everything wasn't as cut-and-dried as your husband described it in his statement. Well, good-bye again and thanks for your cooperation. Have a nice day."

She closed the door and perched on the corner of the desk. The first thought to cross her mind was a question: should she tell Derrick? She hesitated to, it would only lead to another outburst like the first one; to no purpose, other than to let off his steam. And why worry him needlessly?

On the other hand, did she have the right to keep it to herself? She'd never dreamed of deceiving him in anything before; he played straight with her. Oh, they kept little secrets, perhaps, what marrieds didn't? Only nothing approaching the seriousness of this. Still, deceitful though it might be of her, she was actually protecting him, although if he found out, he might not see it that way. Agnes came back.

"Shut the door," said Lyssa. "What I'm going to tell you is really none of your business. But not mine either. The only reason I'm telling you is because we're best friends. I can trust you not to breathe a word to anybody, not even your mother."

"You know I won't."

"Also, if I don't tell you, you won't let up on me till I do."

"You do understand me."

She told her everything. Agnes listened without comment, but when Lyssa was done, she began shaking her head.

"What?"

"He's got no right poking into it as a private citizen. You could have him arrested."

"I don't care about that," said Lyssa.

"You should, we're talking about Derrick here."

"One thing that bothers me, really gets to me, is that Walsh is so damned civilized about it. He isn't certain of anything and as good as admits it. He's going on gut instinct, but going on. What it seems to come down to is he's bound and determined not to carry his suspicions to the grave. It's a king-size loose end for him he desperately wants to tie up."

"Can I tell you what I'd do if I were you? If I were Derrick?"

"Please . . ."

"I'd forget about it. The poor old bugger's full of prunes; he'll go back to Atlanta and dig and dig and find nothing and eventually give it up. I think his problem is he's the one who put the official seal of exoneration on the whole affair back when, and if, by some million-to-one chance, it turns out he screwed up, that's bad. But even worse is if somebody else finds he did. It's the old male ego under the gun, dear heart."

"I never thought of it like that. Still, if he wasn't onto something concrete, why bother pursuing it? No, he's got to have more than a tick under his skin. He spent his own money to fly up from Atlanta, money for a hotel, all his expenses."

"So he's got nothing better to do with his pension. Something else might be driving him—once a detective always a detective, right? He may be officially retired, but in the kingdom of his pride he'll never be off the force. In his imagination he no doubt goes to work every day like he did the past thirty years."

"You think I should tell Derrick about seeing him again?"

"You better. If his nibs ever connects with Derrick and offhandedly mentions it . . ."

"Right. Damn . . ."

An insistent knock rattled the door. It was Ellie Hagen. She looked flustered, besieged.

"We're drawing a crowd, could one of you VIPs give us peons a hand?"

Agnes started out, Lyssa followed but stopped. An opened matchbook lying by the ashtray caught her eye. It advertised Harold's Barbecue on McDonough Boulevard: "Atlanta, GA." Inside the cover a name, address, and phone number had been neatly written in pencil: Gail Warrener Horvath. 13739 Collier Drive, Atlanta. Tel: 1-404-555-6109.

"You coming?" Agnes called, and came back a couple steps. "Whatcha got?"

"He left this." She stuck it in the pocket of her skirt.

"Since when do you collect match folders?"

Lyssa didn't respond. They went out.

~~~ EIGHT ~~~

"Did he show up again?"

She hesitated before answering, barely a second, but sufficiently long to give him his answer. She'd expected him to ask the moment he walked in the door and debated whether she should lie, deny Walsh had come a second time. But of course her expression would have said she was fibbing. And what would be the point of lying?

He had walked in in a good mood, smiling, singing to himself, kissing her affectionately, if too loudly. His smile vanished.

"Son of a bitch . . ."

"Derrick, don't start that again. You really are over-reacting."

He tossed his attaché case on the sofa. "What did he say this time? What reason did he give you for coming back? What did he look like? How did he seem? I mean, was he uncomfortable? Nervous? Did he make you think he realized he was pestering you? Did he—"

"Please! One question at a time. Better, no questions. He was in, he was out. We 'covered' only two things. He asked how you reacted when I told you he'd shown up. I told him I hadn't even mentioned it to you."

"Did he buy it? Of course not. He's no genius, but he's not stupid."

"He asked, I didn't tell him a thing. I figured he was fishing as usual and it was none of his business."

"Good, good; you said two things."

"He said just before he left—I practically threw him

out—he said he'd come to the conclusion he'd been following the wrong tack. That what he should be doing is trying to find the drunk driver."

"Wonderful! Brilliant! What an idiot. He had his chance to find the guy, the whole police force did; stupid rednecks couldn't find their pockets with their hands. He thinks now, after five years, he'll have better luck?"

His expression struck her as intriguing; almost as if he *knew* where Elizabeth's killer had gotten to; better yet, knew he was dead. The only way anyone could find him would be with a shovel, for all the good it would do them.

"So that's that," she said. "He comes to town, has his say, and off he goes."

"Did he say that? Did he tell you he's heading back to Atlanta?"

"As good as. Why would he hang around here? The only reason he came was to talk to us."

"To you. Behind my back."

"I couldn't help him any. I wouldn't if I could."

He had taken her in his arms and was gazing into her eyes. He stiffened.

"What is that supposed to mean?"

"It means, obviously, I'm loyal to my husband."

"I guess. . . . It just sounded like you had some . . . some doubts about me. For the last time, sweetheart, I didn't kill Elizabeth."

"I know that!"

"You don't, you don't know anything about what happened. You have to take my word for it. The thing is, the Metropolitan Atlanta Police Department, the insurance company, and everybody else concerned believed me."

"*I* believe you, okay? What must I do to convince you—stick my arm in fire? You want me to swear on the Bible?"

"I'm sorry. It's him, Walsh. He upsets the hell out of me."

"Why should he? Why do you let him? Let's make a pact. Let's forget about him, never mention his name again from now on. We must have more important things to talk about. Like what would you like for dinner?"

"How about we eat out?"

"We did Saturday."

"So? We're city folk, we're supposed to eat out six nights a week. I've got it, let's go to Blackie's over on Hauser Street and fill up on hot dogs and their homemade relish. I loooove their homemade relish!"

"I don't know, all that saturated fat, cholesterol . . . all those calories."

"Come on, you've got to fall off the health wagon once in a while, to keep your sanity."

"Okay, okay, but I'll limit myself to two."

"I promise I won't eat any more than six . . . eight."

"Pig!"

And just like that Walsh and the accident were dispatched from both their minds. They took the elevator down. Otto flagged a cab for them.

"Blackie's Hot Dogs on Hauser Street," said Derrick to the Asian driver. He could have been Vietnamese, Thai, Chinese. She ran through the countries in Southeast Asia. He had beautiful teeth, flashing black eyes, and skin like ivory.

They settled back.

"Oh . . ." said Derrick. "I almost forgot, I've got to run back to Seattle."

"Oh no . . ."

"Wednesday, just overnight. A couple little glitches in the deal."

"Can't you iron them out over the phone?"

"Afraid not. It's the operating tables. We can't deliver the exact specs we touted. What we can give them are just as good, even better in some ways, but I'm going to have to sit down with them and explain in detail. It's a big, big deal for us, sweetheart, I'd hate to see it fall through because I was too lazy to run back out there. Reggie wouldn't like that. Can you blame him?"

"Overnight."

"Wednesday night, back Thursday afternoon. I'll take a cab from the airport to the store."

Traffic was the tail end of the rush hour, unusually heavy. The driver had to honk his way toward Blackie's. They sat in silence watching him slip skillfully in and out of line, pushing to get them there as quickly as possible. She wasn't that hungry, not for hot dogs. The man was a superb driver. Derrick began whispering, "He's good, he's good." She paid little attention, her thoughts elsewhere, back on Joseph Walsh and the matchbook with Elizabeth's sister's address and phone number on the inside cover. Walsh had left the thing deliberately, of course, even to leaving it open so she had to see the writing. He knew she despised smoking, knew she'd clean up after him. What was he doing but asking her to check his opinions for herself. Don't believe him, ask Gail Horvath. Talk to her, see what she has to say.

Coming home from work, she had taken out the matchbook, rereading the writing inside and squirreling it away in her jewelry box, under a pile of pins and broaches. She could telephone Mrs. Horvath, introduce herself, talk to her, but that would be terrifically awkward. The situation was much too involved to discuss over the phone. She had to sit down with her.

Sit down? Fly all the way to Atlanta just to talk to a perfect stranger about an old man's suspicions? Ridiculous. What was she thinking? And how deceitful could she get? He flies off to Seattle, she sneaks down to Atlanta; for what, to satisfy her curiosity? No, it was much more than that: to dispel her doubt. For doubt she had, despite her love for Derrick, and her loyalty. Or was it suspicion?

If only he hadn't reacted so when she first told him about meeting with Walsh. He all but went berserk, cursing like a stevedore, carrying on all out of proportion to the situation. And insisting he behaved so only because he was so angry with the detective for sticking his nose back into his life.

Only then, as just now when he walked in the door, it wasn't indignation he'd displayed; it was fear. There was no other word to describe the look in his eyes. They all but shouted, "Oh my God, it's dead and buried, now he's going to dig it up and poke and probe until he comes up with the truth and it all blows up in my face!" She glanced sidelong at him. He sat slightly hunched forward watching the driver, evidently fascinated by his skills. Derrick felt her eyes, looked her way.

"What's the matter?" he asked.

"Nothing, nothing . . ."

"Two nothings always means something, sweetheart. You're not still thinking about Walsh, are you?"

"No."

"It was your idea to blot him out permanently. I have already. He's probably back in Atlanta by now."

"I'm sure he is. We'll never see him again."

"Never. Driver, if you take a right up ahead, we can come around one block over from Hauser near Blackie's. We can get out there and walk over."

"Yessir, yessir."

~~~~ NINE ~~~~

A woman constructed along the lines of a refrigerator, flaunting a fortune in jewelry and an unimpressive face too heavily made up, came pounding into L'Image, making straight for a preppy-looking plaid pantsuit in silk and viscose blend, with matching trench coat. Perfect for a woman half her age.

"That's my color," she shrilled, for the whole store to hear. "That's me."

Pantsuit and trench coat were in dove gray and may well have been "her color" but the suit on her would make her look like an overstuffed banker and Lyssa couldn't come within six sizes of her size. Women of her dimensions generally didn't patronize L'Image. The situation called for tact and diplomacy in large quantities, with generous lacings of kindliness and sensitivity.

"Do you have it in eighteen?" the woman asked.

One look confirmed that she'd have difficulty squeezing into a twenty-two and would end up retreating to Bailey's, a shop down the street offering some perfectly lovely outfits for women too girthy for designer fashions.

Lyssa's mind whirled. She hadn't a stitch in the shop in a twenty, let alone refrigerator size. Jenny had just finished at the cash register. She looked up from behind the woman and leered impishly. The phone rang.

"Excuse me," said Lyssa, "that's long distance for me. Would you mind if I turn you over to Ms. Mosconi? Jenny? Ms. Mosconi is our pantsuit expert."

Jenny's face almost made a sound as it fell; she muttered, glared, relieved Lyssa. Ellie had answered the phone. Lyssa marched by her without looking, straight to the rear and the office. Agnes was at the desk going over purchase orders. Ellie did not buzz back for Lyssa.

"We should think about getting in some of those Alaïa sunsuits," said Agnes. "You know, the ones in cotton piqué? They'll sell like crazy."

"It's a little early, isn't it?"

"Lys, I know that outfit. Everything they make flies off the hangers. They'll run out of stock in sunsuits by May fifteenth. We shouldn't wait."

"Do what you think best."

Lyssa plumped down into the visitor's chair. Sight of

the ashtray, cleaned of the single stub left by Walsh, reminded her. She glanced behind her, got up, locked the door. Agnes continued poring over the purchase orders, her granny glasses in imminent danger of falling off, so far down her nose had they slid.

"Stop for a second," said Lyssa.

She told her about the significance of the matchbook, about Gail Warrener Horvath and Derrick's overnight trip to Seattle.

"You're dying to talk to her," said Agnes.

"Hardly dying . . ."

"You should see your face. So what's the holdup? Go buy a ticket, fly to Atlanta."

"It's just that it could wipe the slate clean, clear up everything. I might even be able to check up on Walsh. He could be a flake, he could have Alzheimer's. He could be retired because he's lost it completely."

"He could also be what he says he is. And right on target."

"You think I should go?"

"*You* obviously do."

"Derrick's plane is eight forty-five Wednesday morning. I could catch a flight to Atlanta probably an hour or so after. Only if I do sit down with her *and* try to check up on him, it might take me a couple days, maybe even three. Derrick'll be home . . ."

"Leave it to me, I'll tell him you went t'o New York on a buying trip. Suddenlike. You'll be back . . . whenever you say."

Lyssa sucked in breath between her teeth. "I hate this, lying, sneaking down there behind his back."

"Hold everything, dear heart, that's totally the wrong attitude. You want to clear this up once and for all, the only way is to beard the lions in their dens. Or something. You'll never have another good night's sleep if you don't go. Besides, I'm dying to know if you'll find out anything."

"It's no joke!"

"I'm sorry, of course not."

"You're right, though, it looks like the only way I'll ever get back peace of mind about the damned thing. Only I do hate playing into Walsh's hands. It's almost like following his orders—he leaves her name and address and knows damned well I can't ignore it."

"So are you going?"

"I guess."

"Lys, I'll be honest, I really don't see it as being deceitful. You want to find out for his sake as well as your own, don't you?"

"That's rationalizing and you know it."

"Are you going?"

"I said I was, didn't I? When he gets back from Seattle, he'll be coming straight here."

"If you're not back, I'll tell him you're in New York, simple."

"I'll call you from Atlanta and tell you when I'm coming in. Aggie, you haven't told anybody about this, have you?"

"My orders were to keep my trap shut. To hear is to obey."

"I love you. You're a real friend."

"Yeah, well, your 'real friend' has a lot to do. Would you mind getting out of here?"

"I can't." She told her about the refrigerator. "If I show my face out there, Jenny'll jump on me. In retaliation. Give me five more minutes, she'll finish up and send her customer off happy. You know, she's a genius at letting people down."

The sun came up blazing and beautiful, in a rush to chase the coolness of the night. It promised an unseasonably warm day before the beginning of spring: clear skies, a gentle, friendly breeze, an early sampling of all the similar days to come. It was 7:45. She stood on the terrace looking down, watching the night doorman in his last hour hold the limousine door for Derrick. He looked up and waved and ducked into the car. Off it went.

Leaving her feeling rotten, riddled with guilt. To hell with Atlanta, with Walsh and Gail Warrener Horvath, the whole affair. How could she even think of going down there?

She had her ticket and boarding pass. Her plane was at 11:14, arrival Atlanta 3:18. She had intended to phone Mrs. Horvath, set up an appointment. Agnes had a better idea.

"Send her a wire instead. If she has anything to tell you, she'll be ready and waiting for you. Pacing the floor for the doorbell to ring. Plenty of time to call her when you get in."

Lyssa took her advice. Only now, suddenly, watching the limo vanish around the corner she felt torn. Traitorous. A Judas.

If you don't go this time, you'll go next time he goes away.

"Oh, shut up, Aggie!"

She turned from the railing, leaning against it, arms folded, and thinking. The trouble was Agnes could be right. The idea of following through, flying down there, was producing a highly effective stimulus to her curiosity. It was rapidly approaching a point where she *had* to know. And yet the whole business seemed so outrageously farfetched. Derrick arrange his wife's murder? For her insurance? It was the stuff sinister, sneaky, duplicitous men got involved in, not trustworthy, reliable, devoted husbands. Reggie might do it, but not Derrick. Impossible. Unbelievable.

"So why go to Atlanta?"

Getting on to eight o'clock. She should be at the airport by ten. She'd never been to Atlanta. She'd go, do what she had to, return home. Bringing what? A guilty feeling in place of the suspicion Walsh had injected in her mind? Harsh word, suspicion, only what else could you call it?

~~~~ TEN ~~~~

She didn't firm up her plans for Atlanta until she was on the plane. She thought briefly about inspecting Peachtree Street, reputedly the Fifth Avenue of the south, but this was no pleasure trip. She'd stick to her schedule, which started with checking into the Omni International Hotel. After settling in, she'd call Gail Horvath and hopefully set up a convenient time to get together. Meeting with her was the principal reason she'd come down, getting together with Walsh of secondary importance; perhaps she wouldn't bother with him, although it pretty much depended on what Horvath had to say. Would she support his allegations? Had they talked? Was she bitter toward Derrick over her sister's death? Prejudiced against him? Lyssa'd be able to tell sixty seconds into the conversation.

She crossed her fingers that Horvath would be available that evening. And perhaps, before they got together, she could get over to the *Atlanta Constitution,* research the newspaper coverage of the accident and subsequent investigation, familiarize herself with the facts uncolored by Walsh's interpretation of them. Good idea—it would help her keep Horvath's opinions in perspective as well.

The taxi from the airport to the Omni International was eighteen dollars. She was given a room on the fifteenth floor. She unpacked and sat down with the phone directory; it was getting on to 4:30. Horvath's address and phone number duplicated that which was inside the matchbook cover. She dialed the number. A soft, mellow, slightly southern accent came on.

"Mrs. Horvath? My name is Lyssa Morgan, Mrs. Derrick Morgan. I just arrived in town, and I know this is presumptuous of me, a total stranger, but I'd very much like to talk to you. If it's convenient."

"Derrick Morgan . . . Dear Derrick. How is he? Healthy? Happy? Successful? Dear, dear Derrick. Oh, I did get your telegram."

The bitterness fairly erupted, even though there wasn't the slightest change in tone, not that she could detect. Did she imagine the woman was bitter?

"Could we get together?" Lyssa asked.

"And talk about Derrick? Anytime, my dear. I'd love nothing better. How about dinner this evening?"

"Good, fine. On me."

"Oh no, my pleasure. This is going to be fun. What say to, let's see, how about the dining room at the Ritz-Carleton? On Peachtree Road? Not Peachtree Street. Visitors do get confused. Their food is fabulous and I haven't been there in absolute ages. Is eight o'clock okay? Eight. I'll probably be a few minutes late, I usually am—fashionably so. Derrick, Derrick, oh, this'll be great fun, fantastic! See you . . ."

"Lyssa."

"Of course. Bye for now."

She hung up. Lyssa sat holding the phone, staring at the six holes in the earpiece. Interesting. Gail Warrener Horvath was dying to talk to her. To contribute? Or pick her brain . . .

She freshened up and caught a cab to the offices of the *Atlanta Constitution*. Back issues of the paper were preserved on microfilm. A fluttery, ill-kempt, but gracious elderly lady explained how to use the machine and presently the roll Lyssa'd selected was spinning its way to the first news coverage of the accident: Sunday, December 18, 1988. It described the site, what happened—according to Derrick, the sole available eyewitness—and quoted the chief of police as saying the search for Elizabeth Morgan's hit-and-run killer was under way. The follow-up items in the following week's papers added little information. Detective Joseph Walsh was in charge of the investigation. He evidently had little to say to the news media, no doubt because he uncovered so little. The unsuccessful search for the killer just seemed to peter out. The police went on to other things.

But one thing was clear: Walsh's theories were strictly his own invention. Nothing she could find, and she read every item, supported any of his suspicions. Would Gail Horvath? And if she did, would it be because she wanted to think badly of Derrick? Blame him for what happened? Or for not doing anything to prevent it? What could he possibly do?

If not especially productive, tonight's get-together at least promised to be interesting. Gail sounded flighty on the phone; would she turn out an airhead? Gossipy? With or without malice attached to it? Lyssa had detected an edge of bitterness in her tone or imagined she had. There was yet another possibility: did she like Derrick? More than like? Had she been jealous of her sister? And was she bitter now because the call and mention of his name swept her back five years, to what might have been and never was?

It was 6:40; she'd go back to the hotel, take a shower, call Aggie at home. No, Aggie could wait. She'd only promised to call to tell her when she was coming in. At the moment it appeared it could be tomorrow, she could get in before Derrick returned from Seattle.

Hopefully.

Gail Warrener Horvath was loaded. And very attractive, a blonde hovering around forty-five, slender, in superb physical shape, almost as well endowed as Doreen Carlyle, under her pearls. She wore a gold, emerald, and diamond bracelet that had to have cost a fortune. And a blouson, black with goldtone metallic lace and long black georgette pull-on skirt with a provocative side slit to show off her lovely leg. At the sight of her gushing Lyssa's name and reaching to hug her, Lyssa felt like a peasant, thinking either Gail was badly overdressed or she herself even more badly underdressed.

Gail didn't speak, she sang; her every utterance had a melody to it, even single words, all of the one-syllable ones, accorded a second syllable. The maître d' ushered them to their table. The wine steward materialized, a string quartet was playing Debussy's *La Mer*.

"This is a two-star restaurant bucking tirelessly for three," whispered Gail. "Last time I was here I had the sautéed oysters and the venison and they were heavenly. And the desserts are magnificent. I could eat the whole cart." She giggled. "And my aerobics instructor would hand me my head."

The southern accent came on heavier than over the phone, almost as if she felt obliged to show it off to the visiting Yankee. She ordered them a bottle of pouilly-fuissé, which she confessed she "just adored." Lyssa shunned both oysters and venison and decided on the fresh duck breast. Gail opted for a steak. She leaned toward Lyssa, reducing her voice to a whisper in the manner of a spy preparing to reveal state secrets.

"So you're the second Mrs. Morgan, isn't that exciting. How'd you meet him?"

"It wasn't exactly glorious or exotic; our carts bumped at the supermarket. We got to talking, we had coffee around the corner."

"He called you, you started going out, and voilà! Beautiful . . ."

"That was it."

Gail stared. "I don't blame him, you're lovely. Is he still beautiful? Of course he would be, it's only been five years, he's not one to let himself go. None of the pretty ones do. Are you famished? I am. Let's order."

"Ready when you are."

"Are you a garden clubber? Bridge? Tennis? Do you *do* anything, I mean like actual work? I don't. I do, but not eight hours a day. Don't have to, Mr. Horvath is very well off, so I work on all sorts of charities, balls, fashion shows, auctions, so forth. Noblesse oblige, you know. But I love it. Lizzie and I grew up dirt poor outside of Savannah. A little town you never heard of—Thunderbolt. Daddy raised tobacco; he was awful at it, world's worst businessman, but you don't want to hear about that."

"I wanted to talk about the accident."

" 'Accident'—that's what the newspapers called it. I called it then, I call it now, a stroke of genius. I really must preface all this so you'll know what direction I'm coming from. Lizzie and I were sisters, but about as far apart as Catoosa from Camden County. One's way up in the northwest corner of the state, the other's down next to Florida. Funny how it is with sisters, each of us could get along with Beelzebub himself but not with each other, not since day one. Mind you, we were almost ten years apart, which doesn't make it easy, and we didn't hate each other. At least I didn't hate her; I'm not so sure what she felt. We just disliked one another so intensely, if we were in the same room you could hear a ringing sound. But you don't want to hear about that."

Their entrees arrived.

"Can I ask, do you know a Detective Joseph Walsh?"

"Ex-detective. Oh, you bet we've talked. He thinks Derrick 'arranged' Lizzie's death. Hired that man to smash into the side of their car and kill her. For the insurance money."

"Four hundred thousand dollars."

"Derrick drugged her, she passed out in the car, he stopped at that stop sign, and boom. They say that car hit theirs so hard it drove it sidewise clear across the road half into the ditch on the other side. And if that didn't kill her—broke her neck, so they said at the inquest—

he, Derrick, could have broken it for her, with nobody the wiser."

"Do you think he did?"

"For four hundred thousand? You better believe it. How's your duck? It looks tender. I don't much like duck, I can't handle the grease. I've got a very delicate tummy."

"So you agree with Walsh."

"I'll say this—I always thought there was something fishy about the whole affair. Something strange. Mostly because Derrick never caught the license plate of the car that hit them, couldn't even identify the make. He claimed it all happened so fast. Of course, after he hit them, the driver turned left, speeding off back down Boulevard Road, the way they'd come. So he was behind them and Derrick was fussing over her, so he claimed, and would have had to turn around to get the plate number. Still, if it was me, I would have. Would you? Yes, you would."

"How was their relationship?"

"Now, right there you've got me. I really couldn't honestly say, on account Lizzie and I never saw each other, never talked on the phone. Mr. Horvath and I went to the wedding with Mama. Daddy'd been dead almost ten years. Mama died about six months after the wedding. I'd put her in a nursing home in Savannah, where she had old friends. She died of a stroke. But you don't want to hear about that. What I'm saying is Lizzie and I saw each other for the last time at her wedding. We both thought it was better that way. To this day I can't fathom why she even sent us an invitation. We agreed it was better we give each other a wide berth. We had nothing in common, no interest in getting together. Even when Mama died, the lawyers handled everything, Lizzie and I didn't see each other. To answer your question, I have no idea what their relationship was."

"Where did the four-hundred-thousand-dollar life-insurance policy come from?"

"Lizzie insured herself. She was in the insurance business and she thought life insurance was very important. She was carrying it before she met him. She got it for a great price, being in the business and all. She didn't tell me, Mama did. I gather she quit her job shortly after they were married. I don't know, I'm guessing. Like I say, we had noooo contact. You know something, we didn't even exchange Christmas cards; sisters, can you imagine? But you don't want to hear about that."

"Let me get this straight, you really, honestly believe he arranged to have her killed for the insurance."

"I do, just as much as Joseph does."

"And you're not bitter toward Derrick?"

"Good point. You know the dry white wine the chef uses really makes that duck. It's his secret."

"It's delicious."

"I can't be bitter. I couldn't like her, but I wouldn't wish her dead, that's unchristian. But I'd have to be a five-star hypocrite to hold a grudge against him."

This so astonished Lyssa she started, nearly dropping her fork in her plate.

"You don't think so?" Gail asked.

"It's not for me to say, it's a very . . . personal thing."

"Oh, I'm not pleased he did it; I didn't sit down and write him a thank-you note. That sounds downright vicious, doesn't it? Cold as January ice. No, it's more I suspect he did it, but being as I can't prove it any more than Joseph can, I'm inclined to let it go at that. Do you carry a big life-insurance policy? I don't mean to be nosy . . ."

"No, no. Actually, I'm surprised you didn't ask me before. Half a million."

"That's not small."

"My partner and I are both insured for that amount."

"You're in business?"

She told her about L'Image and Agnes Pelletier.

"Sounds like my type of shop. And Derrick's the beneficiary?"

"Yes. Of course, he's doing very well for himself; extremely well."

Lyssa began telling her about his success at Cambridge and how the company had grown over the past three years.

In an uptown apartment, a man in his early sixties sat with thread in one hand, needle in the other, his bifocals perched near the end of his nose, his lips bunched in concentration, a sober expression gripping his features. Moistening the end of the thread and flattening it between his nails, he guided it expertly through the needle's eye and deftly knotted the thread ends. The topmost button in a row of four at the front of his most expensive and favorite light woolen sweater was missing. He began affixing its replacement, a round, knotted-leather button.

The apartment surrounding him was small: two rooms, kitchenette, bath. Time had left it behind. The man worked by the light of a tassel-fringed floor lamp, of the type unseen in furniture stores for more than half a century. The other furnishings were just as outdated: a sofa that had been secondhand thirty years before; the easy chair he sat in, so old the odor of leather had long ago abandoned it. Books everywhere: dozens, scores of Irish novelists and poets and playwrights predominating. On a mahogany sideboard sat framed photographs of two stern-looking policemen in uniform separated by a picture of a woman in a cracked walnut frame. The curl in her hair and her small, penetrating eyes resembled the sewer's. Four departmental citations were mounted on a red-velvet-covered board displayed to one side of the pictures. The rug was threadbare. The front room and bedroom were separated by an amber-beaded curtain; the bed was unmade. Above the headboard a large crucifix was attached to the wall, all but lost from view in the gaudily flowered wallpaper. To the left of the front room was the bathroom, the door open. A small gateleg table serving as a liquor station stood to the left of the door. On the kitchenette stove sat a simmering pan of canned vegetable soup.

Around and around the thread joining button to material, the man wound the remaining thread; he then pushed the needle through two more times to secure the button and bit free the needle. He held up the sweater to examine his handiwork. Good job, correctly positioned, no binding, nothing to distinguish the new button from those below it. He stood up, removed his vest, replaced it with the sweater and, double-checking to make sure the thread was slotted in the groove at the edge of its spool, restored the spool, the needle stuck in it, to the cookie tin in which he kept his sewing essentials.

In the kitchen he turned off the gas and poured about half the soup into a large cup. Tasting it, he decided it needed pepper—no salt—and shook in a few grains. He was enjoying his soup, looking out the window at two starlings flitting about outside, thinking he should replenish the supply of breadcrumbs he kept on the outside sill for the birds, when a knock sounded at his door. He straightened, listened, to make sure he hadn't imagine it. The knock was repeated. He wiped his mouth with his napkin and, bringing his soup with him, went to the door.

"It's me, Joe," said a muffled voice. "Gerry Connolly, from the second floor."

"Just a sec . . ."

He unlocked and unbolted the door and swung it wide, smiling a greeting. His visitor burst in, pushing him backward, setting his soup sloshing, spilling, and slammed the door behind him.

"What the . . . You're not Ger—"

"Shut up."

"You!"

"You recognize me? Good for you."

Up came his visitor's right hand, in it a gun with a screwed-on silencer. The older man blanched, the tip of his tongue finding his upper lip; he began trembling.

"Wait. . . ."

"I've been waiting, time's run out."

The older man's eyes grew huge, he fought to breathe, he turned to flee the deadly black eye confronting him; the other laughed and fired. The second slug followed the first into the back of the man's head, tunneling, mashing his brain; he fell heavily and lay still. His murderer rolled him over with his foot. The dead eyes stared straight upward. The murderer cast about, spied the open bathroom door, went in, straightened his mustache at the mirror, pulled the brim of his felt hat lower, and went out.

In the dining room at the Ritz-Carleton, Buckhead, a few blocks away, Lyssa and Gail were still discussing Derrick.

"Getting back to insurance," said Lyssa, "believe me, he's not interested in mine. If he died, I'd get twice as much as L'Image is carrying on me."

Gail shrugged. "You know best. Just the same, I do think he killed her for hers. I really believe that, and not because Joseph does."

Up to now she had been very open, very candid. Lyssa felt obliged to tell her everything: about Walsh's visit to Bellingham, their two conversations; she got out the matchbook and showed her the inside cover.

"That sneaky devil. He wants you to be number three in the worst way."

"Number . . . ?"

"In our little club, don't you see? You, me, him. Wait, wait, are you going to pack up and leave Atlanta worried stiff your life is in danger? Because of what I've said? You really shouldn't. You and Derrick are happy, aren't you?"

"Very. But so were he and Elizabeth."

"Could be. I wish I knew for certain. It could be he despised her. Only was smart enough not to show it in public. I shouldn't speak ill of the dead, specially my own sister, but she wasn't easy to like. If you really want to know, she was a bitch on wheels. I have never, I mean never, seen a human being throw a tantrum like she could when she didn't get her way. From the time she was able to walk. I mean—but you don't want to hear about that. Are you going to have dessert? I am."

She signaled for the dessert cart but, despite the praise she'd heaped on it, didn't find anything appealing and ordered crepes with pears.

"I'll hate myself in the morning for the calories," she sang, "but you only live once. You sure don't have any weight problem. Do you work out? I go to aerobics five days a week and eat like a bird at home. This is a treat for me, so I go all out. I have to be careful, though, I go to so many affairs, fund-raisers, you know, but you don't want to hear about that."

What Lyssa had wanted to hear about she'd heard. Interesting, even fascinating, but classifiable only as suspicion; it was almost as if Walsh and she were feeding off each other, sharing the same suspicions. She glanced at Gail's watch: 9:45. Too late to go and see Walsh? Maybe not; if she saw him tonight, she'd be able to get a morning flight home. Still, why bother looking him up? He'd likely told her everything he knew, thought he knew.

Go see him; she just might get him to open up a bit more. Gail insisted on paying for dinner. They stood on the sidewalk.

"Can I drop you at your hotel?" she asked.

"Thanks just the same, I think I'll walk back."

"It'll take you at least half an hour."

"It's okay, I like walking. I'll probably be heading home tomorrow. I'd like to see a little of the city."

"Loveliest city in the south, Scarlett."

The doorman beckoned the cab at the head of the curb line for her. Gail got in, rolled down the window. A siren sounded a few blocks away. She had to raise her voice.

"It's been a downright pleasure, Lyssa. If you ever get down again, do call."

"I will, I owe you a dinner."

"Nonsense. Give my love to Derrick." She giggled. "On second thought, better not."

Gail blew a kiss, waved, the cab pulled away. Back inside, Lyssa found a public phone. She looked up Walsh's number and was about to call him when she changed her mind. She double-checked his house number. He lived on Hunnicutt Street, off Spring. Outside, she got the next cab in the line and gave the driver the address. More sirens sounded on the way. Heading north, the driver passed Parker and turned onto Hunnicutt Street. The apartment house was about a third of the way up the block. There was a crowd out front, police cars, an ambulance. A TV mobile unit was coming in the opposite end, from Venable Street. Almost as soon as they turned into Hunnicutt, a cop came running up stopping the cab.

"You can't go through, buddy, you'll have to turn around."

"Jesus . . ."

"What's the problem, Officer?" Lyssa asked.

"No problem, ma'am. Just turn around and get out of here before you start blocking traffic," he added to the driver.

She tipped the driver generously, significantly reducing his annoyance, and got out, starting up the street.

"Where you think you're going?" the cop asked. He was young, full of himself, of the authority the situation imbued him with.

"I live up there," she said, nodding toward Walsh's building.

"Ah, you better talk to Captain Holland. That's him, the black fellow up there by the cruiser talking to the reporters."

"Why should I talk to him?"

"Please, just tell him you live there and you're going up to your apartment."

She hurried up to Holland. He was answering reporters' questions. He turned toward her, his eyes questioning. He looked beleaguered, the reporters continued firing questions.

"Captain, I live there . . ."

"Okay, but I'll have to ask you to wait a couple minutes before you go in. They'll be bringing the body down any second now, then you can go up."

"Body?"

"One of the tenants got shot. On the seventh floor." He paused. "You may know him—Mr. Walsh?"

She gasped. "I . . . yes . . ."

"Friend of yours?"

"A good friend. How . . ."

"I was just telling this bunch. We think when one of the other tenants came home, somebody must have walked in behind him or her. Went up to the seventh floor, Walsh opened the door. It's a holy mess up there. I'm sorry."

She nodded, backed away. The crowd was being kept clear of the front steps by policemen standing ten feet apart like storm troopers: legs spread, hands on hips, faces blank. The front doors opened. Two ambulance attendants brought out a gurney, the body covered, strapped to it. Descending to the sidewalk, they rolled it up to the police ambulance.

She turned and started back up the street the way she'd come.

~~~ ELEVEN ~~~

She slept fitfully; she had scarcely known the man, but it was a shock nevertheless. He'd been a detective a long time; somebody he'd put away had gotten out, gotten their revenge. Poor Joseph. The morning papers would be full of it, a cop killing was front-page news; she'd pick up whatever was available before heading out to the airport.

She left a call for 8:00 A.M., got up, showered, ordered up coffee and an English muffin. In her robe, her hair turbaned in a towel, she called the airline and got a 10:25 flight to Detroit, with an hour layover to Bellingham. The best the effeminate-sounding man at the other end could do. Breakfast arrived, she turned on the TV and sat. According to the *TV Guide* there was a one-hour local news show. The commercials ran and the cameras returned to the two newscasters, a pretty blonde and an apelike man with a hairline so low his forehead was all but nonexistent. The girl was speaking.

"Earlier in the newscast we reported the shooting of retired Detective First Grade Joseph Aloysius Walsh in his apartment on Hunnicutt Street last night. We have with us now Mr. Carl Hollings, who for twenty-six years was the police reporter on the *Georgian*. Mr. Hollings, you were a close friend of Detective Walsh's?"

Hollings was a small bird of a man, his jacket a size too large for him, an unsightly mole affixed to his naked scalp a few inches down from the point of it. He wore granny glasses and showed a single gold tooth among the gray natural ones. He sat hunched forward, as if he couldn't wait to speak.

"Joe and I knew each other for more than twenty years."

"The medical examiner's report noted that he'd been shot twice through the back of the head. In typical gangland fashion."

"I don't know about 'gangland'—Mafia fashion. Of course, killers with no connection to organized crime do like to emulate the Mob's hit men. It does at least look like a Mob execution."

"Can you recall, did Detective Walsh ever arrest any mafiosos?"

"He never had anything to do with the Mob. There's twenty-four families in the continental U.S. and the closest to Atlanta is nearly seven hundred miles from here, in Miami, the Trafficante family. Like I said, there's no shortage of people out there who like to imitate a Mob hit. But I have a theory on that."

"Let's hear it."

"Just a theory, mind you. I think his killer was somebody he put away who served his time, got out, and decided to get his revenge. But didn't kill him. To be technical, they executed him. The two in the back of the head. I'm sure the department is checking all his arrests and imprisonments, determining who'd gotten out over say the last year. They'll be picked up and questioned."

"You were his friend; what sort of man was Detective Walsh?"

"A good, loyal friend, a man who never went back on his word; not to me. Honest as the day is long. And tenacious. He never gave up on a case. He didn't solve 'em all—nobody does—but he had a damned fine batting average. He never did get the heavy-duty stuff, not to handle by himself. That's why I can tell you for certain he never brushed with the Mob. He had his share of murders, suspicious accidents, he was up to his elbows in blood for almost forty years. What I'd call a good detective—hardworking, thorough, tenacious. Boy, was he ever tenacious."

"Anything you'd like to add?"

"No, except I hope they get whoever did it. Anybody who shoots people in the back of the head, without even looking in their eyes, should be hung up by . . . A fine man, Joe, I'll miss him. Everybody who knew him will."

"Thank you, Mr. Hollings. Ladies and gentlemen, you've been listening to Carl Hollings, for a quarter of a century the police reporter on the *Atlanta Georgian,* discussing the death of his close friend Detective Joseph Aloysius Walsh, who was brutally—"

The phone was ringing, Lyssa turned off the TV.

"Lyssa? Gail Horvath. Did you hear?"

"Last night. But I didn't know until just now, on the TV news, that he was executed."

"By the Mafia."

"Or somebody imitating them," said Lyssa.

"The paper says it was somebody he arrested who was put away and got out. I don't believe it."

"Why not?"

"Wouldn't that be obvious? Who'd have a better motive?" Gail sounded convinced.

"You're thinking like a policeman, not somebody who's carrying a monumental grudge."

"I think it was the driver."

"Driver?" asked Lyssa.

"You know, the one who crashed into Derrick and Lizzie's car and killed her."

"That's"—she held back the word "ridiculous"—"a terrific stretch, Gail."

"You think?"

"It's wishful worry of the worst kind, really."

"Maybe, but I remember Joseph saying Lizzie's death was the only case he was digging back into. The only one."

Lyssa suddenly recalled Walsh's telling her the same thing. She had pointedly asked how many old cases he had dug back into, ten, twenty? He'd insisted Derrick and Elizabeth's was the only one.

"Lyssa?"

"I'm still here."

"So you think I'm wrong."

"I'm afraid so. Think about it. Walsh was getting nowhere. That's certainly the impression he gave me."

"Me, too."

"He had nothing to go on, evidently no way to locate the driver. No cooperation from the department, from the insurance company. Sooner or later, no matter how tenacious he may have been, he'd have no choice but to give up on it. It's not as if he was on to something or close to something and the killer had to stop him. I mean the driver."

"But that's just it, we don't know. He was very crafty, very good at asking questions, not good at all at answering them. Who knows what he had?"

"I can't make the connection, Gail, I really can't."

"I guess. When's your flight?"

"Less than an hour and a half. I'd better get a move on, I'm not even dressed."

"I'll let you go. I hope we see each other again, it was fun."

"It was and thanks again for dinner. I owe you."

"Bushwah." Gail giggled, hung up.

There was nothing much of substance in any of the three papers. She bought the *Constitution* and the *Journal* at the lobby shop and picked up the *Georgian* at the airport. All the way to Detroit she thought about the situation and this unexpected, wholly bizarre turn. In his career Walsh must have handled hundreds, even a couple thousand cases. Among them there had to be vicious criminals, absolute animals, not to mention nuts. Any one of them could have exacted his revenge. His death had nothing to do with the accident on Belvedere Road that cold December night. Of course, there was still the loose end: the "drunk driver" who'd never been found. But why in the world would he come back and assassinate Walsh? He'd been in the clear for five years, nobody coming near him, no threat to his freedom, why suddenly run into town and do this?

There was no connection. Gail was so far off base it was more than ridiculous, it was science fiction. Lyssa told herself to forget about it, completely. So, what had she accomplished running down to Atlanta? Not a great deal, actually nothing more than Gail Horvath's corroboration of Walsh's suspicions, the two of them sharing the same suspicions. She liked Gail, she was fun, but had an odd side to her. She seemed convinced that Derrick arranged to have "Lizzie" killed, agreeing wholeheartedly with Walsh. But didn't seem at all bitter about it. Lyssa would have been. Still, maybe Gail was hiding it, very skillfully; only why would she?

It was all getting terribly confusing.

~~~~ TWELVE ~~~~

The plane landed and taxied down the runway to its deplaning tunnel. Air traffic was unusually heavy; incoming flights were stacked up practically to the stratosphere, so it seemed. Her plane landed eighteen minutes late, after arriving seven minutes early. While waiting for her connecting flight, she telephoned Aggie at the store. The flight to Bellingham was scheduled to land at 3:59; Aggie promised to pick her up at the airport.

"What happened? What did you find out?"

Aggie obviously hadn't heard about Walsh's murder; she wouldn't have, it was local news.

"Not much. Don't worry, I'll tell you everything."

"When is he due in?" asked Aggie.

"'He'? Do you mean Derrick? Damn!"

"What?"

"I just remembered, he's due back late this afternoon. He could easily beat me to Bellingham. He'll come right to the store. If I'm not there and you're on your way to pick me up . . ."

"No problem. Jenny and Ellie'll tell him you had to run to New York, you're coming in, I went to pick you up. Just don't leave your flight-ticket carbon around the apartment where he might see it, for God's sake."

"I hate this deceiving him."

"You'd hate it more if you never went down there, never found out what you did find."

"Not much."

"So . . . You found out there wasn't much to find out, isn't that important?"

The operator cut in asking for payment for the next three minutes. Lyssa said good-bye and hung up.

Aggie stood leaning against her Peugeot waving both arms. She came running up to Lyssa, practically snatching her suitcase from her. It was 4:22. Lyssa glanced at her watch.

"He's back, he must be at the store. . . ."

"Will you stop being such a worrywart? He may not get in till six. You said he said late afternoon. All right, five o'clock. Talk, tell me, I won't interrupt."

"I'll bet."

Lyssa told her everything, practically from the moment the taxi from the airport let her off at the hotel to when Gail Horvath hung up and she started to dress to leave.

"She's screwy," said Aggie. "There's no connection between his being murdered and the thing with Derrick and Elizabeth. The driver did it, what a load of bull."

"I know, I agree, but you must admit it's weird. The timing. Walsh talked to her, he comes up here talks to me, goes home, and is murdered."

"You don't look too good."

"Just beat."

"Is this dumb thing starting to get to you?"

"Aggie, watch your driving, you'll get us both killed. Stop cutting people off."

"They drive too slow. You want to get to the store, don't you? Answer the question."

"I guess it is. It's crazy, one minute I feel like I'm just being nosy, sticking my nose into Derrick's past. The next I wonder what really happened so badly I get knots in my stomach."

"How are you sleeping?"

"Rotten last night. It hit me so hard. I was on my way up to see him. I could have come half an hour earlier and been in his apartment when the killer walked in."

"You could have, but you weren't."

"I hate this—killing, blood, suspicion, the way Derrick flips when I so much as breathe Walsh's name. That's the one thing, you talk about overreacting. . . ."

"You going to tell him Walsh is dead? What am I saying, you can't. Where's your ticket carbon?"

Lyssa dug it out of her handbag, crumpled it, buried it in the ashtray.

"Let's talk about New York," said Aggie, accelerating, pulling round a truck, braking too hard so she could slip back into line.

"Stop it! I'm nervous enough without that!"

"Okay, okay. All right, you went to New York to see a fashion show. Two. And to talk with the Calvin Klein people about . . . about their screwing up our last order. Stuff like that, whatever else you can think of to chew up a few hours. Let's see, you only would have been there from around four in the afternoon to ten this morning. About the same as Atlanta, actually."

"Does American fly between New York and Detroit?"

"Pick any airline, what difference does it make. He won't see your ticket. He won't try to pin you down."

Lyssa sighed. "Neither of us has been to New York in two years."

"You think he'll be suspicious? I don't. Just emphasize the problems you had to go there to solve. Or something."

"Or something."

Derrick didn't get home till nearly seven. After L'Image had closed for the day. She was waiting at home. He came dragging in, dropping his suitcase, tossing his attaché case on the sofa, and plopping down heavily. Removing his jacket, he wrenched off his tie.

"Boy, the rush-hour traffic in this town is murder. Would you believe my plane got in at five-ten? I got a cab at twenty of six. I walked the last twenty blocks from Dial Avenue."

"Can I have a kiss?"

"I'm sorry."

He kissed her tenderly, pulling her down beside him.

"Kick off your shoes," she said. "Want to take a shower?"

"In a little bit. I'd just like to unwind."

"How did it go in Seattle?"

"Fine, except—as it turned out—we really could have done everything over the phone and with the fax machine. They're nice people, not terribly sophisticated, not in my opinion, but not stupid. Very friendly. They practically bow and scrape."

"Did it rain?"

"Not a drop."

"Did you have to take your Bronchodane?"

"More often than here both times. I don't know whether it's pollen, mold spores, what it is. The hotel's across the street from Woodland Park. If I ever have to go back, I'll have Maggie make me a reservation someplace nowhere near trees."

"The breeze carries the stuff."

"I know, I know."

"You okay?"

"Fine. Got anything for supper?"

"I just got back from the supermarket. How does brook trout, a baked potato, string beans, and a salad sound?"

"Terrific. I could eat 'em frozen. They had that goddamned lasagna on the plane coming back. It tastes like plaster."

She had been served lasagna. Funny, when she tasted it, plaster had crossed her mind as well. He took a shower. She felt like one, but held off; for some reason not altogether clear to her, she was reluctant to get into the stall with him.

In God's name, why not?

~~~~ THIRTEEN ~~~~

Two days passed uneventfully. Friday. Taking a late lunch hour—it was almost three—Lyssa walked around the corner down Main and across Fleming Avenue to the little, ancient, out-of-town newspaper store that provided an income to an old woman who apparently never bathed, smelled to high heaven, and dressed like a Gypsy, even to gold chains and numerous rings surrounding her chubby, dirty fingers. She wore filthy gloves without fingers, evidently to show off her rings. She had no visible teeth, she spoke broken English. Lyssa guessed she came from some Eastern European country. Her little store, with its bare board floor and walls concealed by ceiling-high racks filled with papers from all over the world, reeked of her.

"Have you today's *Atlanta Constitution*?"

"Yesterday's an' today's, which?"

"Both."

The little eyes ignited, the smile revealed her naked gums, she stood on a stool and got down both papers.

"Two-fifty."

Distance lent exorbitancy, Lyssa thought as she paid. And fled, standing on the corner drawing in a cavernous breath of fresh air. Thursday's *Constitution* carried the news that an elderly man, one of Walsh's fellow tenants, had approached the police to tell them that a stranger had followed him inside when he came home shortly before the time of the murder established by the medical examiner. The man had been waiting between the outer and inner doors by the mailboxes, had mumbled something about forgetting his key, and held the door for him after he opened it with his key and was restoring the key to his pocket. The witness lived on the second floor. Entering his apartment, he'd seen the man ascend to the third floor. He described him as about six feet tall, fairly young, with a mustache and felt hat, the brim "pulled halfway down his face." He admitted he thought he looked suspicious, but hesitated to ask who he wanted to see. He was quoted as blaming himself for "Joe's death." He and Walsh seemed to be about the same age and had probably passed each other on the stairs often enough to form a stronger-than-nodding acquaintance.

On the front page of Friday's *Constitution* were two pictures, one of Walsh and alongside it, the same size, a police drawing of his suspected assassin. Unfortunately it showed little of the man's face, with the hat brim pulled down and the mustache, likely false, covering most of the center of his face, so luxuriant was it.

Six-foot, light complexion, slender hands, a raincoat with the collar turned up, despite the fact that the weather that night was clear, with no threat of rain. Not much to go on, but definitely the killer.

"Executioner," she corrected herself.

If the man who'd let him in had been on the ball, he would have asked him who he wanted to see. He was a tenant, he had every right to know. That way he'd at least have gotten the killer to talk a bit more. He never should have let him in, but that was easy to say. The witness had to be about twice his age; if he hadn't let him in, the assassin would have forced his way in and probably knocked the older man cold in the process.

One thing Lyssa could not understand. Why had Walsh let him in? If he'd knocked and/or called out, Walsh would have come to the door. He'd normally ask him to identify himself, the man would have to say something. Maybe he pretended to be a close friend. If so, that had to mean he knew Walsh. Or not a friend, but someone who knew all about him and mumbled the name of one of his friends.

And yet it did seem strange that someone with Walsh's experience, a policeman, wouldn't be more careful about whom he let in, especially after dark. At that, maybe the killer posed as one of his closest friends and Walsh was so glad to hear his name he couldn't wait to open the door. Never thinking that if it really was someone he knew, they'd have buzzed him downstairs and he'd have let them in.

Maybe the killer didn't want him to know he'd come in the front way, maybe he identified himself as a neighbor? Who could say how he worked it? He got the results he was looking for; mission accomplished. Filling her lungs, holding her breath, she went back inside.

"Would you do me a favor and save me copies of the next seven days of the *Constitution*?"

"Sure, only you pay in advance. I don' wanna get stuck."

How she could get "stuck" was a small mystery to Lyssa, but the odors were already closing in. She took another fetid breath and held it as inconspicuously as possible. It was a lovely day out, why didn't the woman take pity on her customers and leave the door open?

"The daily is one-twenny-five, that's six-fifty. Sunday is two dollahs."

Lyssa handed her a ten-dollar bill. "Keep the change."

"No, no, I don't take tips, I don' take char'ty. I owe you one-fifty."

She paid her in nickels and dimes. By the time Lyssa got out she was close to asphyxiation. Recovering, heading for the sandwich shop up the street, she reminded herself to leave each day's paper in the office at the store. Come in on Sunday, pick up the paper, read it in the office, dispose of it there.

Lunch was a limp tuna sandwich and tea. Back at the store, she phoned Gail Horvath.

"My, my, isn't this a pleasant surprise so soon. . . ."

"How are you?"

"Just fine, just fine."

"Anything new on you know what? I read the items in yesterday's and today's *Constitution*."

"Me, too. There was something interesting in the *Journal*. They claim more than one person saw the suspected killer. Somebody saw the police sketch in the *Constitution* and the other papers and came forward and claims they saw the fellow leaving—coming down the steps and walking off toward Spring Street. His description didn't add much, but did match Mr. Conolly's."

"That's the tenant who let him in."

"Yes, poor fool. You think he would have been more careful. Joseph'd be alive today."

"I doubt it. If the killer didn't get him Tuesday night, he would have come back. As often as necessary."

"I guess."

"I just wanted to call and check, I hope you don't mind. The *Constitution*'s the only Atlanta paper I can get up here."

"Call anytime; you're lucky you caught me, though, I was on my way out to a meeting. Daughters of the Confederacy."

"Thanks, Gail."

She hung up.

Derrick came home from work in a foul mood. She tensed, wondering what had happened. He set her mind at ease immediately. It had nothing to do with Walsh. The IRS was making tentative inquiries about some aspect of the company's finances. Derrick's reaction put her in mind of Doreen's description of Reggie when he received the upsetting Sunday-night phone call.

"The bastards intend to put us through the wringer."

"Corporate taxes . . ."

"What else?"

"It could be personal income."

He was getting angrier by the second. "Corporate! Corporate!"

"Darling, don't shout. If you want to shout at somebody, try Cochrane."

He stiffened. "How do you know about Cochrane?" He narrowed his eyes, assuming an expression bordering on vicious.

"You told me."

"I did like hell."

"You did, or Reggie did. Cochrane was fired. So he blew the whistle. Didn't he? He must have. Derrick, I'm not exactly ignorant about such matters. Disgruntled chief accountants who get fired know how to get revenge."

"I didn't tell you about Cochrane."

"Then I overheard you and Reggie. What's the big deal? More importantly, what's going to happen?"

He sighed and relaxed. "I don't know."

"Reggie must be really upset."

"Upset? He was closeted with two tax lawyers and Weintraub, the guy who replaced Cochrane, all afternoon. When he came out at five, he looked gray as a fish."

"Will the company . . ."

"Go under? I don't think so. Every outfit runs into trouble with the IRS at one time or another. I don't know what's going on. Reggie didn't say, I didn't ask."

"You've a right to know, everybody who works there does."

He eyed her jaundicedly. "Lys, Cambridge isn't a cozy little sorority like L'Image."

"Don't go putting us down, we pay our taxes."

As soon as it was out, she knew she shouldn't have said it. And didn't need his expression in reaction to confirm it.

"I'm sorry, that was a low blow."

"Forget it. I shouldn't be shouting. *I'm* sorry."

He kissed her. She grabbed him, kissed him tenderly. And thought about Doreen; Reggie would be coming home to her about now. How would he behave? She felt for her.

They lay naked. He was kissing her lightly all over, little feathers of love touching, igniting warmth, lifting. The soft sound of his lips was the language of his love; neither needed to speak, neither had any desire to. When he found her mouth at last, her heart jolted into a thunderous beating. She began to pant, her hand sliding down to grasp his erection. Immense, spike hard, throbbing mightily in her fingers. With her free hand she pushed his shoulder, gently urging him to mount her. But he remained on his side, his right arm across her heaving breasts, his mouth now nuzzling her neck and under her ear. She squeezed his erection and drew a breath in sharply.

He was over her, their bodies separated, his eyes gazing adoringly down into hers. Slowly, down he came; she guided him into her. Little by little he entered, slowly, teasingly, with infuriating slowness, until she bucked, taking him deep inside. And cried out with joy.

She woke from a sweet dream: a garden at twilight, a pond, a solitary swan gliding across it, just the two of them. She groped for him, but he wasn't there. The room was in darkness, the door ajar showing darkness in the hallway. The luminous dial of the nightstand clock read 1:42. Slipping into her robe, she went out. She could hear him tinkering with something in the study. She made her way through the darkness to the open door, the wedge of light cast by the desk lamp. Reaching the door, she looked in, gasped.

Spread on the desk in front of him were the parts of a pistol. He had a rag and a can of oil and was cleaning them.

"What are you doing with that?"

"Cleaning it."

"Very funny. Where did you get it?"

"Bought it."

She had come in; she sat in the red leather chair in the corner. The room was a combination study/library, the books sharing shelf space with bric-a-brac.

"Would I be nosy if I asked what for?"

"Protection, darling."

"From what?"

He set down the barrel he had been reaming. "Lys, I didn't want to tell you, but I guess I have to. I should. I was mugged in Seattle."

"My God . . ."

"Oh yes, by two stalwart, alarmingly efficient citizens with eight-inch knives and attitudes. They got four hundred and five dollars, they also got a good chunk of my pride in myself as a man. It was about nine-thirty at night. I was on my way back to the hotel, they ambushed me, 'surrounded' me, demanded my money. Or else."

"God . . ."

"I thought my heart would jump out of my chest. I was shaking. Nobody else in sight, of course. I set down my attaché case, got out my wallet. One grabbed it, took out the money, threw the wallet at my chest, and took off. Laughing uproariously. I'm only a man, Lys, I've no right to assume how a woman feels after she's been raped, but my guess is something like how I felt standing looking after them, hearing them laughing. Not as bad, not nearly, but . . . 'raped,' in a sense. I stood there utterly helpless. I can tell you I've never felt emasculated in my entire life. Not till the other night."

"And that thing . . ." She nodded at the disassembled pistol.

"Before I took a step, I vowed it would never happen again."

"And a gun will prevent it."

"Yes."

"Will you pack it on your hip like Wyatt Earp or in a shoulder holster?"

"I hate to say this, but I wish you'd been there. You might not be so cavalier about it."

"I'm not being 'cavalier' about 'it.' I am about that thing."

"I intend to keep it in my attaché case. Along with my wallet. Why not—the case goes everywhere I go, certainly when I'm on a trip. When somebody else tries to mug me, I'll tell them fine, you can have every cent, only it's in the case. It's locked. I'll have to get out my key. I'll set it down, kneel, open it, get out my wallet with my left hand."

"And the gun with your right."

"Exactly."

"Clever. Then what, shoot them?"

"I won't have to. They won't have guns, these two had knives, I told you."

"Muggers carry guns, too. What's it going to be, a shoot-out? You've never fired a gun in your life."

"I have. Sweetheart, we live in tough times, in case you haven't noticed. Everybody carries a gun these days."

"I don't."

"You've never been mugged."

"I still wouldn't."

"Wait'll you are, it may change your thinking."

"It's stupid."

"Not the way I intend using it. Of course, I won't shoot anybody."

"Except in self-defense. You make it sound like the whole country has become Dodge City."

"No, just Seattle, and every other big city. You don't approve. I'm sorry."

"I'm sure, as if you need my approval. Only don't you have a problem? First off, don't you need a permit?"

"It's in the works."

"And how do you propose to carry that thing aboard a plane?"

"I'd never get it through security. I'll do what others do—mail it three or four days before I leave. When I get there, the package'll be waiting."

"Leave it, come back to bed."

"I'm almost done cleaning it. I'll put it back together and be right in."

"Do you have bullets?"

"Yes."

"Well, do me a favor, would you? Please don't practice around here. And try and be careful. Don't go killing yourself."

"I promise I won't even shoot myself in the foot."

She got up and walked out.

At breakfast he informed her that his acquisition was a used Colt .38 super-automatic. It weighed thirty-nine ounces and the overall length was eight and a half inches.

Nine shots. He described it as a "cannon" and regaled her with technical specifics: the rifling, groove diameter, bore diameter.

It took him two cups of coffee to realize she wasn't in the least interested; indeed, it turned her off completely.

~~~~ FOURTEEN ~~~~

Saturday's *Atlanta Constitution* carried a three-column report by the paper's police reporter on the Walsh case, a summation of all that the police knew or were willing to reveal. Two other people claimed to have spotted the killer, both at the airport the next morning. The authorities had to be taking their information with a grain of salt. Common sense dictated that by the time the killer got to the airport the next day he'd have to be long out of his disguise, such as it was. Actually, not a bad disguise, simple and eminently suitable to the occasion.

The obvious was acknowledged, that the killer was now miles from Atlanta. Ballistics disclosed that the two bullets entering the victim's brain at close range were .38 caliber. Like Derrick's new toy. Ballistics admitted that close examination of the cartridges, their grooves and other markings, was of no value, not without the murder weapon, which the police held out little hope of recovering.

Retired Detective First Grade Joseph Aloysius Walsh was buried with full departmental honors and a lengthy eulogy by the mayor. No fewer than thirty-one criminals, all but seven murderers, had been apprehended, tried, convicted, and imprisoned by Walsh in his last year and a half on the force. The twenty-four murderers were still behind bars, most doing life. The remaining few were back on the street, two of the seven preparing to go to trial on new charges shortly. The seven free men had all been questioned; all had alibis for their whereabouts on Tuesday night.

Lyssa sat at the desk in the office rereading the article for the fourth time, and concluded that the killer could not possibly be anyone Walsh had arrested. Anyone apprehended prior to his last eighteen months on duty would not have waited this long to exact revenge. His killer could only be someone fearful of getting caught, who either knew or assumed that the old man was closing in on him.

She guessed that he had had a good deal more to work with than what he'd disclosed to either her or Gail Horvath. He'd sat down with them just to pick their brains, with no intention of telling them what he was onto. And it was beginning to look like Gail was right when she suggested the "drunk driver" had murdered him.

She decided to come in tomorrow and pick up the Sunday *Constitution* she'd already paid for, and that would end it. She'd phone Gail in a week or so; Gail would know if there'd been any break in the case.

One thing troubled her; if the killer did turn out to be the driver, it would confirm Walsh's suspicions: putting Derrick behind the whole "arrangement."

She got out scissors and cut out the article, as she had all the previous ones, clipping them together and burying them in her lingerie drawer. Why she bothered, she didn't exactly know, except that the murder, the timing of it, still intrigued her. If was almost as if the killer knew she was coming to Atlanta to see Walsh and had to eliminate him before they could get together.

"My God, talk about stretching it!"

Agnes filled the doorway. "What are you talking to yourself about now?"

"Nothing."

"I'll bet. Mind my own business."

"Derrick's bought a gun."

Agnes rolled her eyes. "Oh boy . . ."

"He told me he got mugged in Seattle. He's determined it won't happen again."

"He 'told you.' Are you implying you don't believe him?"

"I believe him. He's no liar. They took over four hundred dollars, every cent he had on him. Only they left his watch, the one I gave him his last birthday. The black Movado. It was no Rolex, but it wasn't cheap. You must have noticed, it had a sapphire crystal. Why would they take his money and leave his watch?"

"That *is* strange. It's so easy to take the watch, too. And don't they usually? Maybe he wasn't wearing it, maybe he left it back at the hotel."

"He wears it from the time he gets up in the morning to when he goes to bed."

"Did you ask him why they didn't take it?"

"No. I didn't give it a thought till this morning, when I saw he was wearing it at breakfast. I guess I didn't think about it because I was so shocked at seeing him with the gun."

"More and more people are carrying them. Lots of women."

"I guess. Maybe I'm just behind the times."

"Me, too. Oh hell, I forgot, your friend is outside. Mrs. Carlyle."

Lyssa brightened. "Doreen!"

"What a bod. Why does God give everything to some and nothing to people like me? Why not share the wealth?"

"There's nothing wrong with your figure."

"Not if you like small breasts, nonexistent hips, no behind. And second-rate legs."

"Knock it off."

Doreen greeted her with a broad smile, but it failed to camouflage the worry in her eyes.

"What's the matter?" Lyssa asked.

"Can you split for a little? For like coffee?"

"Sure."

Doreen had on lamb's-wool knit separates—pull-on pants and cowl sweater in rose angora, a preposterously wide-brimmed straw, and spike heels. She looked adorable but definitely concerned about something. They commandeered a corner booth in the deli up the street from L'Image and ordered coffee. Doreen set her hat on the seat beside her and leaned forward, continuing to whisper.

"Remember me telling you about that phone call Reggie got when I was fixing the flowers outside the study? Last Sunday night."

"You don't have to whisper."

"I'm scared. I always whisper when I'm scared."

"Nothing's going to hurt you here, except maybe the chili."

No smile came. If anything, she looked even more worried. "He came home last night like a wild bull. He walked in, and the look on his face—I was afraid he was going to trash the whole house. Campbell—he's the butler, sort of, man of all work, you know—took one look and ran."

"The IRS."

"How'd you know? Oh God, oh God, oh God! You didn't tell Derrick, you promised!"

"I didn't. He walked in last night and told me."

"It's awful, even worse than I thought. Reggie has to go to Washington, D.C., with the lawyers and talk to somebody, I don't know who. He says it's a frame-up; he says the company pays every nickel they owe in taxes, on time, no finagling, no cheating. Oh Lee, I'm glad that Cochrane wasn't standing there, Reggie would have beat him to death. The way he carried on. God, my ears ached.

I kept backing away from him, I thought he was going to swing on me."

"He wouldn't do that, no matter how mad he gets."

"He wasn't mad, he was wild! He got all purple. I thought he'd burst a blood vessel. I've never seen anybody get mad like that. My daddy had a temper, he could blow his top over nothing, but not like Reggie last night. He didn't settle down till almost midnight. I lay awake most of the night. He fell asleep, but I was afraid he'd wake up screaming, yelling, and belt me, without meaning to. Lee, it's horrible, I'm scared."

"Relax. Try. Think about it, it may not be as bad as he thinks. He did tell you it was a frame-up."

"Who knows? If it is, it could be straightened out, couldn't it? It could. So why should he get so upset? Maybe it can't be straightened out."

Good point. Lyssa suddenly found herself wishing Derrick told her more about what went on with the company. If he was in the habit of telling her things, he'd tell her about this. It wasn't exactly the end of the world; if Cambridge was in really serious trouble and ultimately went belly-up, he'd find another job. He was good, he worked hard. One of the other medical-surgical equipment companies would snap him up. And he certainly was in no danger of being arrested; he was a vice-president, but he had nothing to do with company finances.

Most husbands bored their wives silly with shoptalk; most wives knew almost as much about what went on inside corporate America as their husbands. Not her. Which was annoying; wasn't she in business herself? Wouldn't she be more intelligent, more receptive, more understanding than a wife who knew nothing about business?

"I don't know what to do," said Doreen, her eyes glistening with tears. "He went in this morning; he told me when he left he'd be home around six or so. What if he comes home like last night?"

"He won't. Believe me, the worst is over."

"Just starting, you mean."

"I mean he won't carry on like that again, he's gotten it off his chest." Lyssa sounded like she was trying to convince herself as much as she was Doreen. "Drink your coffee. It'll pick you up, you'll feel better."

"I don't want it. I just wanted to talk. You're about the only one I can talk to."

"What specifically did Reggie say about Cochrane?"

"Nothing, he just called him the dirtiest names, some I never even heard before. I wouldn't dare repeat one. He must have something on the company or he wouldn't . . . you know . . ."

"Blow the whistle."

"He'd be asking for trouble, saying bad things, getting them in trouble, without anything to back it up. Isn't that so?"

"That's hard to answer. He could be one very vengeful individual, he could be driven, he could be a nut case. Just hang in there till Reggie gets back from Washington. Who knows—we all might get lucky, maybe they'll solve the whole business. When is he going?"

"A week from Monday. The only reason I know, I saw his plane ticket when I hung up his jacket. God, I don't know if I can hold out that long!"

Lyssa couldn't understand why Doreen was so concerned for her safety; Reggie might yell and carry on like all men do when they lose control and for some reason feel it necessary to regress to prepuberty and behave like little boys. But it was hard to imagine her in any physical danger. Perhaps it was merely that she saw him as powerful and herself as weak, vulnerable, and so conveniently available as whipping boy. Lyssa did all she could to persuade her that "this, too, shall pass," but when she realized she was repeating herself and nothing seemed to be helping, she gave up. They had left the deli and were approaching the store.

"You're a true friend, Lee. This has really, really helped. I feel better."

So Doreen claimed, but her eyes said otherwise. They stood out front. Doreen eyed a gold lamé evening dress in the window. It glittered like a golden waterfall.

"Maybe I should buy something," she said. "Make me feel better. Shopping always picks me up."

"What woman doesn't it?"

She sobered. "Maybe not, maybe when the bill comes in, there won't be any money to pay it."

Around four in the afternoon, Agnes was in the office unpacking and inspecting a shipment of summer dresses, and Lyssa, Ellie, and Jenny were out front with customers when a man in coveralls carrying a toolbox came in. The football-shaped patch on his back identified him as an employee of the Bellingham Telephone Company. Over his breast pocket was the name Bert. He was slender, dark, and dragged his feet when he walked. His beard was in its first sparse stages of growth. It promised to effect little improvement in his nondescript features. He approached Jenny, touching the peak of his cap.

"Got to check your phones, miss."

Lyssa excused herself from her customer and came over. "What for? They work okay."

"It's the cable. I have to check every phone in the block. It's kinda complicated to explain." He consulted an abused-looking sheaf of papers on a clipboard. "Two phones, right? Excuse me."

He picked up the phone by the cash register, punched a number, and spoke.

"Two-five-nine, two-five-nine-four-one-one. Check. Check."

He hung up; everyone, even the customers, standing rigid, staring at him, resumed what they had been doing. Lyssa rejoined her customer, a well-preserved, once-beautiful woman in her late sixties who dressed with no concessions whatsoever to her age, a fact that was apparent from her stunning red-and-white-striped cotton and Lycra jacket and skirt. Agnes came out.

"What's going on? Our phones work."

"It's the cable," said Jenny.

Bert went into the office. Agnes moved to the phone by the register, picked it up, listened, set it down, shrugged. Moments later Bert reappeared.

"I checked your box out back, too. You're fine."

"We know," said Agnes.

He smiled through his scraggly beard and left.

⟶ FIFTEEN ⟶

Lyssa and Derrick decided on Sunday-night dinner at Sushi Ray, a Japanese restaurant not far from his office. She was not overly enamored of Japanese cuisine, but he loved it, everything, "the squirmier, the rawer, the better," as she put it. As long as the menu offered tempura, she could go along without complaint.

She still couldn't figure out Walsh's murder. Why had he been killed just before they got together? Could it possibly have anything to do with her? Despite every conscious effort to keep suspicion clear of her thinking, she could not help wondering if, for all his protests, all his indignation, Derrick had indeed arranged Elizabeth's "accident." Giving in to this speculation was stupid, it was unfair, it was destructive. It could harm, could destroy their relationship. Stupid, because it pointedly ignored the findings of the insurance company. Lyssa was no expert on life insurance, but everyone knew that no insurance

company paid on any policy if there was so much as a
mote of suspicion that all was not what it should be. She
had once heard that a company refused to pay because a
widow failed to get a doctor's statement confirming the
time and circumstances of her husband's death in time to
be processed. There was a thirty-day deadline, she failed
to meet it, the company balked at paying. They claimed
the information, actually a stipulation, was clearly stated
in the policy, and when the husband signed the policy,
he agreed to every word in it. The widow sued and lost.
The person who'd told Lyssa the story contended that the
company was stealing; she agreed. But it refused to pay
and the law found in its favor.

The ceiling in Sushi Ray was so low she instinctively
ducked walking in. The place was crowded, dimly lit, and
sitting cross-legged with your shoes replaced by paper
slippers was not her idea of comfort. But before leaving
the apartment, she had sworn to herself she wouldn't complain about anything. Tonight they would be Japanese.

A porcelain doll of a hostess bowed, smiled, and led the
way in mincing steps to their table. It was near a distant
corner. En route they passed two private dining rooms;
both were in use. As they passed the second a burst
of laughter drew Lyssa's attention. The entrance was a
latticework screen permitting a full view of the interior.
She was walking between the hostess and Derrick; curiosity prompted her to turn her head. Ten or twelve couples
were seated around a T-shaped table. Next to the couple
at the head of the T, she spied a familiar face. Reggie
sat next to a beautiful redhead. He was nuzzling her
and running his hand down her bare shoulder to within
reach of her breast; up and down, up and down, getting
a little closer to it each time. From her blank expression
the redhead wasn't even aware he was touching her; she
was too busy drinking. The others at the table poked fun
at him.

Lyssa turned back to Derrick; he, too, was looking.

They continued on to their table, were seated, given their menus.

"What the hell . . . ?" she began.

"Take it easy. Maybe Doreen couldn't make it tonight. Maybe she's ill. Maybe she's . . . in L.A., visiting her family."

"She could be in Timbucktu. That's not the point and you know it!"

"Lower your voice. . . ."

"The son of a bitch, did you see the way he was carrying on?"

"Maybe she's an old friend; maybe she's married to the guy on the other side of her."

"Are you serious?"

"Honey, people are looking. . . ."

"The son of a bitch."

"It's none of our business."

"That's just like you, like every man. Toss it off, ignore it. While Doreen sits home watching TV, worrying about him, wondering how the late-Sunday meeting is going. Rooting for him . . ."

"Okay, okay, you've made your point. He's cheating on her. He'll be leaving here in twenty minutes, going to some hotel and jumping into the sack with that . . .that . . ."

"Whore!"

"Shhh. What do you want me to do about it? What can you? So you don't like it—"

"I hate it! I hate him!"

"Shhh. Good, fine, only there's nothing you can do. It's their business, their problem, if it is a problem."

"What do you mean 'if'?"

"I don't know, maybe Doreen sleeps around."

"Oh boy. Oh boy, oh boy, if that isn't just like a man! Shift the blame, spread it between them."

"Can we please just drop it? We're supposed to be here to enjoy dinner, not bicker over something that's none of our business."

"The bastard, how could you work for somebody like that?"

"Give me a break, am I my employer's keeper?"

"I'm sorry, it's like I'm blaming you. It's just so upsetting."

"I know. See anything you like? Tempura, right? With vegetables and miso soup."

"What's that?"

"Soup. I don't know, they make it with fresh misos. I guess. . . ."

She laughed lightly in spite of her lingering anger. "I'm game. Order for me." She got up.

"Where you going?"

"Do you really have to ask?"

There were two wall phones separated by a clear-plastic panel just outside the ladies' room. She looked up the Carlyles' number and punched it.

"Hello?"

Doreen. She hung up. What a stupid thing to do! What would she say to her? Your husband's here with some whore, I just thought you'd like to know? Poor woman, she cared so much about him and he, obviously, didn't care at all. Not for his first wife, not for her. Disgusting!

"The bastard!"

Their soup had arrived when she got back to the table. She had thought about ordering a drink when they first sat down, but decided against it. Now she could use one, something good and strong. Passing the dining room a second and third time going and coming back, she could see him still carrying on with his redhead, the others laughing. Egging him on? Pushing him into infidelity? As if he needed help!

"How about a drink?" asked Derrick.

"No."

"Maybe some wine?"

"I don't want a drink."

"Okay, okay." He started on his soup, stopped, set down

the spoon. "Are we going to have a good time tonight or aren't we?"

"We are, I promise."

She told him about Bert and the phones, for want of something better to get into a conversation. They were halfway through their salads when a young couple approached, led by the hostess. The girl had on a white silk blouse and black linen suit. Her accessories were perfect, she knew how to dress. They bore down on the unoccupied table beside theirs. Derrick saw her studying the girl and turned to see.

"Maggie!"

He got up, flinging down his napkin, nearly upsetting his salad in his haste.

"Darling, meet Maggie Donovan."

Lyssa stiffened. *Good God, you, too!*

"My devoted and gifted secretary and lady of all work. Maggie, this is Lyssa." He laughed. "You've heard me speak of her."

"Mitheth Morgan." She held out her hand displaying her engagment ring. "Delighted to meet you. A pleathure. May I introduth my fianthé, Derrick Flynn? Derrick and Derrick, what a cointhidenth."

Maggie sat beside her, their backs to the mirrored wall. "Thith ith a thurprith, Mitheth Morgan."

"Lyssa . . ."

"I've been with Mithter Morgan three whole yearth, and to think thith ith the firth time we meet. You really should come up to the offith."

"I would, if I were asked."

"None of the wives come to the office," said Derrick. "No family, girlfriends, boyfriends. The brass thinks outsiders are distracting. We do have our medieval rules."

Derrick Flynn had yet to utter a sound; he smiled a lot, he seemed personable, was reasonably good-looking: dark blond hair, serious eyes despite being too easily amused, a nose a trifle too long and pointy, but handsome mouth and jawline. According to Maggie, he was "studying to be an engineer." This revelation prompted him to speak for himself for the first time.

"I'm at MIT, home for a break just before finals."

They ordered and talked almost nonstop, the two men, the girls. Lyssa liked Maggie Donovan. She was cute, very sweet, with the pale skin of the Irish, freckles, requisite red hair. The real thing, not like Reggie's whore. One thing did strike Lyssa as odd. After suggesting she come up to the office, Maggie dropped the subject like something too hot to hold. In reaction to Derrick's speech on the subject of visitors? Even treating it in the offhand manner he had, it came out sounding like a warning. Cambridge Medical and Surgical Equipment certainly was a curious outfit, in a seemingly ever-increasing number of ways. Derrick had never asked her to meet him at the office. Wives met their husbands at the office when they went out at night all the time, got acquainted with their secretaries, satisfied their curiosity about them, saw the business in operation, got to know the employees not sifted through their husbands' opinions and prejudices, got to see what their husband's desk looked like, everything.

"That place is still in the nineteenth century in more ways than one," she commented out of the blue and resentfully.

Derrick stopped talking to Derrick and eyed her. "I'm sorry, I don't make the rules."

"Reggie . . ."

"And his brass."

"He seems to do a lot of things peculiarly. How does he stay on top there?"

A funny look came over Maggie's pale face. She eyed her boss.

"It's his company," said Derrick. "When the ball and bat are yours, you're entitled to call all the shots."

"You own L'Image, don't you?" Maggie asked.

"In partnership."

"I've never been in, I'm ashamed to thay. I couldn't afford to buy a thing."

"You come see us, I mean it."

"I walk by every day coming and going from work."

"So come in. Please. You'd be surprised at some of the prices."

"Everythingth dethighner, way out of my league. You should thee, Derrick, everythingth beautiful. If I win the lottery, I'll buy out the whole thtore."

"Let me buy you ten tickets," said Lyssa, and got a laugh. "I'm going to watch for you passing from now on. I'll drag you in."

"Oh, you won't have to, now I'm invited. I'm dying to."

Lyssa and Derrick were starting on their dessert when she caught sight of Reggie's party leaving. He walked with his arm around his date, talking too close to her ear. Lyssa's earlier resentment flared in her stomach and she gritted her teeth. Derrick looked her way with a puzzled expression, turned, saw, turned back. Maggie, busy eating, did not look up.

~~~ SIXTEEN ~~~

They lay in bed. She had not brought up the subject since leaving Sushi Ray. Now, for some reason, as her eyelids grew heavy and she was preparing to drop off, he elected to.

"Look at it this way, it's his life, he does as he pleases."

"Obviously."

"You've come to know Doreen better than me, but

you've no idea what their relationship is. Do you? He's almost thirty years older than she is, they may have an agreement. . . ."

"Please, spare me, I'm really not interested." She propped herself up on one elbow and switched on the lamp. "Why is it you feel you have to alibi for him?"

"I'm not alibiing. . . ."

"It sure sounds it."

"Sweetheart, face it, people are what they are. You may not like how they behave, in certain cases, but they don't care. It's none of your business."

"I like Doreen. . . ."

"Me, too."

"You don't know her like I do."

"Didn't I just say I didn't? Does that mean I have no right to like her?"

"That's not what I'm saying and you know it. Let's just drop it."

"I'd love to. You're the one who keeps harping on it."

"You started it."

"Please, Lys, turn out the light?" She frowned and did so. He turned on his side, hugging her back to his chest, his forearm across her breasts. "Love you."

"I love you."

"So there," he added. "You're tense." She consciously relaxed. "Better."

He kissed her neck lightly then rose and turned her on her back. And began to make love. His erection came swiftly and they were sharing a lingering kiss when he suddenly drew his mouth from hers and stared perplexed.

"You're still tense. Can't you put him out of your mind? At least for now?"

She wasn't thinking of Reggie Carlyle, but could hardly tell him that. She *was* uptight, a little, enough so he noticed. God forbid he know the reason. Stamped inside her eyelids was Walsh's face, beside it the drawing of his presumed killer. "Presumed"? She thought about the clippings taken from the *Constitution* lying in the corner of her lingerie drawer a few feet from the foot of the bed. If Derrick ever found them . . . Of course, why would he go into the drawer? There was nothing but her underthings, unopened packets of panty hose, panty hose she had worn. Still, it might make sense to dispose of the clippings, except for the two pictures and maybe the lengthy article that summed up the case she'd cut out of last Sunday's paper; but if she saved them, the best place to hide them was still in the drawer. So why not save everything?

Better yet, get rid of everything.

"Excuse me," he said, "did you hear what I said?"

"Of course."

"Can't you relax? Try . . . ?"

She kissed him. "Yes, definitely."

They made love. It was no good, it was near disastrous; she thought so. Their timing was completely off: he was too eager, she wasn't at all eager, in spite of all she tried to do to conceal it. He lay with his hands behind his head, elbows poking upward, staring at the darkened ceiling.

"That was beautiful," he murmured.

"I'm sorry."

"It wasn't you."

"It was."

"My God, are we going to argue about it?"

"I'm not arguing." He sighed. He said nothing further. Kissing her cheek, he patted her shoulder and lay back, and in minutes was asleep, breathing steadily, effortlessly: the sleep of a man with a clear conscience, she thought. His conscience was clear, it had to be. Had to be!

Late in the afternoon on Tuesday, Derrick phoned her at the store.

"I hope I'm not interrupting anything. I called to tell you I won't be home for supper."

"Problems?"

"Not really, it's just a bunch of us have to work late. There's a big presentation coming up for a medical center down on the Gulf Coast. It shouldn't be too late."

"Midnight?"

"That's *too* late. I should get home before eleven."

"Will you get a chance to eat?"

"We'll have dinner brought in, sandwiches, deli, you know."

"I'll keep your side of the bed warm."

"You keep yourself warm, love, after that debacle the other night we've got some catching up to do. We've got to shape up our act, Mommy."

"Right."

He got home at ten after eleven. She was already in bed, watching the eleven o'clock news. He shut it off and sat on the edge of the bed and kissed her.

"Let me take a quick shower."

"Mind if I join you, stranger?"

"I'd love it."

For some reason she could not identify she was infinitely more relaxed tonight than she'd been Sunday night. Completely, deliciously relaxed. Thinking back, maybe she was upset over Reggie, so that it tightened her up. It had nothing to do with Walsh and Atlanta and the accident on Belvedere Road going on six years ago.

She had no way of knowing at the moment, of course, but that wasn't the case. Actually, the bliss she acknowledged and was enjoying, stepping into the shower with him, feeling the comforting spray caress her back and shoulders as he held her and kissed her, was grounded in ignorance.

~~~~ SEVENTEEN ~~~~

A slender, balding man in his late fifties peered through thick lenses at the computer screen before him; it was filled with numbers. On the stand to the right of it lay an open folder. He was engaged in checking the numbers on the screen against those on the top sheet in the folder, his enormous eyes flicking back and forth between paper and screen. He suddenly stopped working, set down his ballpoint pen, stretched and yawned and, leaving the computer on, got up and went to the open window to look out at the darkened heavens, the swarming stars in the Milky Way, the nearly full moon split horizontally by a slender cloud.

The studio apartment was spartanly furnished and extraordinarily tidy. Even his work station was almost preposterously neatly arranged: six identical ballpoint pens lying side by side in perfect order, the folder cover with the word "Cambridge" neatly lettered on it in red felt pen. The computer and printer were free of fingerprints and, despite being nearly four years old, looked new. The most fastidious cleaning lady could have walked in and bustled about feeling for dust in the most out-of-the-way places and found not a speck. Magazines in a stand alongside a BarcaLounger were stacked upright according to date, and the oldest among them looked as new as the most recent issue.

About his person the man was just as fastidious. He wore a clean dress shirt with the cuffs buttoned; he wore a tie and his jacket. His shoes gleamed. With him and in his surroundings, order was absolute, cleanliness reigned. Had he been married, his wife would doubtless have been held to the most stringent standards of housekeeping. Fortunately he was a bachelor, thereby sparing some woman the demands he placed upon himself.

In the kitchen he took a clean teaspoon from its drawer, washed it thoroughly, took down a clean cup and saucer, washed them as well, and removing the softly whistling teapot from the burner, placed a tea bag in the cup and poured in the water. Studying his watch as he did so, he dipped the tea bag ten times in the cup; not nine, not eleven, over a period of exactly fifty seconds. He disposed of the bag, washed out and dried the teapot, and sat down to tea, unfolding a linen napkin and setting it on his lap. He customarily used neither sugar nor milk. He tested the tea, found it slightly hot for his taste, and put the cup aside. Again he consulted his watch. This time he watched the second hand circle the face twice, blew on his tea three times, and adjudging it ready, began sipping it. A faint smile crossed his plain, unmemorable face. It always worked. One minute was not enough, three minutes was too long, the tea became tepid.

His doorbell rang. He set his cup down, refolded his napkin, placed it alongside the cup, and got up.

"Who is it?"

"Special delivery," said a muffled voice. "From . . . let's see, U.S. government. Internal Revenue."

The man smiled, his huge eyes brightening. "Slip it under the door."

"I'm afraid you'll have to sign for it."

"Oh, very well." Unlocking and unbolting the door, he jerked it open. "My tea's getting cold. . . ."

The man filling the doorway had no envelope, no package of any kind. He wore a raincoat with the collar turned up and a felt hat with the brim pulled sharply down, all but concealing the upper half of his face. The lower half began with a flourishing mustache. From his coat pocket he drew his right hand; in it was a gun with a silencer.

"Ssssseeeee here. . . ." began the perfectionist.

The man closed the door behind him. He said nothing, instead motioning with the gun for the other to move toward the rear of the room, to the open window. The perfectionist stood with his back to it; his eyes fixed on the gun, he was shaking badly, his hands upraised, his sallow face gone bone white with fear.

"Whoooo are you?"

No response. Again his confronter gestured with the weapon, instructing him to drop his hands. No sooner had he done so than the other raised his right foot, shoving it forward, pushing him brutally hard in the stomach. He cried out, a gagging sound, doubled forward, and wedged between the upraised window and the sill, his legs and head keeping him from falling out.

With his free hand, the other man pushed his head downward and outward, sending him tumbling out.

He screamed all the way down to the brick courtyard seven floors below. Looking out, the man could see him lying on his back, his limbs flung outward awkwardly, his head lying at an unnatural angle, his neck snapped. His necktie lay over his face, partially concealing it. The man closed the window, studied the computer screen briefly, turned off the computer, removed the floppy disk, took it and the folder out with him. On the kitchen table the tea sat cooling in its cup.

Once arrived, suspicion like cancer tends to grow, often with alarming rapidity. Countless factors invariably contribute to its maturation. Regardless of how single-mindedly and how strenuously Lyssa fought against believing that Derrick had, technically speaking, murdered his wife, she could not dispatch the dragon. It came, it went, at will. It happened to be nowhere near her when she got a call from Doreen shortly after lunch the next day. Recognizing who it was even before

Doreen identified herself, Lyssa felt her heart sink with sympathy for her. She was such a good soul, she deserved better; what did she need with a man twice her age who cheated on her, lied to her, took it out on her when things went awry in business. Psychological abuse could be more painful, more insidious than physical abuse.

"Lee, have you seen today's paper?"

"It's back in the office, I think. I haven't had the chance."

"Go back and take a look, I'll hold."

"What is all this?"

"Just please go on back, get it out, and we'll talk. This won't take long, I promise, but it's something you should know."

"Why all the mystery? Doreen, tell me."

"Please?"

Back in the office with the door closed for privacy, she sat at the desk with the *Bellingham Press* open in front of her. "I'm here, shoot."

"Look at page seventeen, the obituaries."

Lyssa rattled pages hurriedly to the obituaries and read. "Cochrane . . ."

"Read it aloud," insisted Doreen.

"George Francis Cochrane, former resident of Bellingham, died last night in a fall from the window of his sixth-floor apartment at two-thirty-five Bly Avenue in Elgin. Mr. Cochrane was fifty-nine years old. Born and brought up in Bellingham, he was a certified public accountant who worked free-lance and was also employed by a number of firms in central Michigan, most recently, Cambridge Medical and Surgical Equipment in Bellingham. Mr. Cochrane retired last January. He was a bachelor, a member of the Knights of Columbus, and communicant of St. Joseph's Church in Elgin. He was also a member of the National Association of CPAs and an officer in the state chapter for the seven years preceding his death. He is survived by two sisters."

"It says he fell," said Doreen.

"It says."

"You think somebody pushed him?"

"I don't know, Doreen, I wasn't there."

Doreen prattled on, speculating over the "coincidence": Cochrane's dying just before he was to testify to the IRS. Lyssa only half listened; Derrick rose in mind, the after-hours business meeting, his not getting home until after eleven. Glancing over the obituary, she noted that it failed to specify the time of Cochrane's death. She caught herself. Good God, what was she doing!

"Lee?"

"I'm still here. You're right, maybe now the company's off the hook. Evidently he was all the IRS had."

"He was the one making all the waves."

"Reggie must be breathing easier."

"I'll say, he was in a great mood when he left for work this morning. Kidding around, relaxed, like his old self. I almost asked if he was feeling okay. I mean up to this morning you never saw such a grouchy bear."

"This morning . . . Cochrane died last night, how could Reggie know? Was it on the morning news on TV?"

"It must have been. He always watches the news while he's getting dressed. He came downstairs a different man. What a change, amazing."

"Amazing."

"I just thought you'd be interested. The poor man, how could anybody fall out a window? I know little kids do, but a grown man? Maybe he was drunk. Maybe he jumped, suicide. Maybe he was . . . what's the word?"

"Despondent? Over losing his job? You don't believe that. I'm sure the police are investigating. As a rule, they don't mention if there's anything suspicious about a death in the obituary. If this was suspicious, it'll be in another part of the paper tomorrow, the next day."

"I'll let you go. Maybe I'll see you tomorrow. I feel like shopping. You know, celebrating. Oh, I don't mean because the poor man died. Because . . . because Reggie won't have to go to Washington. I don't think he will. He wouldn't be so happy if he still had to go, would he?"

"No."

"Bye bye, see you."

Lyssa sat with her hand on the cradled phone until Agnes looked in. Then came in.

"You look confused, anxious, slightly shocked, all at the same time. What's up?"

"What time is it?"

Lyssa glanced at her watch; they spoke at the same time.

"One-fifty."

"She gets out of work at five," said Lyssa, thinking out loud. "Five, ten minutes to get ready to leave, ten minutes to get here, walk by . . ."

"Are you okay? You sound like you're flipping."

"Derrick's secretary, Maggie Donovan, walks by here going and coming from work. She should be coming by about five-twenty. I have to catch her, we have to talk."

"About what, atomic secrets? You should see your face."

"She loves our stuff, I asked her to stop in."

"Is that why you're so serious? You might sell her a blouse?"

"I'll tell you all about it after I talk to her. What time is it?"

"About forty seconds since the last time you asked. A long time till five-twenty."

The longest three and a half hours in memory, as it turned out. Lyssa purposely stayed out front in the store from 5:05 on. Five-twenty came and went with no sign of Maggie. She still hadn't shown when Lyssa left for the day.

~~~~ EIGHTEEN ~~~~

Too many coincidences: Walsh's being murdered while she was in Atlanta, Derrick's new toy, a .38, the same caliber, according to the forensic people in Atlanta, as the two bullets that had killed the detective. Cochrane's conveniently falling from a window just before he was to present his damaging evidence against Reggie and Cambridge to Internal Revenue, Derrick's late meeting the night Cochrane died. None of them incriminating but, all taken together, more than enough to keep her suspicions afloat.

That evening she and Derrick had dinner at home: New York bay scallops, baked potato with sour cream, mixed vegetables, garden salad. He was relaxed, in a good mood, prompting her to recall that ever since the business about Cochrane had come to light, he'd been a little uptight. Or did she imagine it?

"You've a birthday coming up," he said.

"Don't remind me."

"The big four-oh."

"I'll be thirty-three, as if you didn't know."

He frowned. "Are you sure? I could swear it was thirty-two."

"Don't be an ass."

"What do you want for your birthday?"

"Nothing."

"Come on, you must have something you've got your eye on."

"Not really. What do you think, women watch the

calendar and start window-shopping thirty days before the big day?"

"I'll surprise you, like every year." He grew serious. "I love you, Lys, I adore you."

"I love you, as if I have to tell you."

"I like hearing it."

She loved him to the max, as the kids phrased it. He was the fuel that fed her flame, the agent that turned it up. They were happy and lucky; life couldn't be better; certainly on analysis it couldn't. They had each other, their health, their work, their common interests. She didn't much like his absences on trips, but that was his job, a big part of it, not unlike millions of others, and had to be put up with. As far as that went, some husbands were away weeks at a time. He was never away more than two or three days, often no more than overnight.

All of which was before; now a change in her feelings toward him was under way: subtle but definite, beyond her control, fed, engineered by forces over which she had no control. Wives suspect husbands of cheating on them, perhaps the most devastating blow to any wife's self-esteem. It had to be heartbreaking to love someone and suddenly discover you were second choice, that you'd been pushed aside by some stranger. Faced with such a situation, women were so terribly helpless, usually so powerless to combat it.

He wasn't cheating on her, he was too ethical, too honest to stoop to such a thing. What she suspected of him was far worse, and dangerous. To her. And yet what, specifically, did she suspect him of? Killing Walsh? Killing Cochrane? How could he kill Walsh when he was two thousand miles away in Seattle? And who said Cochrane was killed? He could very well have been drunk and fallen out of his window. So it was superbly well timed, from Reggie's, from Cambridge's point of view, but it could still be coincidence.

But that was the problem, could have been, might have

been, this insidiously pervasive doubt, uncertainty.

"What are you thinking about, sweetheart?"

"Nothing."

"Amazing, you always say that when you have something particularly heavy on your mind. Level with me— is it you resent my asking? Or just that it's none of my business? Never is."

"I have no secrets from you, if that's what you're implying."

"I'm not implying anything, just making an observation. How's your steak?"

"A little tough."

"Mine's delicious. You're a good cook, Mommy."

"We have a good stove."

One candle flickered, as if lightly moving air passed through it, missing the other candle, leaving it burning steadily. The music coming softly from the stereo was Delibes's *Coppélia*, which she loved. The terrace windows were open, letting in the warm night air.

Suspicion, incipient fear of him. Not here, sitting opposite him, not in the living room, talking, only in the bedroom, with the light turned low or in darkness. When they were close, when his arms were around her, when they made love. Surely the worst time of all. Then and only then did she tighten up, unable to conceal it. He felt it and it puzzled him. Clearly something was upsetting her; next he would begin questioning her. Sunday night, he blamed himself, insisting he was the cause of the "failure" of their lovemaking. He was being generous; she was the sole problem and he knew it.

He would want to make love tonight; they never went more than two nights without it, and the mood was right, if they could sustain it. She sighed inwardly. He had gotten onto talking about the food and failed to notice her feelings of the moment in her expression. She tried smiling as she nodded and could feel the falsity of it.

She dreaded getting into bed. Battling to relax was all

wrong; if anything, effort only made her more uptight. Worse, she was beginning to hate herself for it. How could she do this to him? Accuse him of all sorts of transgressions without having the decency to put any of them into words. It was exactly what she was doing: accusing, judging, punishing him.

There was one way out of it. Tomorrow for certain she'd get together with Maggie; she'd know if he was at the late-night meeting until it broke up just before eleven. Of if he ducked out early. The secretaries had to be there. Or did they? Maybe not; maybe the executives relied on a recording machine, maybe Maggie didn't know anything about the meeting. Still, even if she wasn't required to attend, it was possible somebody's secretary was pressed into service. She could ask Maggie to check with whomever it was.

No, she couldn't.

Damn, it was getting more complicated by the hour. He had stopped talking about the dinner. Excusing himself, he went to the stereo and turned up the music.

"May I have this dance?"

He held her and kissed her soulfully. She gave it her all in response, but it was playacting. It wasn't that she couldn't abide his touch, it hadn't yet gotten to that. But she resisted, on occasion practically shrinking from his hands. She deliberately became the aggressor to forestall his mentioning it.

But from his first kiss on, it was a disaster. When it was over, she sensed that his patience with her was beginning to thin. One night, Sunday, was tolerable; continuation of the same was more than unexpected and a disappointment. It upset him. He didn't assume blame this time, didn't question, did not get angry; he kept it all inside. He kissed her good night and fell asleep.

NINETEEN

Lyssa got to the store at her usual time—10:00 A.M.—too late to catch Maggie Donovan on her way to the office. After a hideously long and uneventful day that she spent on pins and needles, five o'clock came around at last and she began counting the minutes. It wasn't until twenty past when, from her outpost by the cash register, she spotted Maggie walking by. Out she ran.

"Are you just going to walk past?" she asked.

"Mitheth Morgan, how are you?"

"Fine. We're supposed to get together, remember?"

Maggie looked adorable in a navy-blue suit with brass buttons and white sailor. Her belt looked six inches wide and was inexpensive, showing hairline cracks around the buckle. She came in somewhat timidly, Lyssa noted, as if entering some secret chamber, forbidden to all but royalty and the rich.

"I confeth, I wanted to come in, I wath tempted, but I didn't thee you."

"Maggie, this is Agnes Pelletier, my partner in crime. Aggie, Maggie Donovan, Derrick's office brain."

"Oh, Mitheth Morgan." Maggie tittered and waved away the suggestion.

"Lyssa, Maggie, from now on."

"What are you looking for?" Agnes asked.

"What am I not in thith plathe. Everythingth tho beautiful. I know I can't afford buttonth, let alone anything to wear."

Agnes excused herself, setting out for a customer who'd just come in.

"Before we start," said Lyssa, "let's get one thing straight. Whatever you see strikes your fancy, don't think about price." She grinned and lowered her voice. "We mark everything up at least a thousand percent. So everybody thinks."

"Thtill, the priceth are thcary."

"Don't be scared. How about this?"

She showed her a three-button ivory wool jacket with rhinestone buttons and a sprinkling of rhinestone studs.

"It'th heavenly."

"It goes with practically everything."

Maggie eyed the tag: $300.

"Oh."

Again Lyssa lowered her voice. "Seventy-five."

"Oh! Oh, look at that!"

Maggie all but sprinted to a silk blouse with dark blue filigree across the bodice and surrounding the cuffs.

"Forty-nine," whispered Lyssa.

"But it thayth one ninety-nine."

"Don't believe everything you read. Want to try it on?"

"Could I? It'th my thize."

"Take it back, let's see how it looks on you."

Off she ran with the blouse. Agnes came back.

"Aren't you setting a dangerous precedent? Selling stuff at cost, plus we lose the shipping and handling we paid?"

"I'm not about to make a habit of it."

"She may think you want to."

"Trust me, she's walked by a dozen times since I asked her to stop in. You saw, I had to practically lasso her to get her through the door. She won't abuse it, she's not the type to. She's young, attractive, cute, she's underpaid. Let her live a little."

"Whatever you say, Fairy Godmother."

Maggie came back.

"Perfect!" exclaimed Lyssa. "If I didn't know better, I'd think you walked in here wearing it. It's you!"

"It'th expenthive."

"Thirty-nine dollars."

"You said forty-nine."

"My mistake, thirty-nine."

"Really, Mitheth Morgan, I couldn't take advantage of you."

"Please, we take advantage of everybody who walks in the door. You work hard, long hours, you're underpaid, you're entitled. Tell me something confidentially, is Derrick a slave driver?"

"Oh no, heth the thweeteth man, tho kind, and a perfect gentleman."

"Doesn't he make you work late?"

"Jutht oneth in a while. There wath a big important meeting the other night. He wath there."

"Till it ended?"

"Oh yeth, he had to be, he wath pretty much in charge."

Lyssa's heart lifted and sang; she felt mildly staggered by the good news. But almost at once hated herself for suspecting he had anything to do with Cochrane's death in the first place. How in heaven's name could he? How could she stoop to such unfairness? The poor darling . . .

Maggie looked disturbed. "Did I thay thomething out of line?"

"No, no, not at all. Let's see what else we can find. Go back and take that off and I'll look around."

Lyssa found a lovely denim skirt while Maggie was in the dressing room. When she emerged with the blouse over her arm, her eyes lit up. Lyssa went back into the dressing room with her. The skirt also fit her beautifully.

"Derrick is terrifically fond of you," she said. "You really are his right arm. Secretary, file clerk, telephone operator, travel agent . . ."

"That can be a big hathle, getting hith plane ticketh. Would you believe I wath on the phone for almoth two hourth arranging that quickie trip he made down to Atlanta?"

Lyssa reacted stunned.

"Atlanta . . ."

"But there wath one to Dallath latht year that wath the biggest headache you ever thaw."

On she prattled, before charging her two purchases, thanking Lyssa again and again, and leaving.

~~~~~~ TWENTY ~~~~~~

It was 5:38, Lyssa had drifted back to the office to sit alone and digest Maggie's revelation. Agnes came back.

"Was she able to give you anything worth your bribing her?" Lyssa sat motionless, staring into space. It was as if she was unaware someone had come in. "Lyssa?" Agnes snapped her fingers. "It's me."

"He went to Atlanta. He told me he had to make a hurry-up second trip to Seattle, but instead he went down to Atlanta. He was there when I was. He killed Walsh."

"Now wait a minute, you don't know anything of the sort."

"That was his only reason for going."

"Dear heart . . ."

"He's the missing felt hat and raincoat and phony mustache the neighbor described. It all fits."

Agnes locked the door and sat on the edge of the desk. Lyssa went on, talking in a daze. "He practically went wild when I told him Walsh came here to see me; almost as bad the second time. He was deathly afraid he'd uncover the truth about the accident. He had no way of knowing how close Walsh was getting. He had to play safe, had to kill him, don't you see?"

"What about the other one, the accountant?"

"Cochrane. I don't care about him. Besides, the night he died Derrick was in a meeting at the office; he didn't leave till it broke up just before eleven. He . . . wait. . . ."

"What?"

"Maggie never did say what time it broke up. Only that he never left. Don't you get it?"

"I don't get anything, it all sounds like gibberish."

"That meeting could have ended at ten, giving him plenty of time to get out to Elgin."

"So you're saying he killed Cochrane, too. Who's next? Lyssa, you're jumping to conclusions so fast, so hard you'll break your legs. Take a break from railroading him and think a minute. Suppose he did go to Atlanta and was there when what's his name—"

"Walsh."

"—was killed. Does that automatically mean he did it?"

"He had motive enough to kill him."

"Then he must have had it when Walsh came here to Bellingham. Why didn't he kill him then, save himself a trip? Don't you see what you're doing? Forcing everything to fit neatly when, from what I see, nothing fits. Dear heart, if what you've told me were hauled into a courtroom, the judge would toss it out the window. That's how thin it is. It's water."

"Cochrane's not important, it's Walsh. I have to call Gail Horvath."

She set a hand on the cradled phone.

Agnes sighed in exasperation. "I'm going. I'm going." She paused in the doorway. "Just promise me one thing. Promise me you won't light into him when he comes home tonight. It's not fair, you don't have one iota of proof."

"You don't know what I know about this whole mess."

"Whatever you know or think you know isn't proof. For the past couple weeks you've been acting like Eliza crossing the ice with the hounds at her heels, looking behind you, alternating between frantic and suspicious and most of the time a little of each. You're on the verge of cracking up."

"I've got to make this call."

Agnes threw up her hands and slammed the door, leaving Lyssa in privacy. She got out her address book and dialed Gail Horvath's number. The answering machine came on, droning instructions. She hung up. Then called a second time.

"Gail, it's Lyssa Morgan, call me at the office: five-one-seven. five-five-five-two-seven-one hundred. I'll be here till seven. Whatever you do, don't call me at home. We have to talk, have to!"

The store closed at six; Agnes came back to check on her before leaving for the day.

"You plan to sit there till morning?"

"I'm waiting for her to call back."

Agnes cocked her head sympathetically. "Cheer up, Lys. Trust me, you're manufacturing the whole sorry mess. He's incapable of murder."

"Nobody is."

"He's your husband, Chrissakes, you love him; he adores you. See you in the morning."

"Right. And thanks, Aggie, for caring."

The phone rang, she snatched it up.

"Lyssa? Gail Horvath. I just came in the door."

Agnes stood in the doorway. Lyssa looked up at her. Agnes threw up one hand, signifying she understood, and withdrew. Lyssa hurriedly told Gail about Derrick's being in Atlanta on the night of Walsh's murder.

"I gather you think he came down and killed him," said Gail.

"Exactly. It all looks so cut-and-dried. . . ."

"I'll give you that, but it could be coincidence."

"How I wish. Only the way I figure, he didn't go down there to tell him to keep away from me. By then Walsh was done with me, as things stood we'd never have seen each other again. I think Derrick went down to find out what he knew, beat it out of him if he had to. Walsh either told him or didn't. Either way, Derrick had no choice but to shut him up."

"That's possible. . . ."

"You don't agree."

"I don't know, it's that simple. What will you do? How will you face him tonight?"

"I . . . haven't thought about it."

"You better, you're going to have to. I can't tell you what to do, but I wouldn't flat out accuse him. If you're wrong, you'll wreck your marriage, all the trust, the faith you've built up in each other. If you're right, he might kill you."

"I'll have to play dumb, at least for the time being. Anything else come to light on the case?"

"It's dead. And buried by the police, I gather. They're back to mugging complaints, stolen cars, and business as usual. There hasn't been a murder since poor Joseph. We're due."

They talked a little more and Lyssa hung up. It was 6:11. Derrick would be home by now. She'd better leave.

"God . . ."

TWENTY-ONE

Otto the doorman greeted her as she stepped out of a cab.

"Mr. Morgan just went up, Mrs. Morgan."

"How are you, Otto?"

"Getting deaf." He grinned behind his white walrus mustache. "Mit all the zirens all day. It's like zomebody's out to burn down the zity."

She stood staring unseeing at the closed elevator doors. She was getting uptight in bed, he had noticed, now she'd be so from the moment she walked in and their eyes met. She had to get a grip on herself. She thought back to her conversation with Gail; she didn't seem at all surprised when Lyssa told her Derrick had been in Atlanta the night Walsh was murdered. Lyssa had expected some kind of reaction—it was like dropping a bomb—but Gail had taken it without any change of tone. Of course, she was blasé about everything; taking the news in stride was no effort. Likely because being a thousand miles away, she was in no danger herself.

And Aggie, she'd practically read her the riot act for accusing him; railroading him, was the way she'd put it. Of course, all she knew about the situation was what she, Lyssa, chose to tell her, and Aggie chose to base her defense of Derrick on what she knew about him, her own impression of him. And she'd always been crazy about him.

The elevator arrived, an older couple got off. She started; the man looked very much like Walsh, even to his suit.

He saw her staring and smiled thinly. She smiled back to allay his embarrassment, however slight, and boarded the elevator. The doors closed; she took a huge breath and watched the numbers ascend.

"Whatever you do, whatever you say, be fair. Fair!"

That wasn't the immediate problem; disguising her shock at learning he'd been in Atlanta, that he'd blatantly lied to her about Seattle, was the job at hand. The door was unlocked for her. She walked in to find him in front of the TV watching the news, sipping on a diet soda. He had changed into slacks and a T-shirt and was barefoot.

"Sweetheart, I was starting to worry. . . ."

"Sorry I'm late. A big shipment came in about five of six. It was either stay and check it out or do it in the morning. I'd rather face customers tomorrow."

"Tired?"

"Kind of."

"Let me fix you a Scotch." He snuffled.

"I'd love one. You okay?"

"The big A's been kicking up a little today."

"Did you have your stuff with you?"

"Yeah. I hate to overdose on it. I used it all day, but very sparingly. The goddamn pollen count must be four hundred." He handed her her drink. She sat and sipped. He leaned over and kissed her. "Let's start over. I should have kissed you when you walked in the door. You look worried, problems with the shipment?"

"Not big."

"We'll have a bite, go to bed early." He winked. "And see what develops."

"You're in a good mood today."

"No reason not to be, except for the damned pollen. Business is good, my job's secure, it looks like we're going to swing that deal for New Century Laser."

"I thought you were leery about that one."

"Not with our acquiring it. I was just wondering where we'd get the money. Reggie got it."

They made supper together; he continued in a buoyant mood. It helped relax her. That was the big thing, she thought, fight like hell to get relaxed and stay that way later in bed. Fight like hell?

Halfway through the meal she found herself thinking about Walsh. She hadn't gotten to know him well enough to judge him as a human. He was reputedly honest, conscientious, hardworking. People who kept working in the same line after retirement were usually more industrious than the average. But under the soft-spoken demeanor, his almost apologetic approach, did there lurk the vicious doggedness of the implacable Inspector Javert in *Les Misérables*? Had he been out to get Derrick at any cost? Even to fabricating evidence to build his case against him? That sort of thing wasn't common, but did happen. Had Walsh decided on the day he retired that he'd devote the rest of his life to putting Derrick behind bars? And over time had he become monomaniacal about doing so?

What *had* happened that night? It was hard to believe Derrick walked in and brutally shot Walsh. What then? Did Derrick try to reason with him, had they gotten into an argument, had Walsh threatened him with imminent arrest, had Derrick panicked or lost his temper and then shot him? Had he threatened to and Walsh laughed, provoking him to pull the trigger?

No. The detective had died from two bullets in the back of the head, a cowardly execution, the signature of a Mob hit. Derrick was no mobster, he had nothing to do with any gang, much less the Mafia. He had no Sicilian blood.

Still, the manner of Walsh's death did preclude all possible scenarios except premeditated murder. That was a fact and she had no option but to accept it. And that night after his return, she'd found him in the study cleaning his pistol. Doesn't one always clean a gun after it's been fired? And only then? That cock-and-bull story about being mugged in Seattle, the muggers taking over four hundred dollars, his reaction, humiliation, indignation, it'd never happen again. He'd sold it all to her.

"Darling?" he asked.

"Yes?"

"What's wrong, and don't say nothing."

"That shipment, we were supposed to receive a dozen crown appliqué sweaters, we got two dozen. *That's* why the figures were way off!"

"Eat."

They watched the ten o'clock news and took a shower together. She did her best to be compliant and must have succeeded; he didn't take further exception to her mood, didn't repeat his question as to what was wrong. Only in bed it became a different matter entirely. Try as she was might, she could not suppress her mounting fear. Imagination transformed him into a stranger and a threat. She could not relax, his merely touching her with his hand, caressing her arm or shoulder, caused her to tighten up. Once, when he slid his hands up her arms to her neck to frame her face to kiss her, she flinched.

"What the hell is the matter with you!" he burst out. "You're behaving like I'm a rapist, getting ready to attack. Goddamn it, I hate this!"

He got up and began pacing, oblivious to his nakedness, suddenly, in seconds, consumed with anger.

"We're man and wife, in total privacy. If we can't relax here, can't do it right, for Christ sakes where can we?"

"Stop swearing, calm down."

"Just shut up and listen." He stood at the foot of the bed, instructing with his upraised finger. "Shape up, 'darling,' get a grip, straighten out, or we'll have to do something drastic. I refuse to go on like this. Am I being clear? And don't go giving me that crap about problems with fucking sweaters. Something's going on in your head and it's screwing up our sex life! Screw that up and you screw up our marriage. I don't want that and I should think you don't either. This is the last time it goes like this, understand?"

He snatched up the blanket.

"Where are you going?"

"To the guest room, where do you think? I'm obviously not welcome in our bed. 'Not welcome'—that's a laugh. You can't stand being in the same house with me! Good night, love, sweet dreams."

She thought about getting up and begging him to come back, drag him back, if necessary. But thought better of it. She spread another blanket, got back into bed, and tried to sleep. She might just as well have tried to hold her breath all night.

She lay awake till the sky turned gray and the sun rose.

"Jesus, Mary, and Joseph," groaned Agnes. "Did you get the license number before you passed out?"

"That bad?"

"You look horrendous. What happened? I know, it's none of my business. Can I make a suggestion? How about you go home and get some sleep?"

"I'm okay. I'll be back in the office if I'm needed."

"Stretch out on the desk, why don't you? There should be a couple old *Women's Wear Dailies* you could use for a pillow."

"Be a pal, get off my back."

She managed to doze off in the chair for about twenty minutes. The phone woke her. Her watch read 10:50. It was Derrick. She tensed. He'd left the apartment before she did, their last exchange had been his ultimatum, the night before, when he went slamming out to sleep in the guest room.

"Lys? I . . . apologize. I behaved like a stupid punk."

"You did have good reason."

"Not to act like that. Look, how about meeting me at the zoo. We can have hot dogs or something. We can talk.

There's something I've been holding off telling you, and frankly I'm ashamed of myself. Can you get away, say around one?"

"Sure."

"We can meet inside the tropical-bird house. You know the building, the one where they shoot cool air up to keep the birds from flying out; the jungle setting."

"One o'clock."

"Again, I apologize."

"It was my fault. The way *I* acted started it . . ."

"I finished it." He half laughed self-consciously. "In spades. See you, Mommy."

A dour-looking shoebill stood on one rigid leg, the other bent backward, appraising them over its mottled, reddish, curiously shaped bill. Next to it a saddlehill stork, its head and slender neck jet black, its red-and-black-striped bill poking from under the cover of a white visor, where it joined its head. It almost looked as if the two of them were in conversation when the Morgans caught their attention and invited their curiosity. Derrick finished his hot dog.

"Look at that big guy's beak, you could open beers with it."

The dimly lit jungle was filled with tropical birds: toucans in abundance, vultures and storks, and a monkey-eating eagle, its menacing face surrounded by a cinnamon-colored ruff of feathers. Calls vied and echoed and the darkness where Lyssa stood looking into the setting felt like the interior of a vast cavern. Derrick finished wiping the mustard from his fingers with his napkin.

"I almost forgot," he said. "Confession time."

"Let's get some daylight."

The glare of the sun set Lyssa squinting. The zoo was mobbed with schoolchildren, the younger ones hanging on to balloons and carrying on noisily, the older children behaving like sedate seniors. Embarrassed by the little ones? They moved to the railing overlooking the crocodile pit. Two starlings sat on the studded back of a huge, mud-encrusted male partially embedded in the bank.

"I didn't go to Seattle a second time, Lyssa."

She caught herself; she almost said, I know.

"I went to Atlanta."

"I thought you had to go back to Seattle to straighten out something about operating tables?"

"I lied. I . . . didn't want you to know I went chasing after him."

"Walsh."

"Yes. I went down to talk to him. About the accident, Elizabeth, all of it. I went with the intention of finding out what track he was following. Oh, I know he was looking for the drunk driver, a whole different tack. Which I thought ridiculous, as you know. If he didn't find him five years ago, how could he possibly expect to today? Anyway, that's all meaningless now, with him dead.

"I got there early in the day and walked around all day rehearsing what I was going to say to him. How to approach it, you know. After dinner I took a cab to his place. When I got there, a crowd was beginning to gather out front of the apartment house. Police cars were arriving. It turned out somebody had gone up to his place and murdered him not ten minutes before. Walked in, killed him, walked out and off the face of the earth, apparently."

The two birds deserted the crocodile's back and it trundled down the bank into the muddy water, submerging, elevating its snout, swishing its tail gently.

"Why didn't you tell me you went to Atlanta?"

"To be brutally honest, I didn't think it was any of your business. I mean it all happened before we even met."

"Is that any reason to lie? And so creatively. That business about being mugged . . ."

"I was. It happened just like I told you, only on my first trip to Seattle."

"Really?" She larded her tone heavily with doubt.

"So you don't believe me. Have it your way."

"What I don't understand is why you didn't tell me about it when you got home. You waited till you got back from Atlanta to tell me about Seattle?"

"I probably wouldn't have told you at all if you hadn't walked in and found me cleaning the gun."

"Another secret . . ."

"Now, just a minute. I've admitted I lied about Atlanta; because I didn't want to get into a discussion of it."

"Because it's none of my business."

"I'll admit I had no intention of telling you about the gun, only because I didn't want to upset you. I know how you feel about guns."

"So this is what it's come to. We're starting to keep secrets from each other."

"What are you keeping from me?" he asked.

She had turned around to talk with her back to him. She whirled about.

"Are you trying to be funny?"

"I'm sorry, darling. Bad joke." He put his arm around her. "The bottom line is when there's something I know you don't approve of or might upset you, I don't tell you. What would be the point? Don't tell me there aren't things that have happened to you you haven't kept from me. Isn't that normal for married couples, even people who love each other as deeply as us?"

He was right. And uncanny; he seemed able to read her mind about Atlanta, answering the unasked questions. It was certainly a reasonable explanation, but was it the truth? She could see no gain in pressing him on it further, firing questions in volleys, as if deliberately trying to trip him up. That he'd resent and have every right to.

So he'd gotten to Walsh's just after the shooting, turning his trip into a wild-goose chase. It did make sense, though, from a wholly different angle. If she were he and she'd been in the accident and Walsh came out of the woodwork five years later to talk to Derrick, she'd be thrown off balance, especially when he came back a second time. And to prevent its continuing, she'd probably fly down there to beard him in his den, settle the damned thing once and for all. Walsh was disinterring old bones; Derrick wanted him to give it up, leave it where the police and the insurance company had buried it.

"What would you have said if you'd gotten to talk to him?" she asked.

"I'd have asked him to give it up, obviously. I'd have done my best to persuade him to. I don't mean strong-arm him, I mean threaten to sue him. Sue the city, they're responsible for him."

"He was retired, remember?"

"They still have a responsibility; he worked in the department more than thirty-five years. With or without their authorization he was still working. I wanted to settle it, Lys, I wanted it over, not dragging on and on, him drifting in and out of our lives. I wanted us rid of him for good."

That, he could have phrased better, she mused. Having apparently covered the subject to his satisfaction, he dropped it. She was happy to; she, too, was satisfied. And the best part was that she hadn't had to drag it out of him. They were nearing the cat pit: lions, tigers, and a solitary leopard lounging about sunning themselves, oblivious to the children lining the railing gawking at them, demanding their attention. Her thoughts went to Cochrane and his oh-so-timely fall. Cambridge was off the hook, Reggie was happy, Doreen relieved; everyone, even Derrick, seemed to gain something by the poor man's passing.

They stopped by the railing. Directly below, a huge male Bengal tiger lay looking up, looking straight at her. It stared at her, its hypnotic eyes riveting, teeth gleaming, slaver dripping disgustingly from its massive mouth. Was it hungry, was it tasting her? Had it been a man-eater in its dark jungle domain? That would be its secret.

She thought about divulging her guilty secret to Derrick, her trip to Atlanta, only that could open a whole new can of worms and accomplish nothing. As he'd just now said, every couple keeps some secrets from one another. She would have to keep hers. It nettled her conscience, slightly, and perhaps would in the future, but that she could live with. Last night's rancor was spent, the problem solved, their relationship back on track. She squeezed his arm affectionately, gazing into his eyes. His arm around her, he hugged her. They headed for the main entrance.

"Let's get us a cab," he murmured. "I'll drop you off at the store."

"Wouldn't you rather go home?"

"Yes, yes, by all means." He slapped himself in the forehead with his palm. "What am I thinking? Excellent idea, Mommy."

They stopped to kiss; two small boys coming the other way pointed and laughed. She broke the kiss, pecked his cheek, they went on.

⸺ TWENTY-TWO ⸺

Doreen invited the Morgans to Saturday-night dinner. There would be two other couples, "business friends" of Reggie's.

"The Carlsons and the Smiths, both from out of town. New York, I think, maybe L.A."

Doreen had stopped by the store on her way to meet Reggie for lunch, looking lovely in a two-piece suit of scarlet wool crepe. Definitely her color, scarlet; the jacket was studded with goldtone nail heads around the neckline and around the sleeves. When Lyssa saw her walking in, for some reason she thought of Maggie Donovan and her superb taste in clothes and distressingly limited budget, and wished Doreen were two sizes smaller so she might might shower the secretary with her designer hand-me-downs.

"We'll sit down to dinner at eight," Doreen went on. "But that doesn't mean come at eight, of course. There'll be drinks and stuff before. I wish you and Derrick could come around six."

Lyssa smiled. "Isn't that a bit early?"

"I don't know those women, I just know I'll be a nervous wreck. I'm not much at entertaining, not what you'd call the grand hostess. I know lots about the receiving end, but not much about the giving. It's important to Reggie I be the perfect hostess, only I'll sure need help. I know which fork goes where but . . . oh, Lee, you do understand."

"Of course. We'll be there at six. I will. I can't promise Derrick'll be ready that early. He plays golf Saturday afternoons, if the weather's decent."

"Oh, we won't need him. Just you, for moral support. I do so want everything to be just bee-yoo-ti-ful. For Reggie. He said to me it's real important to make a good impression on them."

"You'll knock their socks off. What do you plan to wear?"

"That's a secret. It's wild." She frowned. "Maybe too wild, I'll have to check with Reggie."

"Wear your Victor Costa, the one you wore to our dinner. The silvertone metallic two-piece, the one with the dirndl skirt. You looked gorgeous in it."

"You really think? I'll do it. Oh, look . . . bee-yoo-ti-ful!"

She fairly lunged toward a tunic-length crewneck pull-over, knit with large cables and airy mesh, with wide ribbing along the edges.

"I love it. . . . I love the color—shrimp."

"Coral."

"Bee-yoo-ti-ful."

~~~ TWENTY-THREE ~~~

Lyssa and Derrick got to the Carlyles at 6:05 Saturday evening. Reggie greeted them; he seemed surprised at their early arrival. Slightly but plainly taken aback.

"The others won't be here till seven."

"We're early, I know," explained Lyssa. "I thought Doreen might need an extra hand."

"She's upstairs putting on her face. Dorey! Doreee'! Company!"

"Be right down."

Lyssa loved the house. It was old, it was grand, it reeked of dignity, gentility. The only real drawback she could see was that on overcast days the dark paneling in both living and dining rooms must make it desperately gloomy: candles at high noon. Had it been her house, she would have ripped out every stick of paneling in favor of wallpaper in light colors. And replaced the clumsy girandole chandelier with something modern. There were also patriotic touches about the place that she thought tasteless, obviously Reggie's contribution: an eagle mirror that all but shouted *e pluribus unum,* carved American flags in the fireplace mantel, less than subtle reminders that the residents were patriotic Americans. Lyssa recalled Doreen's telling her when she moved in she hadn't changed a single thing. Reggie liked his first wife's decorator's taste; his second wife diplomatically let well enough alone. There were some beautiful pieces: twin back-to-back sofas one could be swallowed up by, so comfortable were they, with Boussac prints; she loved the striking Clarence House damask on the regence chairs at the dining-room table. In the dining room, the gloomy paneling was brightened by a group of nineteenth-century prints of the ports of France and a lovely regence gilt mirror, but their presence failed to draw attention from a gilded wooden U.S. eagle, accorded one entire wall. Lyssa could almost hear drums rolling in unison. The occupant of a glass case in the study set the patriotic tone: a life-size figure of a minuteman in full uniform.

"Where is everybody?"

It was Doreen coming down.

"In the study, honeybee," called Reggie.

She came in looking radiant; she was beautiful, decided Lyssa: extraordinary figure, gorgeous complexion, the bone structure of a professional model, without flirting with anorexia. Her smile was like the sun coming up after a solid week of rain.

"Isn't she stunning?" Reggie asked. "Sometimes I think I should take Mr. 1776 out of the case and put you in. Permanent display."

"How would I breathe inside there, Reggie?"

"You wouldn't have to, just stand like you're standing now and look smashing."

Evelyn, the maid, bustled about fine-tuning the dinner preparations. Lyssa caught the distinctive smell of roast beef wafting from the kitchen. The Carlsons and Smiths showed up together around quarter after seven. Arnold Carlson didn't look at all Scandinavian: he was big, bulky, dark-complexioned, a handsome head of dark hair beginning to show gray at the temples. He had a slight speech impediment, a faint lisp, not to be compared with Maggie Donovan's. Mrs. Carlson, Annie, was a handsome older woman who struck Lyssa from the outset as being

a snob. Glancing about the house, she looked critical.
Carlson had to be in his midfifties, she was at least six
or eight years older. The contrast was emphasized by the
Smiths. He was Carlson's age; his wife couldn't have
been more than thirty. She was pretty; not striking, like
Doreen, but undeniably attractive. She looked cool, well
cared for, a petite brunette, the sort of woman who sits
with her mirror more than two hours a day every day
of her life. When she opened her mouth, it sounded like
she had a small potato lodged in it and that she had
almost mastered the art of talking around it. Her southern drawl put Gail Horvath's to shame. Lyssa's attention
went back to Mr. Smith; he didn't look like a Smith, he
looked distinctly Italian or Albanian, something close to
the Mediterranean Sea.

Evelyn served cocktails in the drawing room. Doreen
was standing behind Reggie's chair, Lyssa sitting across
from her, sipping a whiskey sour, Derrick beside her.
Doreen looked straight at her, knit her brows, and made a
slight, barely discernible movement of her head. She obviously wanted to talk. She nodded to Lyssa and excused
herself.

"Let me check on dinner," she sang.

The moment she walked out Lyssa got up and followed.
Derrick and Reggie were too busy talking to the others
even to notice. Lyssa found Doreen not in the kitchen
but in the study. She stood running one hand aimlessly
up and down the glass case. When Lyssa came in, she
closed the door.

"Anything wrong?" Lyssa asked.

"I don't know, but it's weird. It's that Mr. Smith."

"What about him?"

"His name's not Smith, he's Anthony Minervino. They
call him Tony Boots."

Lyssa grinned. "You make him sound like the Mafia."

"He is. . . ."

"Doreen."

"I'm telling you, Lee. He doesn't recognize me, but I do him. No mistaking that face, those eyes. I saw him in Harrahs in Vegas must be four or five years ago. He wasn't with her, what's her name—Harriet? He was with some hooker and his bodyguard. He's a big deal in the Licata family, in L.A."

"Are you sure?"

"Sure as I'm standing here."

"Do you think he recognized you?"

"No, we never got introduced or anything. I was playing the slots with a couple girlfriends when he walked by. He didn't look toward us. One of my friends, Tina Drago, she pointed him out, told me all about him. He's a killer. What'll we do?"

Lyssa patted her back comfortingly. "We don't have to do anything. I'm sure he's not going to pull a gun and start shooting up the place."

"I'm serious! He's bad news. What's he doing here?"

"Reggie invited him."

"How does Reggie know him? We don't know anybody with the Mob. What's going on? What's he doing here in my house? I'm scared."

"Take it easy, he'll be gone in a few hours. You'll probably never see him again."

"I hope. Guys like that make my flesh gallop. They really are scary, I mean ten times worse than what you see in the movies. They looove to hurt people. You look at them cross-eyed out in Vegas and next thing the cops are digging around in the desert looking for your bones. There's tons of people buried out in the desert. The stories you hear . . . I love Vegas, but those creeps ruin it for everybody. They walk in and it's like a black drape drops down over everything. Tony Boots—to think he's going to sit down and eat my roast. I just know I won't even be able to look at him."

"Come on, Doreen, he won't bite. Just put what he does, what he is, out of your mind. His wife seems nice. . . ."

"She's bottomland trash, I know the type, believe me. I bet she doesn't even know he's in the rackets. Most Mob wives don't know what their husbands do. The mistresses know more than the wives. I'd sure hate to be in her shoes."

"When you sit down at dinner, sit at least one chair away from him on the same side. That way you won't have to look at him."

"That's a good idea, let's go back."

They started for the door. Doreen stopped.

"Only one thing. What *is* he doing here? How come Reggie knows such a bum? You think they're doing business?"

"Ask Reggie."

Doreen shuddered. "As if I'd dare. That man's got more secrets from me than a street dog's got fleas."

He does, reflected Lyssa. She patted her back and they set out for the dining room.

﹏﹏ TWENTY-FOUR ﹏﹏

The roast beef, all the food, was superb. Only one slight hitch from appetizer to coffee. Evelyn raced back and forth to the kitchen and appeared close to collapse by dinner's end. Reggie still complained. Campbell, the butler, was on a week's vacation, and the house, certainly the dinner, proved more than Evelyn could handle alone, as hard as she worked. Doreen calmed Reggie after he snapped at Evelyn and he came out of the incident apologizing to her, to his guests, mumbling through his sheepish grin.

Dinner was strange. Mrs. Carlson and Mrs. Smith sat like mannequins while their husbands talked briefly about baseball, the relative merits of all the New York Yankee third basemen back through the past half century, and when this subject was exhausted, they had nothing further to say. Derrick, sitting between Doreen and Lyssa, talked in low tones, but when the others ceased, so did they.

Lyssa studied Annie and Harriet; neither had uttered a sound since sitting down. They put her in mind of well-trained show dogs sitting like stone on the sidelines waiting to be put through their paces. It was eerie, and when the three men fell silent as well and Derrick, Doreen, and she followed suit, it became even eerier. From the main course on, the only sounds were the clicking of silverware, the soft sound of liquids being poured, and the occasional clearing of a throat. It was as if everybody had been struck dumb. Lyssa decided that while she and Doreen were off in the study the men, excepting perhaps Derrick, had gotten into an argument. About baseball? About something. She could feel the tension. Out of the corner of her eye she studied Reggie. Head bent slightly, silver in hand, he fed himself small portions steadily, almost rhythmically. He lowered his face even further. Then raised it, setting down knife and fork. His expression was affable, the suggestion of a smile playing at the corners of his mouth, but it had to be put on, for his eyes burned. What was wrong? What had happened?

The tension sustained itself throughout dinner and the remainder of the evening—and the silence. The situation discouraged Lyssa from breaking the silence with a compliment on the dinner, with any sort of comment. After dinner the men fled to the drawing room for brandy. Reggie closed the door, leaving the four women standing staring at each other.

"Well . . ." Doreen burst out spiritedly. "Anybody want to play Monopoly?"

STRANGER IN MY BED • 139

Their expressions told her they weren't interested in Monopoly. She escorted them into the living room.

"Did the fellows have a . . . Is something wrong?" she asked Harriet.

"Business," she said, and shrugged in a manner that implied "you know."

Doreen looked to Annie for explanation, Annie looked away. Doreen was right, Lyssa thought, the little she herself had seen of Mob wives in the movies suggested these two were precisely that.

"What does Arnold do?" she asked Annie.

"He's in finance," was the vague answer.

"And To—" she began to Harriet, and caught herself. "And Frank?"

"He imports things," responded Harriet. "Ah think."

You think? You don't know? Curiouser and curiouser. Doreen finally managed to get a conversation going with the two of them. Lyssa did her best to contribute. Not a particularly interesting or edifying topic for discussion: the weather. Still, it was something to break the silence.

Lyssa took off her jewelry, hung up her dress, and plumped down on the edge of the bed in her slip to remove her panty hose.

"That was a fun evening," she murmured.

He stood at the dresser taking off his cuff links, restoring them to their place in her jewelry box.

"Believe me, it could have been a lot worse."

"What happened when Doreen and I were out of the room? Something must have, and the way you four locked yourselves in after dinner. It was like you were in there planning World War Three. Business, I know. So what happened? Why the ice all evening?"

"I really don't want to burden you with Cambridge's problems."

"Hey, mister, Cambridge's problems are our problems."

"Not really."

"Why don't you ever want to talk about the business? All this time, four years with Reggie and Cambridge, I could type up on a postage stamp what you've told me about your work. I tell you everything."

"What's to tell? It's not the most fascinating job. It's so close to bean counting, sometimes it drives me up the wall with boredom."

"You've never said that before."

"You want me to share my boredom with you, is that it? Sweetheart, if I don't tell you anything, it's only because it's not worth telling." He stood over her, his hands on her shoulders; he leaned down and kissed her. "If I was in show business, if I was a brain surgeon, I'd talk your ear off. Lots of jobs are interesting, just not mine. Okay?"

"So what's Cambridge's problem?"

"New Century Laser, the company Reggie wants to acquire and was all set to, until tonight."

"What happened?"

"It's a question of financing. Arnold and Frank are . . . Never mind, let's just drop it. Let's get our robes on and go out and sit on the terrace for a while. It's still early. I don't feel like bed, do you?"

She rose and embraced him. "Yes."

ᔕᔕᔕᔕᔕ TWENTY-FIVE ᔕᔕᔕᔕᔕ

Doreen was at her vanity buffing her nails when the phone rang. It was Sunday night, about 9:30. She turned and stared at it on the nightstand. It rang twice, a third time; Reggie picked up downstairs. She wondered who it could be at that hour and remembered Cochrane and the threat of problems with the IRS, the trip to Washington that was canceled, Reggie's near-violent reaction to the phone call.

She picked up. Very gently, easing her index finger under the receiver to keep the bar from snapping up, making a sound.

"Listen to me, Rags, Frank and I talked to him like fucking Dutch uncles, okay? He sat there like stone, like always. You know how he is. He makes up his mind and that's that."

"That's not that, goddamn it! It can't be."

"You can get the bucks someplace else."

"He's clogging up the pipe on us. I gotta have this outfit!"

"You can handle the flow, you can handle twice as much. You're good, you can handle anything."

"Don't fucking stroke me, Arnold. We need that fucking company!"

"That's his whole point. He doesn't see that you do. Hey, set up a dummy outfit. Get the lawyers to draw up incorporation papers, everything legit. . . ."

"Fuck that, that's playing with fire. You know how close Cochrane came to cutting our fucking legs off for just that type of thing. Does he know?"

"He knows."

"Fuck him!"

He slammed down the phone. Doreen hung up. She resumed buffing her nails. Minutes later he came upstairs. Hearing the way he climbed the stairs, she could tell he was livid. He came pounding in.

"Sons of bitches! Fucking bastards!"

"Can I do anything, honeybee?"

"Shut up! How the hell could you help in anything? Look at you, you're shit. A fucking pea-brained broad, there's millions of you running around loose. *You* help me?"

She frowned and sniffled. "That's not fair. Just 'cause

you're mad, you take it out on me. . . ."

He stood rigid, glaring at her, gradually softened his features into a stare. Then came toward her smiling.

"You're right, you didn't do anything. I'm sorry, okay? I apologize. Here, give me a fucking kiss."

Monday morning Lyssa was at work when the phone rang for her.

"Doreen Carlyle," said Jenny, covering the mouthpiece.

"I'll take it in the office."

"She'll be right with you, Mrs. Carlyle."

Agnes stared as Lyssa swept past her. In the office she kicked the door closed and picked up.

"Lee? Something's going on, something terrible!"

"What now?"

"I'm being serious. It's Cambridge."

"Not the IRS."

"No, it's that company they were going to buy."

"New Century Laser."

"That's the one. They can't buy it. Somebody won't let him."

"The present owners, no doubt."

"No, somebody Arnold and Frank know told them to tell Reggie it's all off. I don't understand. He's president and chief . . . chief . . ."

"Chief executive officer."

"That's it. So how come he's letting somebody else tell him what to do?"

"I wouldn't know."

"I mean if it was just a question of the money to pay for the company, couldn't he go someplace else? Like to a bank or some other person? Why would he hit the ceiling if whoever Arnold and Frank talked to put the kibosh on the deal? So he doesn't get the money from him, can't he get it someplace else?"

"Doreen, from what you've said, you don't really know

what's going on. I know even less. Derrick tells me nothing."

"Reggie, too. But this is serious! God, he was mad."

"I'll tell you what's serious. You talking to me like this over the phone. Your phone could be bugged."

"Could it! It couldn't, why would Reggie bug his own phone?"

"I'm not thinking of Reggie. Maybe the law. I don't know, maybe you're right, that doesn't make sense. Look, just sit tight. As you say, maybe he'll get the money elsewhere. Maybe he'll just pass. Whatever the case, don't let it upset you like this."

"It upsets me 'cause it upsets him. Man, does it ever! But I'll do like you say, just sit tight. Maybe it'll all come out in the wash. You think?"

"It has to. Cambridge is no different from any other business; everybody has their ups and downs. How about lunch this week?"

"I'd love it. How about today?"

"Ah . . . sure. Come to the store about one."

"With bells on. I feel better already. Talking to you always makes me feel better when something's going wrong. You're a real friend, Lee. See you."

Lyssa sat holding the phone, studying it in detail. Doreen had every right to be curious, to be worried. Welcome aboard.

~~~~ TWENTY-SIX ~~~~

Derrick sat at his desk in his spacious office. Outside, out of his sight, Maggie was working at her computer. Across the way the elevator doors parted and a slender, dark-complexioned man emerged. He wore a jacket, denims, and dusty work shoes. From his face depended a nearly fully grown beard. He dragged his feet as he made his way around the secretarial pool heading for the open door of Derrick's office. He nodded a greeting as he came in.

"Close the door, Bert," said Derrick. "What's up? What have you got for me?"

Bert sat heavily, dug in his inside pocket, and brought out a tape cassette.

"I don't know if this is for you or Mr. Carlyle. I guess you better be the one to decide."

"Let's hear it."

Bert inserted the cassette in the player, turned it on.

"Turn down the volume."

A familiar voice came on. *Lee, something's going on, something terrible.*

What now?

I'm being serious. It's Cambridge.

Not the IRS.

No, it's that—

"Kill it," snapped Derrick. "Roll it back, give it here."

Bert did as he was instructed. Derrick sat staring into space, tapping the cassette against the palm of his hand.

"Okay," he said finally, rising from his chair. "You

better get back to your room."

"Right. Good-bye, Mr. Morgan."

"Good-bye, Bert, and thanks." He managed a grin. "The check is in the mail."

"Oh, I don't worry about you paying me."

"Only kidding."

Derrick watched the doors part, the elevator accept Bert, and continued tapping the cassette against his palm. Then he lifted his phone and dialed 111. Reggie's secretary came on. Derrick asked to speak with him.

"What's up, Derrick?"

"You got a minute?"

"For my favorite employee? Always. Your house or mine?"

"Would you mind coming down here?"

"You sound serious. You don't want to tell me over the phone?"

"I can't."

"Give me a few minutes. I was in the middle of dictating a letter."

"Close the door, Reggie."

The cassette was ready to roll. Derrick turned it on and leaned against his desk to watch Reggie's reaction.

Not the IRS.

No, it's that company they were going to buy.

New Century Laser.

Reggie's expression had been placid, if somewhat curious, when he sat down. But now, less than ten seconds into the conversation, his cheeks were crimson, threatening purple. His lower lip quivered, sweat gleamed on his broad forehead, his knuckles showed white on the arms of his chair.

"Shut it off!"

"Shhh, Reggie."

"I'm all right, I'm all right." He was suddenly out of breath, fighting for oxygen. His eyes had become huge.

"This came from that bug you had that guy put in your wife's office phone, right?"

"Where else? Doreen and Lyssa are getting to be good friends."

"Too fucking good . . ."

"I thought you'd like to know."

"You're goddamn right. Listening in on my personal calls, the one I got Sunday night, the nerve of the bitch! She's nosy as shit, you know. Well, this cuts it. She's dead meat!"

He got up to leave; he was shaking.

"Wait, wait, what are you going to do?"

"What do you think. Are you stupid?"

"Now just take it easy, don't go off half-cocked. Think about it. Put yourself in her place. She doesn't know what goes on any more than Lyssa."

"They're not supposed to know!"

"Shhh. She loves you, Reggie, she's crazy about you. And worries about you. Lys worries about me. So Doreen got nosy."

"I'll rip her fucking nose off and shove it down her throat!"

"Calm down, think rationally. She didn't mean any harm, she didn't do anything. So she was curious—"

"She's got no fucking business listening in on me. I don't give a shit if I call up the phone company for the time of day, it's none of her business. She's dead!"

"Stop talking like that."

"Wait'll I get home. What time is it?"

"Getting on to three."

"I'm leaving. Tell your girl to call Phyllis upstairs and tell her I had to leave. Tell her if anything important comes in, she can reach me at home."

"Sit down!"

"Who the hell you yelling at, you son of a—"

"Reggie, Reggie," he cut in. "Please sit. Just for a minute, hear me out. She loves you, she worships you, and she's good for you, you know she is. You should see yourself, you look so proud with her hanging on your arm. You're a different man since you married her. You were dying on the vine with Carol. You said so yourself. You married Doreen and you're happy as hell. She's made you happy for the first time in your life."

"I don't give a shit about any of that. She fucked up, she's going to have to pay!"

Out he stormed. Derrick threw up his hands. Maggie appeared in the doorway, her eyes questioning.

"It's nothing, nothing. . . ."

His eyes wandered to the phone; he thought about calling Doreen, warning her. But he'd be out of line sticking his nose into it. She'd made a mistake, now she'd have to make amends. Amends? That was a soft way of putting it. Expiate her crime was more like it.

"If only he'll give her the chance to."

Maggie had returned to her desk. She leaned across it to look in.

"Nothing, Maggie, nothing."

~~~~ TWENTY-SEVEN ~~~~

Evelyn was in the foyer dusting when Reggie barged in.

"Mr. Carlyle, sir, you startled—"

"Where is she?"

"Mrs. Carlyle went out earlier, I believe into town to have lunch with Mrs. Morgan."

"Shit, when is she coming back?"

"I expected her back before now. Perhaps she stopped to do some shopping—"

"Where's Campbell?"

"Eric's not due back till Wednesday, sir."

"Good, good. Okay, you can leave now."

She stared at him, nonplussed. He got out his wallet.

"Here's twenty, thirty bucks. Go shopping yourself, go buy a hat or something."

"Why, sir . . ."

"You understand? I want privacy. Go change into your regular clothes. Make it fast, okay?"

"Yes, sir. Right away."

She left about ten minutes later. He paced and fumed and smashed his fist into his palm. Again and again he stopped at the front window to look out. Doreen's red Mercedes finally appeared, pulling into the turnaround. He watched her get out and remove a large dress box from the rear seat. She was in a happy mood, singing to herself.

"Bitch!"

He stood waiting in the living room. She came in singing, setting down her purchase, removing her sailor in the foyer mirror. He approached. She saw him in the glass and started.

"God, you scared me, what are you doing home so early?"

He strode up to her, drew back, slapped her resoundingly. She staggered back against the table under the mirror, her hat falling to the floor. Up came the back of one gloved hand, going to her cheek.

"You bastard . . ."

"What? What did you call me?"

"Nothing . . ."

She shrank from him, her eyes darting left and right, looking for the best way past him.

"You said bastard!"

Again he struck her; she fell, narrowly missing striking her head on the edge of the table. She scrambled about on the floor, her eyes enormous, brimming with fear.

"Reggie, you're hurting me. . . . What did I do?"

"Don't give me that shit, don't play the innocent with me, you fucking nosy bitch! Get up! I said get up!"

He kicked her in the side; she screamed and doubled over. Grabbing her by the hair, he dragged her across the floor and into the living room. And struck her a third time, this time with his fist, catching her at the point of the chin. She started to scream, but it cut short as she passed out. He slapped her face lightly.

"Wake up, bitch, you're not hurt. You don't play possum with me. Wake up!"

She was out cold; he got her up onto the sofa and stood, fists on his hips, glaring down at her. Then he went into the kitchen, rattled a pot from a cabinet, half filled it with water, and returned. She was still unconscious. He dashed the water in her face. She groaned feebly and came to.

"Reggie, my side's killing me, you broke my ribs."

"That's not all I'll break. Get up!"

"I can't . . . I can't move. It hurts so. Please, please, calm down, tell me what I did to make you so mad."

"You think this is mad? You haven't seen nothing!"

He drew his fist back and smashed her as hard as he could in the face. She could not muster the strength for a scream; all she could do was groan in her mounting agony and pass out.

~~~ TWENTY-EIGHT ~~~

Sunlight brightened the two windows and splashed across the floor, almost but not quite reaching the bed. The room had been painted a pale green, entirely, even the door, which whooshed almost timidly when opened and closed. Lyssa had brought a bouquet of spring flowers, the nurse had gone for a vase. Doreen's head seemed to barely dent the pillow, as if she were lying rigid, fearful of moving a single muscle. The expression on the visible portion of her battered face suggested she dared not move, dared not even take a healthy breath; instead she sustained herself with a series of rapid, shallow inhalations.

Her head was wound in a bandage down to her neck, leaving only one eye and the cheek beneath it, her nostrils and her mouth exposed. Her left arm was broken and had been placed in a cast and suspended in midair by a pulley cord. Four ribs on her right side were fractured, but as the nurse had just finished telling Lyssa before leaving to get the vase, broken ribs, as a rule, were permitted to heal without taping, to ensure proper realignment. This, in the long run, was preferable, but it required the patient to "live on painkillers." Doreen's upper lip was badly swollen on one side, causing her speech to be slightly slurred. Her visible eye was blackened and the white filled with blood; her one cheek showing was bruised and badly swollen.

Lyssa sat staring at her, alternately sending forth waves of sympathy and wondering where the wild animal who'd inflicted this damage and pain had gotten to, mentally putting herself in his place. Tiring of beating her, possibly becoming bored with the effort against no resistance, Reggie had left her where she lay and stormed out of the house. Evelyn had found her, called an ambulance, she'd been rushed to the hospital, and when Reggie came back to find Evelyn alone, what was his next move? He'd no doubt poured himself a drink, eaten his dinner, watched TV, gone to bed. Gotten up this morning, gone to work.

One thing was certain; he had yet to call the hospital. That was one of the first things Lyssa had asked about upon arriving herself. He hadn't visited, hadn't even called, couldn't care less. Doreen had done something to trigger his anger, he'd punished her, and that ended it, evidently; to his way of thinking. Easy, even logical to assume such a view. She wasn't a wife; such a status didn't exist in his view. She was chattel, "a movable article of property," like a prized car he had acquired to show off, to tell the world, especially the men of the world, that he had the wherewithal to acquire such a beauty. She had no rights, no privileges, nothing beyond what he gave her. Had she been a dog, she would have been permitted to run loose in the yard, to bark at birds and small animals, she would have been fed, given a place to sleep, cared for when ill.

The nurse returned. A motherly-looking woman with soft, sympathetic brown eyes. From her expression when she looked at Doreen, it was easy to see she despised the monster responsible—but would resist the temptation to comment. Doctors and nurses must see many such cases and can offer sympathy, but professionalism demands that they withhold comment. This Lyssa decided while watching the woman arrange the flowers in the clear glass vase with a small chip missing from the lip. But she was wrong. Hawkins, the name on the small black plastic plate pinned over one mountainous breast, let "professionalism" be hanged.

"Her husband did this, the son of a bitch. Sick, that's what he is. He should be in Worthmore in a straitjacket in a padded room. Son of a bitch!"

Lyssa glanced at the woman's watch depending from a fob under her name tag. It was 9:44. Evelyn had telephoned her just before she left the store the previous afternoon, telling her she had just called for an ambulance and "Mr. Carlyle's gone out." Evelyn sounded extremely upset, saying she was afraid Doreen would die before a doctor could get to her. As it turned out, according to the nurse, she'd never been in danger of dying, but the pain she was suffering had to be excruciating. As soon as Lyssa hung up on Evelyn, she phoned the hospital. Doreen had not yet arrived. She called a second time minutes later and was told she was unconscious, no visitors till morning at the earliest. Hawkins had finished arranging the flowers; she stood staring down at her patient.

"With every breath her ribs send pain shooting in every direction, poor child. Do you know her husband?"

"Yes. And yes, he's a wild animal."

"Sick in the head is what he is; he should be in Worthmore. Don't stay too long. She's fulla painkillers, but they only do so much. She's hurting like she never hurt before, poor child."

She gave the bouquet one last adjustment and left. Doreen was awake.

"Lee . . ."

"Shhh, don't talk, you don't have to."

"It's okay. I can talk okay, it's just the breathing. It feels like my whole side's been stove in. Like somebody hit it with a sledgehammer."

Somebody?

"Is it bleeding?"

"No."

"Good, I can't stand the sight of blood and here I am bleeding in sixteen places, I'm sure. Feels like I am."

"You're not, you're just bruised and broken."

Just?

"I'll be okay, it'll take a few days. I'll bounce back real fast. I'm in real good health, you know. I'll spring back. Oooooo . . ."

"Take it easy. Doreen, listen, you know you're going to have to press charges against him."

"Against Reggie?"

"I'll call the police for you, somebody'll come, they'll bring a stenographer or tape recorder, whatever, and you'll give them your statement. Tell them everything from beginning to end."

"I can't. I can't."

"You have to. He nearly killed you."

"No, he'd never have, he loves me. He's always telling me how much he loves me."

"He may still kill you."

"No! Ooooo . . ."

"He could do this again anytime. You recover, you're a hundred percent, you cross him or he imagines you do, and he'll start in all over." She leaned closer, lowering her voice. "And next time he could very well kill you. We have to prevent that. There can't be a 'next time.' He was out of control, he had to be."

"That's just it, he didn't know what he was doing."

"Next time you may not be so lucky."

"But there won't be a next time. I'll never never listen in on his phone calls again, I swear. I only did because of Saturday night, those people, that Minervino, Tony Boots. I was deathly afraid Reggie was getting, you know, involved with him. He's such terrible bad news, Minervino, I mean. I'm just always so in the dark. When you never know what's going on with your husband, in his business, with the people he knows, it's terrible. Just awful. It's like . . . like being deaf and living in fear that you won't hear when somebody yells fire or . . . or look out, he's got a gun. Maybe not deaf, maybe more dumb. You find yourself imagining all sorts of things when you don't know anything about what he's doing. Bad, bad things. You worry. I know wives are supposed to worry, but if I only knew what goes on, what I should be worrying about. I'm not making sense, am I? I feel so light in the head, I feel like I'm floating in the air. But I can't tell the cops about it, I just can't."

"You've got to."

"But he's my husband. And it was my fault."

"That's ridiculous. You didn't do a damned thing!"

"I did. Because, like I said, I'm getting so worried about him."

"Listen to me, I'll be leaving in a few minutes—"

"No, don't go! Please . . . Ooooo."

"I have to. You need your rest. I'll be back this afternoon."

"Promise?"

"I promise. But please listen, I'm going to contact the police. I know a Sergeant Hugh O'Fallon, he's very nice. When L'Image was broken into and robbed a couple years back, he investigated, he caught the two men responsible. He's a good man, intelligent, super-conscientious. And the furthest thing from a male chauvinist. He'll be sympathetic—hell, he'll be outraged. He'll want to help. He'll come, you'll give him your statement—"

"They'll arrest poor Reggie, oh God, no! I can't do that to him."

"You've got to."

"I can't, I can't! Ooooo."

"Take it easy, don't get upset." She was the one upsetting her, Lyssa thought. "I'll be back."

"Don't call the cops, please don't. I don't want to drag them in. Please . . ."

Lyssa left.

She got to the store at ten after ten.

"Derrick called," said Agnes, striding up to her as she entered. "He wants you to call him at the office. It sounds urgent."

"Okay, okay . . ."

"What's going on? You should see your face, you look like you've been fighting tooth and nail with somebody."

Lyssa took her aside and told her about Doreen.

"The bastard!"

"Shhh. I'm calling the police."

"If you don't, I will!"

"She doesn't want me to."

"They never do. Wives are such idiots. If my husband beat me up, I'd see the son of a bitch hanged. I'd buy the rope. She must be so full of medication she can't think straight. That's why she's objecting."

"I don't think so, but I'm going ahead anyway. Because next time he'll kill her. And as sure as we're standing here, with him there'll be a next time."

The cash-register phone rang. Agnes picked up.

"For you, Derrick."

"I'll take it in the office."

"Lys? Where have you been?"

"At the hospital."

"You know . . . ?"

"The maid called me last night."

"You never said a word."

"I know, I was in no mood to discuss it. With anybody."

"I understand. Anyway, I talked to Reggie. He told me what happened."

"You mean he told you what he did to her."

"A terrible thing, terrible. He says so himself. He's conscience-stricken, he kept saying over and over, 'I don't know what came over me.' "

"My heart bleeds for him, the bastard. Animal!"

"Okay, okay. He nearly killed her, he admits it. And he's sorry, sweetheart, you never saw anybody so contrite. He sat there telling me and the tears were rolling down his cheeks. He said he'd give anything for it to have never happened. But it did, he did it."

"And he's sorry. Good, great."

"He wants to make it up to her, only he doesn't know how."

"I've an idea. Why doesn't he get himself a gun and unload it in his temple?"

"Lys, please . . . The man is crushed. He's afraid to go to the hospital."

"He doesn't want to see what a thorough job he did, is that it?"

"Come on, sweetheart, give him a break—"

"Give him a break! I don't believe I'm hearing this. I'll tell you the break he'll get. She's pressing charges. They'll arrest him, he'll be tried, found guilty, put away. Hopefully for twenty years!"

"She's not going to press charges. She's not exactly brilliant, but she has to know better than that."

"She's pressing charges—get him off the street and behind bars where he belongs. Anything else you want to talk about?"

"Listen to me. If you love her, listen good. You're her friend, about the only friend she's got around here. You can talk her out of it."

"What?"

"I don't have to draw pictures, you know what to say. Granted, he made a big mistake, but she's going to have to call a halt right now before *she* makes an even bigger one. Talk to her, Lys, explain to her."

"You."

She hung up.

~~~ TWENTY-NINE ~~~

Hugh O'Fallon, Sergeant, Metropolitan Bellingham Police, was about thirty, ruggedly handsome, ruggedly built, but soft-spoken and possessed of the type of smile so clearly the beacon of good feelings that his merely turning it on inspired confidence and trust in anyone who asked his help. He had helped L'Image, had made no rash promises that he'd be able to recover the apparel stolen by the thieves who'd broken in, but had done so; he delivered. And Lyssa had every confidence that he would again, for Doreen.

O'Fallon brought with him a small tape recorder. Lyssa stood with her back against the patient's door to prevent anyone's interrupting them. The sergeant sat in the visitor's chair by the bed. Lyssa had introduced them. She had brought O'Fallon there, leaving him outside for a few minutes while she went in alone to tell Doreen he'd come and to persuade her to cooperate. She warned, she begged, she pleaded, she came close to threatening, but Doreen continued reluctant to bring charges against Reggie. Still, talking to her, Lyssa gradually got the impression that Doreen was beginning to lean in the right direction. Lyssa decided as well that it was an effort of some courage on her part. Doreen did feel responsible for what Reggie had done to her, she loved him, she was loyal, she admitted outright she fully intended to forgive him. But more than any of these things, Lyssa could sense that she was mortally afraid of Reggie, and if he didn't kill her the next time, he'd no doubt try to the moment she set foot in the house. If she, Doreen, pressed charges.

"I already told Lee I don't like this at all," she announced to O'Fallon the moment he sat down, before he could utter a syllable.

"You'll feel disloyal toward him," said the sergeant. "I understand. I've seen cases just like this. And do you feel as if you caused it, or at least contributed?"

"I caused it, period."

"Mrs. Carlyle, there's no question you may have done something to make him angry, but nothing to justify his beating you so brutally."

"He . . . lost his temper."

"Everybody does, but few take it out on others to this extent. Mrs. Morgan is absolutely right and you should keep this in mind. He did this to you. It's done. What does that say to you?"

"He . . . what?"

"That he'll do it again. And next time . . . I don't have to say it, you know what could happen. He's capable of it, he probably enjoyed every minute of it."

"No! Reggie's not like that. You don't know him. You don't either, Lee. He lost his temper, can't either of you understand that? I made him lose his temper!"

"Tell me what happened," said O'Fallon. "You left your car in the turnaround, you opened the door, walked in. . . ."

Doreen related the whole story; Lyssa heard the details for the first time. She listened aghast, catching her breath again and again, prompting O'Fallon to look her way occasionally. When Doreen was finished, he turned off the tape recorder.

"Now, that wasn't hard, was it?"

"What?" Doreen asked blankly.

"You've made your statement."

"I didn't, you asked me what happened, I told you."

"It's what happened, which is what your statement would be—the facts laid out clearly, in proper sequence. I'll have this typed up, you'll have a chance to read it and make any corrections, any changes you want, then you sign it. We'll get a couple nurses to witness it."

"No. No!"

"Doreen . . ." began Lyssa, coming forward. "You've got to."

"I don't, you can't make me. I can't do that to him!"

O'Fallon gestured capitulation.

"Give me a minute with her, Sergeant."

He shrugged and started for the door. He whispered on the way by, "Good luck."

"Doreen," began Lyssa, "if you don't press charges, if you don't let the police do their job, I'm telling you here and now, I wash my hands of this whole sorry mess."

"Wash your hands of me, you mean, don't you?"

"Does he own you? Are you his slave? You let him get away with this, do you know what you'll be doing? You'll be giving him license to treat you like a dog!"

"He wouldn't."

"Face it, for all his power, all his money, all his bluster, he's a coward. If you stand up to him, he won't lay a finger on you. But you knuckle under this time and from now on he'll make life miserable for you. You could end up committing suicide."

"That's a terrible thing to say, and I thought you were my friend—"

"I am, damn it! Don't talk, listen, please. I'm trying to help you help yourself."

"No." Doreen looked away. "You don't like Reggie. I could see last Saturday night, I noticed for the first time. You look at him when he's not looking at you and you get this funny look on your face, like you're tasting something bad."

"That's nonsense."

"It's true, it's plain as day. For some reason you don't like him. You used to, but you don't anymore. You . . . you want to see me hurt him."

"*That,* Doreen, is a terrible thing to say. All I want, as God is my witness, is for you to do the right thing. Can't you get it through your head? I'm trying to talk you into helping yourself save your life. I seem to be doing a fairly rotten job of it; maybe I better shut up and mind my own business."

"Don't be mad."

"I'm not, I'm frustrated. You frustrate me."

"I'm sorry."

"For the last time, let him get the thing typed up, bring it here, and you sign it."

"I can't."

"Okay."

"Where are you going?"

"You can't, you won't, there's no sense in O'Fallon hanging around. I'll go tell him, I'll be back."

"You're really sore at me, aren't you?"

Lyssa bent, kissed her bandaged forehead lightly, squeezed her uninjured hand.

"I could never be."

Outside, she told O'Fallon.

"It figures," he said. "Eighty percent of them do the same thing, they just don't want to make waves. Don't want to start something they think'll mushroom and make things worse than they already are. They cross their fingers, they recover, they get back together with their husbands, and a couple months later . . ."

"It happens all over."

"Every time. Now's the time to break it off, get a lawyer between her and him."

She shook her head. "It's so damned discouraging. If only she weren't so set."

O'Fallon was staring at her. "You'd break it off."

"I'd see the book thrown at him!"

"I gotta go. If she changes her mind . . . What am I saying, she'll never. You know you get some that while you're talking to them you can read them. She was easy to."

"Thanks anyway, Sergeant, Hugh . . ."

"Anytime."

She watched him walk down the corridor to the elevators then went back inside.

⌁⌁⌁ THIRTY ⌁⌁⌁

Lyssa stood by the window looking down on the parking lot, mindful that her disappointment had to be showing like a waving red flag. Doreen continued rationalizing.

"Reggie and I've got a very strong thing going, Lee. I'd hate to be the one to break it, you know? This was just something that happened, one of those things. Every couple has spats. You and Derrick do, don't you?"

Lyssa turned to her. "If Derrick ever so much as slapped me . . ."

The door opened. It was Reggie, bearing an enormous bouquet of roses. He looked like a small boy, with his tentative smile, his uncertainty over how he would be received. He glanced timidly toward Doreen, cocking his head, masking his face with sympathy. The sight of him so disgusted Lyssa, she despised him so, she could feel her cheeks warm and her heart begin thrashing in her chest as it picked up speed. She wanted to charge at him and beat him with her fists.

"Sweetheart!" sang Doreen.

"Hi, honeybee. Hello, Lyssa."

He moved quickly to the bed, snatched the bouquet of spring flowers from the vase, set them dripping on the serving stand, and crammed the roses into the dirty water.

"They're bee-yoo-ti-ful, Reggie."

"I'll be going," said Lyssa.

"No, no," insisted Reggie. "Stay, I won't be long, I've got to get back to the office. Big meeting. I just wanted to stop by and see how you're doing, honeybee. And tell you how . . . how sorry I am for what happened. I really am terribly, terribly sorry. I've been having trouble sleeping, my conscience is bothering me so. Can you forgive me, honeybee?"

"You hurt me really bad, Reggie."

"I know, I went wild, I didn't know what I was doing. Do you forgive me?"

"If you promise not to do it again."

Lyssa suddenly felt queasy; she eyed the basin on the nightstand.

"I promise," said Reggie solemnly. He crossed his heart as he elevated one hand. "I swear it."

"I only listened in 'cause I was worried about you," Doreen went on.

"Worried?" He seemed astonished and then amused.

"Those men who came to the house Saturday night. That one who calls himself Frank Smith, the one with Harriet. His real name is Anthony Minervino. They call him Tony Boots, he's a mafioso."

"No!"

"He is."

"You're wrong, sweetheart."

"I'd better go," said Lyssa.

"Stay," said Reggie. "Didn't I tell you I'm leaving?"

"I'll wait outside, Doreen."

As she exited, the last thing she heard was Doreen's repeated insistence that Frank Smith was Tony Boots, was with the Licata family, and she was "terribly" worried that

Reggie might be getting involved with the wrong people. Again he dismissed her concern; she was confusing Frank with someone else.

Lyssa sat outside on the bench. He came out minutes later; the sight of him a second time, relaxed, smiling triumphantly?—revived her disgust. She tried to keep it from her face.

"Lyssa, Lyssa, I sure do appreciate your coming to see her. You're a true friend, the only one she's got around here, actually. You've got a good heart. She's going to be okay, right?"

"Eventually."

She almost added, "If you keep your hands off her."

"Hey," he burst out, "don't look so worried, she will: She's young, strong, she'll be her old self again before we know it. God, I don't know what came over me." He glanced at the clock on the wall above the nurses' station. "Will you look at the time, I've got to get back. See you."

Off he sailed, whistling, waving.

Leaving her with a sudden curious thought. Something didn't add up, there was something wrenchingly wrong with the sequence of events. She watched him vanish into the elevator. She pondered. What could it be? It started when he'd gotten the phone call Sunday night. Doreen had listened in, he'd come home early from work the next day, Doreen arrived home from shopping, he was waiting, he attacked her. . . .

"That's it!"

The delay. Why didn't he beat her up the night before, the instant he hung up the phone? Instead they'd gone to bed, everything apparently rosy between them, gotten up the next morning, had breakfast together, he'd gone off to work, not so much as a single harsh word; not until she walked into the house in the middle of the afternoon did the volcano erupt.

After Doreen called the store to tell her about the phone call the night before.

~~~~~ THIRTY-ONE ~~~~~

One might easily have assumed Derrick had suddenly become Reggie's lawyer, so earnest and spirited was
his defense of the man. He started almost the moment
she walked into the apartment. She found him on the
terrace inhaling his Bronchodane and sipping a can of
diet soda.

"You should see Reggie, sweetheart, my heart goes out
to the guy."

"Really?"

"He came back from visiting her at the hospital, sat on
the couch in his office hanging his head, shaking it, saying
over and over, 'What came over me, how could I do such
a terrible thing?' "

"It was easy, darling. Most things people enjoy doing
they find easy."

"That's pretty harsh."

"I'm 'harsh'? Maybe you should visit her yourself, get a
look at his handiwork. And did you say he came back and
sat down on the couch? Funny, I thought he had to rush
back to a big meeting, the bastard. He should be behind
bars. I pleaded with her to press charges."

"You what?"

"You heard me. She refused."

He was leaning against the railing. He shook his head.
He spoke quietly but with a hard edge to his tone. "You've
got some nerve. Hasn't it occurred to you—I mean just
in passing—that no matter how sympathetic you feel . . .
it's between them? It's none of your business."

"So I made it my business."

"The last thing either of them need is cops and lawyers sticking their noses in."

"Don't worry, he couldn't get to first base with her." His eyes widened. "Sergeant O'Fallon. Most wives beaten up don't bring charges."

"You brought a cop to the hospital?"

It wasn't smart of her to tell him so, he might even tell Reggie; when the sexes choose sides, the bonding firms almost instantaneously. Still, she couldn't resist telling. It had nothing to do with either Carlyle, actually, she simply wanted Derrick to know how strongly she felt. And perhaps give him a hint as to how she'd deal with such a situation. Not for a moment could she believe he would ever lift a hand to her, but she saw it as important that he know, if he didn't already, *that she was no Doreen*. To forgive may be divine, but in some cases it was totally wrong.

"Doreen refused to cooperate, O'Fallon left. You look shocked, you surprise me. You should know by now I'm no Doreen, and bless your heart, you're no animal, like your friend and employer. There's just one thing that puzzles me about the whole sorry business. Why did Reggie hold off beating her up? Why wait till the next afternoon? I've a theory."

"You've lost me."

"Just listen. I think their phone is bugged. Funny, I suggested that to Doreen and she said—and I had to agree—why would anyone want to bug their phone? But it is, it has to be, and when she called me Monday morning, they listened in. Reggie didn't hear her listening in the night before. *He was told about it after she called me.*"

"You've got a wild imagination. Bugged phones—"

"Just one, theirs."

"What possible reason would Reggie have to bug his own phone?"

"Doreen, obviously. Face it—he doesn't tell her any more about what he's up to in business than you tell me. That Frank Smith who was at the dinner is actually a mobster."

She told him how Doreen's friend in Las Vegas had pointed Minervino out to her when he walked by with his bodyguards. That he was big in some Los Angeles crime family, she couldn't recall the name, that Doreen recognized him as soon as he walked in the house Saturday night.

"Reggie is up to something he doesn't want her to know about. He nearly killed her to discourage the temptation to ever listen in on his calls again. It should work. Whenever the phone rings in that house from now on, she'll run out of the room."

"She's crazy. And getting you the same way. A mobster, what was his name?"

"Anthony Minervino, Tony Boots. You know they all have colorful nicknames."

"She's been seeing too many movies, too many TV cop shows."

"I don't think so. She may not be the brightest person in the world, but she's not blind and she was very certain when she told me in the study that night."

"Well, it's really between them. There's no point in our even discussing it. Want to eat out?"

"I'd love to."

He held her and kissed her. "Love you."

She loved him, but was nevertheless curious: he'd been in such a hurry to dismiss Doreen's recognizing Minervino out of hand. Of course, he could hardly concede she might be right. Clearly he had no idea what Reggie was involved in, apart from the business. Or did it have to do with the business? Recalling the dinner party, she remembered how Derrick had separated from the other three, especially at the table. Before the weighty silence fell over the evening, he'd been talking to her and Doreen while the others talked baseball. Briefly. And when they stopped talking altogether, he, too, had stopped, as if the silence was catching.

But he really did seem distanced from the others.

They had dinner at Bassini's on Front Street. They enjoyed themselves, returning home and making love till well past midnight. Again and again she found herself thanking her lucky stars that he wasn't Reggie, not because of the beating, but because there was something sinister about Reggie, something she couldn't put her finger on: sinister, deceitful, threatening. Perhaps the impression found lodging in her mind the night they saw him with the redhead at Sushi Ray's; perhaps seeing him cheating created fertile ground for planting all sorts of suspicions about him.

Whatever the case, she disliked and distrusted him and was having a hard time hiding it from Derrick.

~~~~~ THIRTY-TWO ~~~~~

A chamois white plaid tunic sweater lay on the desk; it went with a fluid chamois-color skirt of sueded silk. Lyssa was in the office with Agnes. Agnes held up the sweater, eyeing it critically.

"It's beautiful," said Lyssa. "I love it."

"Me, too, only it's the third one they've shipped us with an imperfection. Look at the buttons."

Pearly golden buttons highlighted the crewneck of the sweater across from the shoulders.

"The right one's way out of line," said Lyssa.

"And look at the left armpit, the stitching goes off line,

comes back. A beautiful mess is what it is. Schleiman in New York expects us to accept this crap. I'm going to phone him and hand him his head."

"I wouldn't do that. He's honest and decent and one of our best suppliers. It probably just slipped through."

"It's the third time."

"I'll call him."

"Promise. I'm getting fed up. God forbid something like this slips through us, somebody buys it and brings it back. So how's Doreen doing?"

"Improving."

"Getting back in shape for round two, right? Amazing, he nearly kills the poor thing for listening in. Can you imagine what he'd do if she steamed open one of his letters?"

Lyssa repeated what she'd said to Derrick last evening.

"I don't get it," said Agnes. "You can hear somebody listening in, the little click when they pick up. Or put the receiver down. Why didn't he beat her up as soon as he hung up? He must have been furious."

"That's the whole point. That's what I tried to tell Derrick. Why would anybody wait till the next afternoon? Unless . . ."

"What?"

"She was very careful, she picked up and didn't put the receiver back down till he did, exactly when he did."

"But you can hear if somebody's listening in. The air, the sound is different."

"I know, but it evidently was a pretty unsettling conversation. He wouldn't pay any attention to that, the 'different' sound. He just didn't hear her."

Agnes nodded. "I suppose that's possible."

"Aggie, I think a third party told him she listened in. I think their phone is bugged."

"Who by?"

"Who knows?"

Agnes shook her head. "That doesn't make sense. If, as you say, Carlyle didn't hear her listening in, how could a third party?"

"Do you know you're right?"

Agnes stiffened, Lyssa stiffened. Agnes's expression altered from puzzled to deeply, gravely concerned.

"She called you here the next morning," she began. "You don't suppose . . ."

"No, impossible."

"We'll soon find out."

Agnes snatched up the phone and began unscrewing the mouthpiece.

"What are you doing?"

"What do you think? If there's a bug, it should be obvious. Look, that little round black thing, what is that? Hang on."

"Where are you going?" Lyssa asked.

"Dear heart, you've got the dumbs this morning. I'm going to check the phone at the cash register. Don't touch that thing."

She came back moments later. "It's a bug, all right."

Lyssa gasped. "It can't be."

"It is."

"Can . . . can they hear us?"

"Not with the phone not working. If it rings, somebody answers, then they listen." She pulled open the desk drawer. "Where's that little tool kit?"

"Wait," cautioned Lyssa.

She took the phone from Agnes and hung it up.

"Give it here," said Agnes. "Here's the kit—screwdriver, pliers—"

"Don't touch it. Whoever's listening in, let them think we don't know it's there. Leave it, I'll just be careful what I say from now on."

"Don't you want to find out who did it?" Agnes asked. "Who's listening in?"

"We already know, that scruffy-looking man in the

phone company coveralls. He was working in here by himself, remember?"

Agnes shuddered. "This is scary."

"I wonder if we can find out where he's listening from?"

"The phone company could. You know, I read about wiretapping. In Sunday's paper. All about how technology is making wiretapping harder. The FBI is complaining. Something about the new fiber-optic lines that are replacing the old lines. It's all getting much more sophisticated. Maybe this works by radio, do you think?"

Lyssa hadn't heard a word, so involved was she in working out the answer to her own question.

"*Where* they're listening from isn't important. What is, is who that fellow with the beard is working for. I think I know."

"Carlyle," said Agnes, "or somebody working for him."

"Exactly. Somebody working for him. Derrick."

~~~ THIRTY-THREE ~~~

It would be simplicity in itself to accuse, difficult to ask forgiveness for what could turn out to be a false accusation. She recalled that shortly after the bug was installed, she had called Gail Horvath, to touch bases. The call had been recorded, she now knew, informing Derrick that she had gone to Atlanta—for what other reason but to see Gail and Walsh. So he knew about her visit before she learned about his. That day at the zoo he'd confessed to her that he'd gone not to Seattle a second time but to Atlanta. Had to confess.

Since he knew she already knew he'd lied, he had no choice but to admit he had and tell her the truth. Or what he hoped might pass for the truth. There followed the Cochrane affair. Doreen had phoned to discuss Cochrane. She'd asked her to read his obituary in that day's paper. She'd alluded to how convenient it had turned out for Cambridge, that the government's star witness against the company should plunge to his death just before the meeting in Washington that Reggie already had his own plane ticket for. And yet, although Cochrane's death, the timing, and the way he'd died seemed fishy to them, the police who'd investigated failed to uncover anything suspicious. Nothing that made the newspaper. How thorough a job had they done?

"Good question, Lyssa," said Lyssa.

All that seemed to come out of Cochrane's death were Doreen's suspicions. Reggie had no doubt heard the tape of their conversation, elected to say nothing to her about it, but when the second tape was played for him, the one in which Doreen expressed her concern about Tony Boots, Reggie's patience gave way.

All of which made sense. But was it Reggie or Derrick who'd assigned the phony telephone man to bug L'Image? Reggie was concerned about his wife's curiosity, not hers. Still, he knew that having found a friend, Doreen would not hesitate to confide in her. What better phone to tap than L'Image's?

But all that had nothing to do with Atlanta. And that had to be the main reason for the bug. Which brought her back to Derrick. He'd ordered it installed to monitor her curiosity about the case; presuming she and Walsh would be in contact? And again, he'd confessed that he'd gone to Atlanta to "talk to Walsh," but only after he heard the tape of her conversation with Gail and learned that she'd gone there. He confessed to protect himself.

Nevertheless she found it hard to accept that the bug had originated with Derrick. It wasn't his style, it was definitely Reggie's. All Derrick had done, as far as she could see, was profit by it: secondhand, in a manner of speaking. Doreen had to be the prime target.

As for Derrick, now she was back to square one: suspecting him of doing away with Walsh because the detective was getting too close to the truth about Elizabeth's accident. He at least suspected Walsh was getting too close. Of course, he could be telling the truth about flying down just to speak with him, arriving at the apartment house just after Walsh was killed. She'd accepted this that day at the zoo, why should she doubt it now?

Because of the bug, the bug. It cast everything in a whole different light. It was deceitful, it was cheating, Derrick and Reggie were.

"Listening in on us, like a party line. Of all the disgusting . . ."

He, Reggie, and Lord only knows who else. One thing was certain, from now on any and all phone conversations between her and Doreen would be made from public phones. At both ends. Doreen was in serious trouble with Reggie, forget his apologies, his roses, and everything else in the way of a peace offering. She had carelessly betrayed herself, telling him, warning him—she assumed—that Frank Smith was Anthony Minervino. As if Reggie didn't know.

And Doreen, poor soul, knew too much.

Lyssa had been sitting at the kitchen table sipping tea, examining the whole complicated and confusing situation, turning it over like a jeweler examining a multifaceted precious stone. Complicated, but no longer confusing. What, she wondered, did Derrick know about Reggie's affairs? Nothing? Everything? She heard Derrick open the front door and come in humming to himself. He filled the kitchen doorway, came in, and kissed her. Then studied her, his expression serious.

"What a face. Tough day in the mines?"

"We have to talk. Sit down, would you like some tea?"

She made him a cup.

"What's wrong now, Mommy?"

"Reggie."

"Ahhhh, this may surprise you, but I'm glad you brought him up." He held her hand, kissed the back of it, squeezed it, continued to hold it. "Darling, I can't tell you what to do, and believe me, I haven't discussed this with anybody, least of all him, but I think it's time you broke off with Doreen. I know you feel sorry for her, you like her, she's cute, she's funny, she's also trouble. She's got a big nose and a bigger mouth. I sat with Reggie while his secretary was on her lunch hour and you should have seen him. He really let his hair down. He loves Doreen, he says himself she's the best thing to come into his life since . . . ever. But he's worried sick about her. You see, men like Reggie Carlyle don't get to the top of the heap without getting a little dirt on their cuffs, rubbing elbows with the wrong people, sometimes downright bad people."

"Are you trying to say he's finally come around to admitting he knows Tony Boots?"

"Whether he does or not isn't the point. What he does is strictly his business. Cambridge is his business, how he runs it is all up to him. He's the driver. Doreen, I'm afraid to say, is rapidly developing into a liability. She's on a collision course. He hates to see it happening and doesn't know what to do about it."

"He can always beat her up again."

"Come on, Lys, this is you and me talking, can't we just put that part of it to one side? The bottom line is she's sticking her nose in and finding out things she shouldn't, things nobody should know, and that can be a very big problem for Reggie. You're her friend, this could even rub off on you. I know how fond of her you are, I know this is a big thing to ask of you, but in both our best interests, I think you should drop all contact with her. Don't call her, duck her calls, after a while she'll stop calling. No more lunches. If you see her coming into the store—"

"You know you're absolutely right?"

"Good girl, I knew you'd understand."

"What you said starting off—quote: 'I can't tell you what to do.' You can't, so don't try. Get this straight, I refuse to turn my back on Doreen, which is what dropping our friendship would amount to. Since you're playing go-between, tell Reggie for me. You can also tell him I'm not interested in his cloak-and-dagger shenanigans with 'Tony Boots' or anybody else in that tribe. Not unless what he's up to affects you. If it does, 'I can't tell *you* what to do,' but my advice is quit. You're capable, intelligent, conscientious, you could catch on with any 'respectable' outfit."

"Not funny, Lys."

"Trust me, I'm not trying to be."

"I've given you good advice. Take it or not, it's up to you."

"Right."

"Let's drop it."

"Good. For keeps, permanently." She leaned across the table and poked out each word, jabbing with her forefinger. "And don't ever ask me to do such an outrageous thing again."

He set his cup down a trifle too hard, glowered, got up.

"Where are you going?"

"Out."

"Where?"

He stared at her, then walked out without another word.

"Have a nice day," she murmured to her cup. "That does it!"

She slammed the table with the flat of her hand. Time to call a halt. Stop deceiving herself: rationalizing, skewing logic, deliberately sidestepping the obvious. He worked for Reggie, he knew everything that went on inside the company. He had to be as deeply involved in whatever Reggie was up to with Minervino and Carlson as the big man himself. Had to be. How could she possibly think Reggie was responsible for tapping her phone? It was Derrick who'd arranged it. Reggie had no interest in Walsh, in what happened on Belvedere Road years ago. Derrick's curiosity as to what his nemesis was up to had to be eating him alive. He had to be just as concerned over her getting together with Gail Horvath.

"Wake up and smell the foulness."

She went out on the terrace, standing at the railing, looking down. A cab was pulling away. She sensed that Derrick had gotten in. Go. She didn't care. Whatever they had, whatever they shared, their love, their friendship, suddenly hung by the slenderest of threads. Let it snap.

Would she ever trust him again, ever accept his explanation of anything? Would she ever again feel safe in his arms, ever again lie beside him in bed and not tighten up with fear? Doubtful. Reggie and Derrick were the team; Doreen and she were merely window dressing, props to lend legitimacy, respectability, to the two of them. To whatever it was they were up to behind the front of Cambridge Equipment. Something terribly wrong, corrupt and dangerous, was going on, and Derrick would no more divulge what it was than he would the truth about Elizabeth's death.

So be it.

There was one other thing, as disturbing as it was obvious. She knew what Doreen knew; her life had to be in just as much jeopardy.

He came home around eleven; she was in bed asleep. He woke her and apologized for doing so.

"It's okay," she murmured sleepily.

He moved to kiss her, she turned her face from him.

"So that's it," he said.

"It's better, for now. I need time to sort things out."

"What things? Never mind. I have to leave early tomorrow. Dallas, for three or four days."

She was sitting up.

"I'll pack for you."

"I'll pack myself."

"Whatever. Don't forget your Bronchodane."

He said nothing further; he set the opened suitcase on the foot of the bed. She got up and went into the guest room and in minutes was asleep. He was out of the house the next morning before she awoke.

⁓⁓⁓ THIRTY-FOUR ⁓⁓⁓

Doreen's broken arm was no longer suspended in mid-air. Wrapped in a new cast, it now rested on her stomach. Her ribs were knitting "beautifully," according to her doctor, and the bandages wrapping her head, concealing most of her face, had been removed. The swelling on her upper lip had gone down, but her blackened eye was turning a sickly yellow.

"I'm feeling better and better. Dr. Plummer says if everything keeps going the way it's going now, I can get up in a couple days and be discharged next Thursday or Friday."

Listening to her enthusiasm pleased, even relieved, Lyssa. The life had come back into her voice and the sparkle returned to her eyes, even the blackened one. Lyssa listened, focusing on the roses Reggie had crammed into the vase after disposing of the still-fresh spring bouquet she had brought earlier.

"Reggie insisted on bringing fresh roses every night when he visits, but I put the kibosh on that. I love when roses get a few days old. They begin to look so . . . antiquey."

"Antiquey."

"Like old-fashioned things, old lace, silk, you know. He comes every night. He's really very sorry, Lee, he keeps apologizing. You know, he's right about one thing. I really believe he didn't know what came over him."

Lyssa did her best to keep the disgust this triggered clear of her face.

"Doreen, you trust me, don't you?"

"With my life. And both my minks. Seriously how could you even ask such a silly thing? I take seriously every thing you say. I do. Like your wanting me to press charges. I thought about it, because it came from you. But I decided I just couldn't. You're not sore or anything, are you? I just couldn't."

"I understand, but that doesn't alter the situation."

"What do you mean?"

"You're still in danger."

"From Reggie? No way. He's apologized and apol—"

"Please listen. They'll discharge you next week, you'll go home and what, pick up where you left off? How can you? What's done is done, you know about Tony Boots. Me, too, as far as that goes. We're in this together."

"In what?"

"Danger. I lay awake last night thinking about Minervino and Carlson's wives. Annie and Harriet, right? Remembering them sitting at the table like two carved life-size figures. Perfectly trained to keep their mouths shut. Be deaf to everything they hear, not even daring to swap gossip between them. You and I should be so lucky."

"You think *they're* lucky? Why, they're just . . . just painted, prettied-up shadows. They don't talk, don't laugh, don't dare let go. They're dead."

"They're alive and determined to stay that way."

"Their husbands don't even sleep with them. They all have mistresses; they trade them like little boys trade baseball cards. I know, my friend Tina Drago out in

Vegas went steady with a button. You know what a button is?" Lyssa shook her head. "A hit man, professional killer. Tina told me, and don't you dare tell a soul, she was with the guy, the button, and three others, and they kidnapped some squealer. They were in New York and they took him up to Westport, in Connecticut, to a barn way out in the country. Tina was there and saw the whole thing. They tied his hands behind his back and made him get down on his knees and they fed him chicken shit off the floor. They laughed and laughed and passed around a pint of whiskey and the guy kept throwing up and Tina said the place began to stink terribly and her boyfriend got nauseous and hurried things up and shot the guy twice in the back of the head. Through the brain, you know? Killed him dead. The two other guys got real sore 'cause they wanted to drag it out."

Lyssa had gotten up and was pacing, half listening, arranging in her mind what she would say.

"Doreen, when you get out of here, don't go home."

"But—"

"Listen! Please. You . . . can stay at my place."

"Your apartment? What would Derrick say?"

"Who gives a damn? Better yet, leave town. I can have Evelyn pack your things, I'll bring them to the airport. Where can you go? Where do you have family? No, that'd be the first place he'd look. Friends. What about out of the country?"

"Please, slow down. I can't, I can't desert Reggie. You make it sound like he can't wait to get me home so he can kill me. That's terrible, how could you? Poor Reggie . . ."

"You're in danger! We both are, don't you understand?"

"I'm not. What are you getting all excited for? It's over nothing, honest. Reggie and I talked about Tony Boots. He said I was to just forget him, forget I ever even heard his name. I promised I would and I will. So it's all cleared up, it's over. He won't bring it up again. Me neither."

"Do this for me, please. Just think about it. Think about Annie and Harriet. They know what they're doing. You and I, we're a little late. I have to get back to the store."

"Will you come tomorrow?"

"Of course. Anything I can bring?"

"Surprise me. You know something, I think I'd like a book."

"Book?"

"To read, you know. I get sick of TV. I haven't read a book in . . . I can't remember when. Bring me one, would you? Maybe something funny. Not a comic book, a real book. Funny. Okay?"

"A funny book. Right. Let me see what I can find."

～～～ THIRTY-FIVE ～～～

Hugh O'Fallon's office was discouragingly tiny and dingy; everything old, thirdhand. The chair she'd been ushered to was granite masquerading as walnut. She'd been informed he was in a meeting "with the captain" but would only be a few more minutes. A few more minutes was getting on to twenty, by his desk clock. The clock was small, a nightstand alarm clock; had it been any bigger, any heavier, it might have caused the desk to collapse, so ancient and fragile looking was it—the right front corner missing a leg, an old telephone directory serving as a replacement. Sharing the desk with the clock was an "in" and "out" box. "In" was full, "out" was practically empty. Hugh O'Fallon was a busy man. She must remember not to take too much of his time. He came in carrying his jacket over one shoulder like a politician.

"Mrs. Morgan, sorry to keep you waiting. How've you been?" He stopped; his jaw dropped. "Don't tell me, Mrs. Carlyle changed her mind. Did she?"

"I'm afraid not. I came about something else. This won't take long."

"It's okay. I'm here to serve the public, you're the public. Love that scarf. What can I do for you?"

"She'll be getting out of the hospital sometime late next week. Going home. Sergeant—"

"Hugh. Can I call you Lyssa?"

"She's in great danger. He'll kill her. Have her killed."

"That's pretty heavy. Why would he, just because she listened in on a phone call? I thought she already paid for that."

"You don't understand, she's become a liability. Even a threat. He . . . evidently is involved in things that are top secret. Things he doesn't want anybody knowing about."

" 'Things.' "

"I can't tell you what, that's not important. She needs police protection around the clock. She's in the gravest possible danger."

"I got the impression you know what she knows. She tells you everything. Aren't you in danger?"

"I can take care of myself."

"Before you go any further, let me explain something. Two things. Number one, she hasn't called us to ask for protection, so this is really your idea."

"She doesn't understand."

"Number two, there's no way the department can provide her with protection. Not in her present situation."

"What does that mean?"

"She's not a witness—"

"I'd like to know what you call it!"

"No crime's been committed. The law doesn't recognize the assumption that a crime *may* be comitted."

"You can't do anything till after she's killed, is that it?"

"I'm afraid so."

"That's crazy."

"It doesn't make a great deal of sense, I grant you. But look at it this way—if all the upright citizens in this town who feared for their lives from one threat or another came to us and we gave them protection, we'd need a force ten times the size of the one we've got. People are very imaginative."

"This has nothing to do with 'imagination.' "

"Okay, okay. As I started to say, if she was a witness to a murder, to kidnapping, any felony, she'd be entitled to protection. A court would order it. But she's not."

"She's dead."

"Lyssa . . ."

"I know it, I feel it. She'll go home, come night she'll go to bed, she'll have an 'accident.' "

"I'm sorry, I honest to God wish I could help—"

"But you can't." She smiled thinly. "I suppose that's better than you won't, for all the good it does her. Thanks for your time, Hugh."

He managed an apologetic, even somewhat guilty look; they shook hands and she left.

⸻ THIRTY-SIX ⸻

He stepped off the elevator on the ninth floor wearing the uniform of a security guard: gun, walkie-talkie, badge, the complete outfit, rendering him indistinguishable from the ten other security guards on the four-to-midnight shift at Bellingham General. But one factor set him apart from the other guards. He was late for work, more than six hours late. The clock above the floor desk read 10:09. The nurse on duty did not look up from her *People* magazine as he passed. One hand reaching up to smooth his mustache, shoulders back, he strode purposefully down the corridor and into the men's lavatory.

There he checked his mustache, the cut of his jib, and reaching into his left breast pocket, withdrew a single cotton glove. Bunching it in his left hand, he appraised his image one last time in the glass and went out, walking farther down the corridor, around the corner to Room 907. Pausing with one hand flat against the door, he glanced both ways, heard no sound of approaching steps, and pushed into the room, into pitch darkness. Inside, he slipped the glove onto his right hand and, with his left, brought out an old-fashioned razor, the type that fits the blade into the handle.

He began singing softly. Flipping open the razor in his gloved hand, he started toward the bed. His eyes were rapidly becoming accustomed to the darkness. He could make out the bed and the headboard and, coming closer, the patient lying on her side, her back to him.

At the side of the bed he reached over her with the razor, holding the blade upright. He squinted, he could barely make out the blade.

Setting the edge carefully against the pulsing jugular, touching it without piercing the flesh, he took a breath and smiled to himself.

The patient stirred slightly, there came the sound of a soft moan. He hesitated. She lay still.

He sliced her throat, deftly, easily, loosing a freshet of blood, spilling in quantity. Retreating a step, moving around to the other side, he groped about, found her right hand and closed her fingers around the razor handle.

He stiffened, listening, and imagined he could hear the gentle pumping of the jugular vein as it sent forth more and more blood from the gash that ran from ear to ear.

He headed for the door and was outside.

~~~~~ THIRTY-SEVEN ~~~~~

The cab that Otto ushered her into in front of the apartment house was a relic. She almost hesitated to get in and the instant she sat down regretted doing so. The seat springs were shot, the leather cracked and ripped, the rubber floor mat showed holes and lay in three pieces on the right side of the differential housing bump. The motor sounded on the verge of giving out; the driver, who had to be close to seventy, also looked to be nearing his end. But having gotten in, she hadn't the heart to get out.

It was a lovely day. She always looked forward to May; everything that came alive in April began showing its beauty, its glory in May. It was 9:56 when she got to the store; she opened up. As she stood checking the cash register, her thoughts went back to last night. It had been as if the guest-room door she closed behind her closed off the past, ended an era.

There was one thing he could do to restore the happiness and contentment that had been the status quo: quit Cambridge. Phone Reggie as soon as he got off the plane in Dallas and give notice. Get out of that place, loaf for a week, maybe the two of them could go away for a time. Come back, hunt for a job. He'd have no trouble. But if she suggested he quit, he probably would have laughed in her face. Or told her what she could do with the idea.

To be brutally honest, she no longer cared what he did. Should she file for divorce? Start the ball rolling today?

On what grounds? Cruelty? What cruelty? She suddenly remembered reading somewhere that the only ground for divorce in Michigan was proof that the marriage had broken down and there was no reasonable likelihood that it could be restored. That seem to fit the situation; it included irreconcilable differences, which appeared to be the core of their problem.

Agnes and Jenny came in together.

"Did you see this morning's *Star Bulletin*?" Aggie asked.

She unfolded the paper under her arm and held it up. Lyssa read the headline of an item halfway down the page on the right: PATIENT SUICIDE AT BELLINGHAM GENERAL.

Her heart leaped and twisted. She gasped. "God in heaven . . ." She read on. "Mrs. Martha Travis, a patient at Bellingham General, was found dead early this morning by a nurse making her rounds. Mrs. Travis, scheduled for gallbladder surgery, was discovered still gripping the razor with which she cut her own throat."

"Isn't your friend Doreen at Bellingham?"

"This was no suicide," said Lyssa. "They don't know what's going on, it's murder!"

Jenny's eyes widened. Not Agnes's; if anything they narrowed slightly, in manifest disbelief. Lyssa went on.

"Don't you see? The killer was after Doreen, he got into the wrong room."

"Dear heart," said Agnes, "simmer down. Of course, it's possible—"

"He did it. It was Derrick!"

Agnes and Jenny exchanged glances. Agnes sent her arm around Lyssa's shoulders.

"Let's go back to the office. Jenny, if you need a hand, sing out. Oh good, here comes Ellie."

Lyssa and Agnes sat in the office.

"He was out late last night, he took off for Dallas early this morning."

"Aren't you jumping . . . pole-vaulting to conclusions?" asked Agnes. "Why in the name of all that's good and holy would *he* kill Doreen Carlyle?"

"For Reggie, her husband."

"From what I can see, her husband doesn't need outside help if he wants to get rid of her. He's already come close. By the way, isn't it time we got rid of that thing in the telephone receiver? Haven't things gotten pretty much beyond that? You seem to think so."

"Leave the bug. Doreen and I can win that one, even if we lose out in everything else."

Agnes was shaking her head. "I've never seen you like this, you're worried sick. You're convinced he, Derrick's, up to something ghastly. So how do you do it?"

"What?"

"Sit across the table from him, make small talk. How do you lie in bed with him at night. Do you let him . . . ?"

"Touch me? The last couple days neither of us is interested. Now that he's gone to Dallas for 'three or four days,' that's not a problem. If he really has gone, he's such a liar."

"Things seem to be getting rockier by the hour. How long do you plan to go on like this?"

"Until we split and one of us moves out. I like the place. I hope he leaves without too much noise. What are you staring at?"

"You're crying."

"I love the son of a bitch! I did. God, but I despise that company, Reggie Carlyle."

"Listen to me. Despite this being none of my business, I've been giving it a lot of thought. We're partners—I should, right? The one thing I can bring to it is objectivity. If you stop and think about it, you're no better off than you were six weeks ago. I'm talking about solid proof against him. My point is, if he were being tried, the prosecution would need solid proof to make its case. Lyssa, shouldn't you, his wife, be extending him the same 'courtesy,' for want of a better word?"

"You don't understand, it's not like that. I don't need a smoking gun in his hand. I've seen enough, heard enough, from Doreen, Walsh, Gail Horvath, my own little voice, to convince me he's up to his eyeballs in everything Reggie's involved in."

"What, specifically?"

"I . . . I don't know."

"The Mafia."

"No question."

"No question but you 'don't know.' Listen, you may be right, but that doesn't make him a killer. So he was out late last night, you've no idea where, what he was doing. But you want to think he sneaked up to that poor woman's room and slit her throat."

"He mistook her for Doreen."

"Okay, fine. That shouldn't be hard to prove," Agnes said. Lyssa looked perplexed. "If he comes back tonight and finishes off Doreen, you're right."

"He's in Dallas, I told you."

"Maybe not. He told you he went to Seattle and instead went to Atlanta. He could be checked into the Paige Hotel crosstown. He could be planning to rectify his error tonight. Knock off Doreen."

"You talk about her like she was some faceless, nameless nothing you've never laid eyes on. But he does plan to kill her. He has to. The question is, how do I warn her? She doesn't believe a word I say. No matter what anybody says, ignorance is not bliss. In this case it guarantees doomsday."

"So go back and talk to your friend O'Fallon. Bounce all this off him. Just for the fun of it."

"Bad choice of words."

"Seriously."

"Maybe that's not a bad idea. They're probably already digging into the Travis woman's history. They'll find she had no reason to commit suicide. Facing a gallbladder operation? That's a piece of cake, isn't it?"

"So I hear. I wouldn't know, I still have mine."

"They'll establish she had no reason to commit suicide and no enemies who hated her enough to kill her. She was a mistake. Doreen's got herself a temporary reprieve. You think I might get Hugh O'Fallon to put a guard at her door? Only one thing—she'll probably have to okay it."

"Talk her into it."

"Sure . . . piece of cake."

~~~ THIRTY-EIGHT ~~~

Luck, like a country road, can turn when least expected. Good luck dropped into Lyssa's lap on her second visit to Sergeant O'Fallon. He invited her to lunch at the diner across from the police station. The place was mobbed, mostly with uniforms. She thought it amusing when a self-conscious, suspicious-looking little man in cap and raincoat came in right behind him. Came in, took one look at the clientele, and left.

The moment they found a booth she began trotting out all her reasons for the belief that the killer had gotten into the wrong room. And would return to rectify his error. O'Fallon took a bite of his toasted cheese sandwich, a bite of his dill pickle, and a swig of coffee. And nodded agreement.

"Very possible."

She brightened. "You think?"

"For a couple of reasons. I have no trouble buying Mrs. Travis as a mistake. That the killer, he or she—"

"She?"

"Women kill."

"He . . . he!"

"That he intended to kill your friend, Mrs. Carlyle, could be open to conjecture, but I'm inclined to lean in your direction. I mean her life could be on the line. We won't need her permission to sit a uniform outside her door. We'll need the hospital supervisor's, but that shouldn't be a problem. You do realize, the killer may figure we'll post a guard. When is she due to be discharged?"

"Thursday or Friday next week."

"Six, possibly seven days. We'll guard her from seven P.M. to sunup, that is to when the full day shift comes on."

"Great!"

"Only have you thought about after she's discharged? We can't very well sit somebody on her doorstep."

"We'll cross that bridge later on."

"When we get to it," he said.

"If . . ."

He grinned. "You haven't much faith in your police. Anything wrong with your tuna?"

"I'm not hungry. You want it?"

"I couldn't."

"Take half. This is good, posting a guard, only could he come on later, after visiting hours are over? Immediately after? The thing is her husband visits her every night."

"Visiting hours are over at nine, I think. We'll make it after. He won't see anybody on her door. There's something else you should think about. A guard may scare the killer off."

"Isn't that the idea?"

He laughed, she laughed. She liked him, enjoyed his company. He was so open, so honest and straightforward. She trusted him, she could count on him.

THIRTY-NINE

Lyssa felt extremely uncomfortable visiting Doreen later that day, and it showed.

"You're biting your lip, Lee. You always do that when you're worried, did you know that? Friends pick up little things like that about friends, isn't that so? Did you hear about last night? You must have. The poor woman, what a way to die." She shuddered. "The morning paper said suicide, but now the rumor's going around it was murder. Of course everybody blows things like that up big as balloons."

"I almost forgot," said Lyssa.

Out of her handbag she brought a gift-wrapped book. Doreen fairly snatched it from her, ripping open the wrapping.

"*Women Are the Funniest People*! I love it!"

She hugged Lyssa.

"I'll read every joke. I hope they're not real dirty. Reggie says I can't take really dirty jokes—I get red all over. I guess deep down I'm a lady."

"Deep down and up top."

Lyssa thought about telling her a policeman would be sitting outside her door from tonight on, but it didn't seem necessary. Why court her objection? She made no mention of it. They talked for over an hour, during which Lyssa grew increasingly more despondent. It occurred to her that this could be the last time she'd see Doreen alive, guard or no guard. What guarantee was there that he wouldn't fall asleep on the job? Would one of the security guards wake him if he did? Would they resent a uniform supplementing their numbers? They would; it was a slap in the face. She wished she could be sworn into temporary service, be armed, and sit outside, her gun in her lap, her finger around the trigger. Let him come. . . .

Doreen was browsing through the book and giggling.

"These are terrible, I love it!"

She read a joke to Lyssa about a hooker, her john, and the judge. She thought it hilarious. Lyssa managed a weak smile.

"Funny," she murmured.

"You don't look like you think it is. I'll find the really good ones and turn down the corners of the pages, and when you come tomorrow, we'll have a ball. You *are* coming. . . ."

"Of course."

Lyssa kissed her good-bye, holding her hand a bit too long, then went out. As she descended in the elevator her thoughts flew ahead to that night. Reggie would visit, there'd be no guard outside, no chair. When he left, the guard would come on. And stay awake.

"Please stay awake. . . ."

It was a temporary solution to just one facet of the problem. Doreen still had to return home. Maybe not, maybe in the time left she could talk her into going away somewhere. She could go with her. Aggie and the girls could handle things at the store. Come to think of it, she hadn't taken a vacation in nearly eight months. She could steal two weeks, a month.

She'd discuss it with Aggie when she got back to the store.

~~~~ FORTY ~~~~

Another idea supplanted the thought of getting Doreen, and herself, out of town. It occurred to Lyssa as she paid the driver and stepped out of the cab in front of the store.

Cambridge Medical & Surgical Equipment. The mystery company. Reggie had total control, despite the presence of a board of directors to rubber-stamp his decisions. He was president and CEO. Of what, precisely?

Aggie was waiting on a customer when she walked in. When the woman took the suit she expressed interest in—a navy cotton ottoman knit with white ottoman inserts at the front of the jacket—to the dressing room to try on, Lyssa took Aggie aside.

"What's that broker's name, the fellow with Sherman, Walters and Baake?"

"Thompson Chambers, Sir Tommy, the consummate WASP, but brilliant and a nice guy."

"He checks into companies' backgrounds, doesn't he?"

"More than checks. You can get a poop sheet on any company you're interested in investing in from any broker, but Tommy does better, lots better. He dissects companies. Finds all the dirt, all the skeletons. Price-earning ratios aren't everything. Who's running the show, who they are, their personal track record, all that sort of thing is important. Inside stuff."

"Can I call him? Would you mind?"

"Why would I mind?" Aggie beamed understanding. "You want to find out about Derrick's outfit. Call Tommy, his personal number's on the Rolodex. You can get him direct."

Lyssa sat flipping through the Rolodex, found Thompson Chamber's number, and was about to punch it when she stopped. Getting out the tool kit, using a small conventional screwdriver, she carefully removed the bug from the mouthpiece. Restoring the cover, she punched the number. Chambers came on. He had a squeaky, high-pitched voice; her first impression was that he'd make a great puppeteer on a Saturday-morning children's show.

"How's Agnes? I haven't heard from her in months. What's she doing, hiding her millions under the mattress?"

Lyssa explained why she was calling.

"Cambridge, Cambridge . . . I know them, they're here in Bellingham, right?"

"I want to know all about them."

"They're not public."

"I know. Can I come over and pick your brain?"

"Sure. How about this afternoon? Say . . . threeish? I'll need a couple hours to dig. I'll see you at three. We're on West Main. Agnes knows. Look forward to meeting you, Mrs. Morgan."

She hung up. When he finished filling her full of Cambridge, he'd probably try to interest her in something. That was okay; according to Aggie, he was an excellent broker, great track record. She might consider investing in some company.

Anything but Cambridge.

She dialed Derrick's work number. Maggie came on.

"He'th gone to Dallath, Mitheth Morgan, Litha."

"I know, but he left before I got up this morning. I just want to know when he's due back."

"I have it here thomeplathe. Here we are, Tuethday evening. United, flight one-oh-three. He'th arriving at eight thirty-nine."

"Thanks, Maggie, come see us."

"I . . . hate to, Litha, I feel like I'm taking advantage. . . ."

"Nonsense, you're not 'taking' a thing. Stop by."

Hanging up, Lyssa thought of calling Maggie right back, find out where Derrick was staying in Dallas. Call there and see if he was registered. No, she couldn't, it would be tantamount to accusing him outright of lying about going. Only it had gotten beyond that. Had he really gone to Dallas?

Or was he in the Paige Hotel here in town?

She called Maggie back, got the number of the Hyatt Regency in Dallas, and called it.

"Mr. what was the name?"

"Derrick Morgan, Cambridge Medical and Surgical Equipment. This is Mrs. Morgan."

"One moment."

She held her breath, her heart thudding. The "moment" seemed like ten minutes.

"Mrs. Morgan? Yes, he checked in about an hour ago. But he's not in his room. Would you care to leave a message?"

"No, that's okay. Thank you."

⸻ FORTY-ONE ⸻

Thompson Chambers's office was a shrine dedicated to Yale University and the Delta Kappa Epsilon fraternity: framed photographs, statuettes of football players, of the bulldog mascot, pennants, ashtrays, all manner of memorabilia of his four years in New Haven. Chambers was a dapper individual, stunningly attired in a Georgio Armani suit and handmade Italian shoes. His fingernails were manicured, his mustache neatly trimmed, his silver hair neatly coiffed, giving him the appearance of a matinee idol beginning to get slightly long in the gleaming tooth. Entering his silver years. His voice, alas, if not shattered, certainly marred the overall impression. It sounded even squeakier than it had over the phone.

"You madam, I am indebted to," he announced as he seated her. "It's been"—pronounced "bean"—"a perfectly fascinating past couple hours. Ever see that old movie *The Gaunt Woman*? Before your time, ancient, circa World War Two. The *Gaunt Woman* was a ship; I get a vision of her drifting at night, mist pouring over her, a secret cargo, danger, mystery."

"Cambridge."

"Cambridge." He consulted his notes. "Medical and Surgical Equipment. President and CEO, Reginald Carlyle. No previous experience heading up any firm I can find. The man came out of the woodwork. In business four, almost five years. Doesn't make money, doesn't lose money." He grinned toothily. "Interesting consistency. Companies go up and up and down and down. Cambridge stays level, earns enough to get by, hasn't lost enough, according to its annual statement, to put it in trouble. Owns three other companies, possibly more. Three is all I can find."

"They're in the process of acquiring a laser-surgical company. Is there a New Century?"

"I'm familiar with New Century—fine company, efficiently run, good product, growing. That's what's so strange here. . . ." He tapped a thick leather-bound book sitting on the corner of his desk. "Every firm in here is an open book. Like New Century. Not Cambridge. They put out an annual report, as I said, of course. They have to, but it could very well be pure fiction. The numbers are certainly suspect. As far as I've been able to make out, the companies they've bought have no backgrounds, no histories, nothing."

"Dummies."

"Dummies. I could go on and tell you about this sale and that one in cities around the country, all apparently legitimate. Funny that—they haven't sold a stick overseas. I could tell you about the board, lots of things, but I gather your interest lies in my overall impression. Is that so?"

"Definitely."

"Mind you, it's just an impression, but an educated one. From everything I've researched thus far, my impression is that Cambridge is like . . . like one of those mock-up western towns you used to see in old cowboy movies. False fronts, nothing behind them but two-by-fours holding them upright. Which leads me to conclude that Cambridge is a laundry."

"A what?"

"They launder money, in copious amounts. They conduct business, they manufacture—in Lansing—fill orders, make a profit, pay salaries, expenses, taxes. Everything looks good, normal. But it's all a front."

"I knew it!"

"And who are they working for? With? I shouldn't have to tell you."

"I don't understand. . . ." She was frowning, shaking her head.

"The Mob."

"I didn't mean that. I know that. What I don't understand is how they get away with it, why the government doesn't come down on them?"

"Evidently because their front looks so legitimate, works so flawlessly, there's no hint of suspicion."

"I know they're tied in with the Mob. That's not news."

She told him about Cochrane. He pursed his lips, tented his fingers, nodding, nodding.

"Interesting. You think it had to do with taxes—nonpayment, underpayment? Could it have been something more? Could that have been the tip of the iceberg? Maybe the fellow, had he lived to tell his story, would have knocked the government's socks off. We'll never know."

"Carlyle was going to Washington at the IRS's behest."

"Behest. You mean they ordered him to come."

"I know he was tremendously upset. Extremely worried. Then Cochrane conveniently died, the pressure was off, he never did go to Washington."

"Whatever the accountant knew died with him. Intriguing, murkier and murkier. You said your husband works for Cambridge. Doesn't he talk about his job?"

"Almost never and then superficially. Something I've always wondered about. I'm a businesswoman. I like to think I'd understand more than the average wife. And show an interest. He knows that, but he's still very tight-lipped. Carlyle is, too. I know his wife well. He tells her nothing."

"Would you like me to keep digging?"

"There's no need, thanks. All I really wanted was for you to confirm my suspicions. You have, in gold. Laundering money for the Mob didn't occur to me, but I had a feeling something strange was going on."

"At the risk of offending, taking advantage of getting you into my lair, may I ask, do you invest in the market?"

"Very little. Like Aggie, I plow most of my money back into the business."

He nodded. He suddenly looked like a wolf that had found the scent.

"And yet Aggie does invest," he said. "She's very conservative—that is, I'm conservative for her."

"What money I have, I've been putting into CDs. Some corporate bonds, not much."

"No stocks. Well . . . if anything should catch your eye, give me a ring." He handed her his card.

"I will, definitely. I owe you."

"Pssh, my pleasure. As I said, it's been quite fascinating. Most of the companies I put under my microscope for interested clients turn out to be dull as dishwater. This has been intriguing—so many questions leap to mind, so few answers available. I wonder how many banks they use. More than a couple, I'll wager."

"Would you say for certain that they're laundering money?"

"Would you say we can expect rain anytime within the next thirty days?"

"Amazing."

"Not really, not these days." The wolf narrowed his eyes and sucked in through his clenched teeth. "What I wouldn't give to have been able to sit down with that accountant and pick his brain. I'd bet my Rolex he was onto something bigger, scarier, than tax evasion. Godfrey, half the companies on the exchanges have tax problems at one time or another." He leaned forward, grinning impishly. "Even this place."

She thanked him and left. Thinking back to Derrick as she stepped out of the elevator and started across the crowded lobby, she wondered *was* he in Dallas or had they sent someone down there to pose as him? A little dog-and-pony show strictly for her benefit. Giving him an alibi for whatever he planned to do here in town tonight.

"He can't, he can't!"

FORTY-TWO

She got back to the store a little past four, going straight back to the office and dialing the Hyatt Regency in Dallas.

"Mr. Morgan is not in his room, ma'am, would you care to leave a message?"

"Would you tell him to call me at the store?"

"The store . . ."

"He knows the number."

"Very well."

"Thank you."

Entering the store, she had breezed past Aggie, who was busy checking receipts. Aggie came in.

"To answer your question," said Lyssa, "I made out fine with Thompson Chambers. He's great—cute, colorful, very informative. He's convinced Cambridge is laundering money for the Mob. Manufacturing and selling medical and surgical stuff, legitimately enough, but with no concern for profit or growth."

The phone rang. Aggie picked up.

"For you. Tommy."

"Mrs. Morgan, interesting footnote to our conversation. The number is seven."

"What?"

"Banks, dear lady. Cambridge has accounts in seven different banks, six out of state. Quite bizarre. A company that size has need for at most two banks. Usually one serves all their needs, a number of different accounts. Seven banks is . . ."

"Bizarre."

" . . . a dead giveaway. Par for the course, for an operation like theirs. Just thought you'd like to know. Icing on the cake, right?"

"Thanks, Tommy, I appreciate it."

"Have a nice night."

She hung up. "What's the best-performing stock in your portfolio? I want to buy some from him."

"Later. What now, what's your next move?"

Lyssa sighed and shook her head. "I don't know as I have one. It's not my game, nor is it Doreen's. The king and his knights and bishops are calling the shots. She and I are just pawns."

"You really think they'll try to kill her?"

"Face it, Aggie, they've already tried. And messed up. What's to prevent them from trying again? Not the cop on guard outside her room."

Ellie stuck her head in. "Customer wants you, Agnes. Mrs. Champion."

"Oh shit, the Queen of Complaint." She scowled. "Tell her I'll be right there."

"I'll take her," said Lyssa.

"Take her to Benton Harbor and drop her in Lake Michigan."

She went out. The phone rang. It was Derrick.

"I just got back from a meeting, you called?"

"Yes, I . . . wanted to apologize."

"Forget it, we both overreacted. You okay? You sound . . . tense."

"I'm okay. I just wanted to talk to you."

"I'm glad you called, sweetheart. I wanted to but—"

"Are *you* okay? How's the asthma?"

"No problem. No pollen down here, leastwise not today. But God, is it hot! It must be a hundred and ten. Anything I can bring you back?"

"Just you."

"I love you, Lys, madly."

"I love you."

"What do you say we take a week somewhere when I get back? Fly out to the coast, maybe Mexico. Think about it."

"I will."

They talked further, he finally said good-bye. She sat staring at the cradled phone. So he really was in Dallas.

᜵᜵᜵᜵ FORTY-THREE ᜵᜵᜵᜵

Doreen Carlyle lay on her side, asleep, breathing easily, her back to the door. It opened, light spilled across the floor. In came a security guard. Turning his back on her, he held the door wide with his left foot and dragged inside the unconscious form of the policeman who had been sitting on guard outside. Dropping him, he glanced out the open door, looking up and down the deserted corridor, then brought in his chair, letting the door whoosh softly closed. Kneeling, bringing the policeman up to a sitting position, the guard set his forearm across the other's front under his chin. Setting his right knee hard against his back, he then set his right upper arm on the man's right shoulder and, gripping it with his free left hand at his own shoulder, raised his right forearm and set his hand firmly against the back of his victim's head.

Pushing his knee forward, at the same time pulling under the chin of the policeman with the crook of his arm and pressing his head with all his strength, he snapped his neck.

Letting the body fall, the head lolling awkwardly, he got to his feet and moved to the bed and the sleeping patient with her back to him. He did not sing; he was not in the mood. His earlier mistake, in confusing Room 709 with 907, was embarrassing, slipshod, an error no one who calls himself a professional should be guilty of. He glanced toward the closed door. Minutes before, he had come strolling up the corridor, passing the policeman, stopping and engaging him in conversation. They talked briefly about the weather, the boredom attending both their jobs, then began comparing their respective weapons. While the policeman was pointing out the practical advantages of his issue .38, the security guard lifted his own weapon high and hammered the man's head viciously, knocking him cold. The rest was routine.

Circling the bed, he approached Doreen face on. Removing a pair of cotton gloves from his pocket, he slipped them on.

~~~~~ FORTY-FOUR ~~~~~

Lyssa put in a sleepless night, thoughts of Doreen, concern for her safety keeping her awake. She got up groggy at seven, made breakfast, watched the TV early news briefly. At five of eight she telephoned police headquarters, asking for O'Fallon. She was advised he would be in shortly.

"Would you please ask him to call Mrs. Morgan?"

She gave the operator her number and hung up. At 8:32, she was almost done dressing for work when the phone rang.

"Lyssa? Ah . . . bad news."

"Oh, my God! No, no, no, no!"

"He killed the cop on guard—the guy was unbelievably careless. He must have been. When Captain Roarke okayed him to sit outside her door, I spoke to him myself. I warned him to be especially careful of security guards. It had to be somebody in a guard's uniform that killed Mrs. Travis. It's the perfect disguise. The only way an outsider can wander around the place without raising somebody's curiosity. I figured that much when Travis was killed. The same last night."

"Mmmmm."

"It doesn't help any, but it shouldn't have happened. I did warn him."

"Her husband did it. Ordered it done."

"There'll be a thorough investigation."

"What good will that do? They haven't turned up anything on Mrs. Travis, have they?"

"They're still working."

"Good for them."

"I'm sorry, Lyssa."

"Can't you arrest him? At least bring him in for questioning?"

"We can, but I can tell you now he'll have an ironclad alibi for his whereabouts last night. The prelim report from the coroner establishes time of death between ten and ten-forty-five. She was . . . strangled."

"God I hate this! Because it's no surprise. To see it coming, to know it's going to happen, is horrible, just horrible!"

"I know, I know." He cleared his throat nervously. "What about you? You're in danger."

"I know, but not like Doreen was. I thought. Now . . ."

"I'd like you to come in and talk with Captain Roarke."

"About what, my suspicions? He'll laugh in my face."

"Did I? He won't, not after last night."

"I know it happened, I knew it was going to. I still can't believe it. It's so easy for them, getting rid of anybody who gets in their way, anybody who poses a threat, real or imagined. You know what the most ironic part of it is? She loved him! I thought she was afraid of pressing charges when he beat her. I suppose she was, but it was also because she loved him and couldn't bring herself to hurt him. Do you believe it? I could kill him with my bare hands! Animals, that's what they are!"

"Take it easy. Will you talk to the captain?"

"I really don't see what good it'll do. The damage is done."

"You'd like to catch him, wouldn't you?"

"I'd love nothing better. I just don't see how it's possible."

"Please think about coming in."

"I will. Hugh . . . ?"

"Yes?"

"You tried to help and you did. I'm grateful."

"It shouldn't have happened. Kozlowski was a good cop. He had three citations, he was no dummy. I was glad when Captain Roarke assigned him. The killer must have distracted him. I'm keeping you, I'm sorry. For the last time, think about talking to Captain Roarke, he's a good man."

"We'll see."

She hung up. What would be the point in talking to Roarke, to anybody? What could they do to stop Reggie, expose the company? That, Cochrane had tried, look what it got him! What in God's name could she do? Poor Doreen, the slaughter of the innocent, married to the Mob.

And yet in all the horror, the blackness of it, one tiny, feeble light was visible: Derrick was 1,200 miles away.

~~~~ FORTY-FIVE ~~~~

The police launched an investigation into the murder of Doreen Carlyle. At the time of her death, established by the coroner, Reggie was in a meeting with four other company officers, which lasted until 11:30. Derrick Morgan, meanwhile, was still in Dallas, not expected back until Tuesday night.

Doreen's wake was held on Monday evening. Lyssa did not attend; she was too upset, enraged, to the extent that she did not go to work Monday. She never left the apartment. On Tuesday, having become resigned to the situation and calmed down, she worked all morning, planing to take the afternoon off to attend Doreen's funeral.

All Saints Episcopal Church was in the suburb of Chase Ridge, about three miles north and east of the Carlyle residence. It was a lovely old granite church partially bound in ivy, surrounded by venerable oaks, accessible by a lengthy series of wide stone steps. Behind the church, on an elevated plateau, was a small, carefully tended cemetery enclosed by the requisite wrought-iron fence. Lyssa took a cab from midtown, joining the throng of people paying their final respects to the deceased: Reggie's friends and business associates and their wives. Climbing the steps and entering the church, she fleetingly felt like a solitary "friend of the bride," (directed to sit on the right by herself while everyone else sat on the other side of the aisle) being not only Doreen's best friend but very possibly the only real friend she'd made since arriving in Bellingham.

The church was crowded, the sides of the alter banked with dozens of floral tributes; the organist plodded through *Abide with Me* while the late arrivals found places. Lyssa sat on the aisle to the right alongside an obscenely fat man who sat patting his brow, face, and neck with a folded handkerchief, alternately wheezing and sucking a tooth. Entering, she had spotted Reggie in the first pew squeezed between two other men, his head bowed, his shoulders shuddering slightly. She could tell it was he by the shape of his bald spot, for he did not turn around, could not see her.

The minister materialized in the pulpit to the left of the alter: tall, distinguished looking, very nearly handsome, save for his square jaw and overly prominent ears. His expression said he was pleased with the turnout and the opportunity to perform. Did he even know Doreen? she wondered. *Was* Doreen a churchgoer? Not a regular, perhaps, but an "occasional"? They had never discussed religion; it could be that Doreen and the minister had never even seen each other. Lyssa recalled that she and Reggie had been married by a justice of the peace.

He had a dreadful speaking voice; an apt description of it would have been "studiously cultivated boring." He managed to wring three syllables out of two-syllable words, four out of three, and so on. It was a delivery that induced relaxation and sleep. In his eulogy he elected to quote from the fifth chapter of Ephesians.

So ought men to love their wives as their own bodies. He that loveth his wife loveth himself.

For no man ever yet hated his own flesh; but nourisheth and cherisheth it, even as the Lord the church:

For we are members of his body, of his flesh, and of his bones.

For this cause shall a man leave his father and moth-

er, and shall by joined unto his wife, and they two shall
be one flesh.

Lyssa could not stop herself from shaking her head,
but managed to stifle most of a groan of disgust. Still,
enough of it emerged from her throat to cause the fat
man beside her to pause in his mopping and look askance
at her. On droned the minister, mercifully finishing and
directing his listeners to exit by the doors behind them,
circle the church to their right, and climb the path to
the cemetery in the rear. She stood in the aisle to let
the others in the row pass by her. And she wanted to
see Reggie pass, wanted him to see her. The crowd
exiting the pews between them blocked her view for a
time, but presently he appeared, moving slowly forward,
head down. Then obligingly raising it, eyeing the ceiling
in, it appeared, appeal to the Almighty to lift the great
burden of suffering from his shoulders before it cracked
his spine. His eyes under his beetle brows were red,
his face also. He looked wretched, a suffering mar-
tyr reaching the end of his tether. Their eyes met.
He tried a feeble smile and waved halfheartedly. He
passed her.

"Bless you, Lyssa, bless you for coming. . . ."

You bastard, she thought, fighting to keep from blurting
it out. She moved out into the exiting crowd. And suddenly felt so acutely bitter, so consumed with hatred for
him that she became nauseated. She could not recall ever
truly, genuinely hating anyone; she had never found the
limit of her capacity to hate. Until now. He was about six
people ahead of her. She wanted to push through, catch
up and attack him; claw his cheeks, his bloated lips, rip
his eyes from his head, scream at him, curse him, expose
him for the monster he was. Monster, murderer, hypocrite.
Murderer, murderer . . .

Pushed along by the crowd, she thought of Doreen and
imagined she heard her high-pitched, happy laugh; she

recalled her sweetness, openness, her little-girl honesty and naïveté and wonder. Her beauty, her great good heart. What kind of world was this, what kind of God who permitted such an outrageous crime? An innocent assassinated and her destroyer allowed to put her to rest like this, under the eyes of decent, well-meaning individuals, lavishing their sympathy on him, feeling their hearts tug at the sight of him grieving, suffering at his "loss."

She was dead and he would live—scot-free, conveniently deaf to his conscience, relieved at her passing, rid of the threat she posed him. As if the poor creature had been a threat.

The minister stood at the head of the grave, the breeze whipping his surplice, tousling his hair. He restored it and swept his audience with his eyes. The gathering stood in a semicircle, all eyes on him. The casket was in position, ready to be lowered. He commented on "man's brief time on this earth," rambled on, flung a handful of soil onto the casket; a few women tossed flowers, he closed his Bible, lowered his head, and asked everyone to pray.

"Almighty God, we commend the soul of Doreen Alice Carlyle to your keeping, to the protection of your everlasting mercy . . ."

Protection? reflected Lyssa.

Reggie roared, stopping the minister's words, and flung himself bodily across the casket, crushing the flowers atop the lid, beating the ground on the far side with his fists, kicking, carrying on outrageously. It took three men to pull him off it. Upright, he couldn't stand, two had to support him. Sad-faced men shook their heads pityingly, women clucked and whispered, sympathy poured toward him from all sides, inundating him.

Lyssa sighed. You miserable bastard . . .

The minister had finished, the casket—the flowers atop it crushed and broken—was lowered, those paying their respects streamed down the hill in pairs and small groups toward their waiting transportation. On the far side of the street a solitary taxi, blazing yellow among all the muted colors, was wedged between two limos. Lyssa descended to the sidewalk and was starting across to catch the taxi when someone tugged at her arm, stopping her.

"Lyssa . . ."

It was Reggie. Arnold Carlson, Frank Smith/Minervino, and two men she'd never seen before stood behind him, all cold-eyeing her. Their wives were nowhere to be seen. Reggie let go of her arm.

"Don't go running off, please? Come back with us to the house. We're having a little get-together, a little something to eat. Please, I want you to join us."

"I'm sorry, I have to get back."

"Please?"

"No, thank you!"

He'd gotten hold of her arm a second time; she jerked free and ran toward the taxi, waving, calling. The driver looked up from his newspaper, nodded, reached back, unlocked the rear door for her. As she got in a man entered the door on the other side. His head down, he failed to see her. He looked up; he was young, his plain face narrow, his complexion dark, like a faded tan. A small round Band-aid was affixed to his jaw under the right corner of his mouth where he'd cut himself shaving. He nodded a greeting, smiling self-consciously.

"Sorry, I . . . Would you mind sharing? I really have to get back to the city. Oh, I'll pay the full fare."

She read the desperation in his eyes and smiled. "It's okay, I can afford my half."

He rapped the Plexiglas. "Okay, driver."

"Where are you going?" she asked.

"Grove, the Buchanan Building."

"I'm just past there."

"So it works out fine. Oh, I'm sorry. Jack Corey." He offered his hand.

"Lyssa Morgan."

"You a friend of Mrs. Carlyle's? I met the lady, I didn't really know her. I know him. Poor guy, what a blow, she was beautiful and they were crazy about each other." He stared straight ahead, his voice taking on a solemn tone. "He was devoted to her."

"Tell me about it. Are you with Cambridge?"

"No, we handle his insurance."

The driver had turned right then left. She swung about to look out the rear window, then ahead; she frowned.

"Driver, didn't you hear? We want to go back to the city, you're heading in the opposite direction."

"It's okay," said Jack, "he knows where he's going."

"But . . ."

He eased back one lapel, just enough to reveal the heel of a gun butt. He grinned and patted her hand.

"Just sit back and enjoy the ride. We'll be there before you know it."

She could see in the rearview mirror that the driver was paying no attention to them. Her heart swiveled. She'd been set up, walking, running into their trap.

"What do you think you're doing?" she rasped.

"Nothing you have to worry about. Relax, we're just taking a little detour. To Mr. C's. He really does want you to join the party."

"Driver, stop!"

He paid no attention.

"I told you," said Corey, "sit back and relax."

His smile left his face; he patted his pocket over his shoulder holster and cocked his head slightly in warning.

"Keep it there," she said icily. "Your manhood. You won't need it, I promise not to hurt you."

He leered; he tapped the Plexiglas.

"Slow it down a little, friend, we don't want to get there before they do."

This was it! Doreen had told her everything she knew, which didn't amount to much. Still, it had been enough to get *her* killed. Now was it Lyssa's turn? Reggie wouldn't dare, not in his own house. Her mind whirled. She never should have come to the funeral, common sense suggested that with Doreen eliminated she would be next. She glanced out at the passing houses, the unfamiliar area. The driver had slowed; at the end of the block he turned left. At the far end of the street Reggie's house loomed behind the hedge walled with tall, blooming rhododendrons.

"Relax," said Corey, "nobody's going to hurt you."

She ignored him.

~~~ FORTY-SIX ~~~

"Lyssa, Lyssa, you changed your mind, I'm so pleased."

A burly man standing behind Reggie laughed uproariously. Reggie himself could not suppress a smile. He looked like a changed man, no more suffering in his face, no tears or any other evidence of grief. Three other men approached, coming up behind him, all of them gaping at her. Carlson and "Smith" stood looking on from the far end of the living room. The seven of them, along with Corey, were the only ones who had come back to the house, as far as she could see. She erupted.

"You pig! How dare you kidnap me!"

"Pig?" He looked offended. "That's not nice." He waggled a finger. "Not ladylike, not you. And 'kidnapped'? Did somebody throw a bag over your head, tie you up?"

"What do you want?"

"Just to talk, just the two of us." He glanced at the men now standing on either side of him, forming a file. "In privacy, boys, if you don't mind."

"I have nothing to say to you and I'm certainly not

interested in anything you have to say to me."

"Oh, in that part of it you're wrong."

"I demand you drive me back to town!"

"I'll see to it, I promise. After we talk. Please don't be upset. If you remember, I did ask you to come in a nice way. You refused, what else could I do? Granted, it was dirty pool. I apologize."

They were in the foyer; she spun around and started for the door. Corey blocked her path.

"Get out of my way!"

"It's okay, Jack," said Reggie behind her, "she's not going anywhere. How? It's three miles into town, you can't get a cab out here. Come on, Lyssa, be nice, cooperate. We'll talk—civilly, no steam, no hard feelings, I get what I have to off my chest, you say what you want, that'll be it. Fifteen, twenty minutes and Jack here'll drive you back to your store in Doreen's car. How's that sound?"

"Good, fine."

"Thatta girl."

"On second thought I do have a couple things I'd like to tell you."

"I knew you did. Let's go into the study, shall we? Is that okay? Or would you prefer the living room? Anyplace you want."

"Just let's get it over with."

"Right. The study it is. Let's go."

The glass-encased minuteman stared at her blankly as she entered and sat in a studded leather barrel-back wing chair. He sat opposite her, slouching, grinning affably, either unconcerned or unaware that he was intensifying her disgust. Disgust with him or fear of him? Both. He clucked, shook his head, shed his smile.

"Poor Doreen . . ."

"Don't start on that," she snapped. "I'm not stupid, I'm not a fool. You had to shut her up."

"You think *I* killed her?"

"You've never killed anybody in your life. You get

somebody else to do it for you. Still, does it matter what I think? Do you really care?"

"I do." He shook his head, sighing in discouragement. "I loved her. I did. Does that surprise you? You could even say I was a little crazy about her. She turned me on. But she had a problem—she was nosy. You know she was. A long nose for such a beautiful face—and a big, big mouth. I'll tell you the truth, something I'm proud of. I never made a lot of demands on her. I let her go her own way. She could throw money around like Mrs. Rockefeller, I didn't care, let her enjoy herself. I enjoyed her enjoying herself. And she could come and go as she liked, I never asked questions, like some guys. One thing I was a stickler about, though. The business, Cambridge. It's my business, my private toy. What I do, who I do it with, the inside of it, is nobody's business, not hers, not yours, nobody's unless I want 'em in on it. That's the way it is, the way it should be, right?"

"I'm really not interested."

"Bear with me, I'm getting to my point. It's a question, just one. What did she tell you? About me, about Cambridge? And don't say nothing, please. You were her closest friend, whatever she found out she had to have told you."

"If you're so sure of that, why ask?"

"I want you to tell me. I want to hear it from you."

"First, I've a question for you."

"No, no . . ."

"Yes, you tell me what I want to know. First. Who did you get to strangle her? Was it . . . Derrick?"

He stared at her; he seemed suddenly to have drifted off. Then he snapped back.

"It could have been anybody. Me, I don't get involved in such things."

Clear-cut admission that he'd ordered her killed, as if Lyssa needed it.

"Well, it wasn't Derrick. It couldn't have been, he's

been in Dallas the past four days."

"Has he?"

She started, her throat tightened, her breath came faster. "I talked to him down here. He's staying at the Hyatt Regency. He's not due back till tonight."

"If you say so."

Panic seized her; she was on her feet. "Where is he? Tell me the truth!"

"Not in Dallas," he sang.

"He never went. . . ."

"Not that I know of. And I'd know, wouldn't I? He never left town, not this time."

"You're lying! I tell you I talked—"

"Liar, pig, boy, you don't think much of me. But Derrick, he's a Greek god, right? Up on a pedestal. You're something, you know so much and you don't know anything. I'll let you in on a little secret. He killed his first wife."

"He didn't. You didn't even know him back then, knew nothing about him."

"Oh no? Give a guess, how long do you think he and I know each other?"

"I don't care."

"Over ten years. I knew him when he started out. Oh, he killed her, all right. No. Let me correct myself—had her killed. But not for the insurance, like that detective, that Walsh thought. *Stupido*. You want to know the real reason why she had to die?"

He leaned forward, his eyes slitting evilly.

"Because she stuck her nose into what she shouldn't have. She eavesdropped on a meeting, private. Stuck her nose in, got it chopped off. You women, what is it with you? What's inside that makes you have to know what's going on with your husbands and boyfriends? And then, even worse, blab about it? It's like . . . like a sickness in you."

"You don't know what you're talking about. Derrick had nothing to do with Elizabeth's death. It was an accident. The police agreed, so did the insurance company."

He laughed until tears glistened. "Amazing, you really believe that?" His face hardened. "All that proves is how smart he is, clever. Lyssa, he had her killed and killed the detective to shut him up."

"That's absurd. He didn't even get to Walsh's apartment till after he'd been killed."

"He told you that? Oh Derrick . . . Let me ask you something. What do you think he does for a living? I mean you're his wife, you should know. Maybe not all about his job, the ins and outs, but what he does. He sells medical and surgical equipment, right? Ha-ha-ha—" He stopped. "What am I laughing at? He does. On the side. Up front he hits people."

"I don't know what you're talking about."

"How about a glass of sherry? There's some right there in that cabinet."

"No, go on."

"You mind if I have some? I like sherry. I like everything, I'm no teetotaler, like Derrick. I don't have his willpower."

" 'Hits' people?"

He poured himself a sherry.

"You sure you don't want one?"

She waved it away.

"Okay, okay. Hits. Come on, don't try and tell me you don't know it means? He's a hit man, lady, he offs people for money. People people want offed. And he's very good at it, a true artist. I'd say he's one of the top five pros in the country. I'm talking professionals, mind you, not people who kill their relatives and friends because they're sore at 'em, or have to get 'em out of the picture because they stand in the way of something they want. A professional takes out people he doesn't even know. Never been introduced to, sometimes never even heard of. He's offered the assignment, agrees on the fee, he packs his bag, goes there, bang bang, and home. Where you going?"

"I don't have to listen to this garbage. I'm leaving, don't try to stop me. I'll walk back to town!"

He was on his feet like a cat, backing against the door. He suddenly looked very formidable. Panic shot through her. She heard him lock the door behind his back.

"You think I'm bulling you? Why would I? I like the guy, I respect him. You got to respect people who are tops in their line. Sit down, there's more."

"I'm not interested."

"Of course you are." He sipped. "You should see your face. You can't wait to hear the rest. Hey, I like you. I like how you made friends with my little girl when she needed a real, true friend. She loved you, she talked about you all the time—how great you were, how sweet, good to her. You're a very good person, Lyssa, straight, loyal. You got a right to know the truth about your husband. I'm telling you the truth. He killed his first wife, he killed Walsh, he killed Mooney, the nut case he hired to ram the side of his car after that party. Then, you know what? The guy tried to stiff him. Stiff Derrick Morgan, can you imagine? They agreed on a price, somehow Mooney found out Derrick stood to inherit four hundred G's, the insurance, he demanded half. Derrick paid him off, two in the back of the head. Six states away that's how come Walsh never found out.

"That one piece of business, he killed three people. He's killed a ton. He did me a very big favor, for ten thousand cash."

"Is that how much Doreen cost?"

"Not her, a guy, you don't know him."

"George Cochrane."

He had been talking to his sherry, enjoying his performance to the fullest. The name visibly shook him.

"How do you know about him? You don't—"

"He was pushed out a window. Convenient, very timely, for you."

He sucked in a breath. "See? You see? That's what I'm

talking about. Is that any of your business? No. Not yours, not Doreen's. Lyssa, Lyssa, you're making it hard for me, you're making it impossible!"

He turned, unlocked the door, and called for Corey. She heard steps run up outside. Reggie whispered to him. Corey went away. Closing the door, Reggie leaned against it.

"We were supposed to have a friendly little talk and then you'd go on your merry way. But you had to go and shoot off your mouth. I don't get it. You're smarter than that. A successful businesswoman and all. I talked to you the first time we met for two minutes and I could tell you had brains. Not like Doreen, God rest her soul."

"Out of my way, I'm going."

"You were—"

"Move!"

"Not now, you know what you've done? You've talked your way into staying. You're my guest. Until he gets here. Who? Who do you think?"

"You'll pay for this, Carlyle."

"Sure, you'll make me. Who's coming? Guess . . ."

⎯⎯ FORTY-SEVEN ⎯⎯

Gripping her arm too tightly for her to shake off, he led her out to the foot of the stairs.

"Derrick won't hurt me," she said firmly. "We love each other."

"I know, I know, he's crazy about you, he's always saying. But that doesn't matter, it won't stop him. His kind—

real pros—don't let anything get in their way, not their feelings for the hit, that's for sure. You know what they say about a good hit man? He can't see faces. He sees the body, the face is blank. He sees the body, picks his spot, and blammo. I guess you have to be like that. You don't think, feel; your mind, your emotions stay out of it, know what I mean? He'll come, he'll close the lid on this thing."

"He won't."

"He loves you, you said."

"What we have . . . you wouldn't understand."

"Hey, don't kid yourself. I do understand; I was just as crazy about Doreen."

"I'm sure."

She turned from him and went on, softening her tone, ridding it temporarily of its disdain.

"She loved you so much. That was the only reason she 'stuck her nose in.' She worried about you and was helpless to protect you."

"I know that. She told me when I visited her in the hospital. Only that doesn't change the situation. Oh, it was nice of her, sure, but Cambridge and all I'm involved in is top secret, like the government, right? And that's the bottom line. Once she started making my business hers, it was all over. There's something neither of you understood. Derrick and I have people over us we have to account to. We operate under very stiff rules, we have what's called a code of silence. *Omerta.*

"You see, it's not what you two found out, it's that you're both naturally curious and it could only go from bad to worse. You're not like Derrick and me, we live with zippers on our mouths. I tried to explain that to Doreen. Derrick explained it to you, right?"

"No, he just doesn't talk."

He bristled. "I don't either! Corey . . . Corey!"

Corey came running.

"Take her upstairs to the third floor. The room down the end on the left, the key's in the lock. Bring it when you come down. When will he get here?"

"Fifteen, maybe twenty minutes, I don't know."

"Fifteen, twenty minutes, you don't know, which? Never mind. Go with Jack, Lyssa, and remember what he's got in his pocket. I'm really sorry it turned out like this. You got to believe that, really and truly sorry."

"I'm sure."

"I am."

"He won't do it."

"Keep telling yourself that. You're not thinking, you don't see your problem. When I tell him all you've told me that you found out about him—"

"I've told you nothing, you've been doing all the talking."

"Ah, you know that and I know that, but he doesn't. And I get to talk to him first."

"Bastard!"

"Bastard, pig, liar, anything else? No? Good-bye, Lyssa."

"Go to hell. And don't be so cocksure. It's not over."

"Till the fat lady sings, right?"

He laughed, turned, and walked off. She could hear his guests talking in low tones around the dining-room table. Corey took her arm; she shook him off.

"Up."

On their way up to the first landing they passed a large, nearly life-size portrait of the Carlyles, Doreen in her wedding gown holding her bouquet. It had been painted from a photograph. She looked radiant, her happiness uncontainable. Reggie's expression made him look like the proud owner of the Kentucky Derby winner. If he loved her as much as he insisted he did, he never would have had her killed. Derrick loved her with all his heart. He'd kill himself before he'd harm her.

They reached the landing, walking slowly in silence down to the next flight up. On the second-floor landing as they turned the corner, like a switch thrown, all the confidence, the certain knowledge that Derrick would not kill her, fled. Displaced by panic and fear. Deliberately assuming the role of blind fool was stupid. She should be planning for the worst. Fifteen minutes, possibly less, and he would arrive. Waiting for him so she could talk to him would be more than risky, it'd be insane. Her only chance was escape.

They reached the room at the end of the corridor; the key protruded from the lock. Corey opened the door.

"In."

She hesitated. He pushed her in, locked the door.

~~~ FORTY-EIGHT ~~~

Inside she whirled about, tried the door: instinctively, not thinking. He had locked it immediately and left, taking the key with him. She turned. The room was larger than she had imagined, rectangular, with two large windows overlooking the grounds below, and just outside the one at the left, a white birch—huge, old, the bark yellowed with age and peeling on its surface. Black branches like buggy whips studded the trunk. The tree stood at least ten feet from the window. Did she dare to jump from the sill to it?

No, more like twelve or fifteen feet. She cast about; dominating the furnishings was a Regency-style painted canopy bed. There were pleated wall coverings. On the wall to the left of the bed, which separated the windows, hung an eglomise portrait of a woman in a pale blue gown, her dark hair piled up under a feathered hat. There was a chinoiserie table, on it a Lalique art-deco lamp. A lovely, warm room, but the impression of its beauty and taste dimmed as she pondered her situation.

Standing at the window with no tree obstructing her view of the ground below, she raised the window and peered straight down. At least thirty-five feet down to the lawn and about fifty feet toward a gazebo and the fence beyond. Flagstones led to it, with pachysandra edging the way.

She began going through drawers, searching for nothing specific, anything that might held her escape. Jerking drawers wide, fumbling through their contents, slamming them shut. In a drawer in one of the nightstands she found a box of matches: *Bassini's Restaurant, 24 Front Street, Bellingham.*

Recollection of her dinner with Doreen came snapping back. Her uncle Carleton and his gin. Brian Carlyle, the now-prodigal son, Reggie's drinking, her jobs: drugstore clerk, costume-jewelry-counter clerk, manicurist. Hairstyling school when she was eighteen. It all came flooding back; she could see Doreen's face, the happiness in her smile, the joy she exuded.

"Bastard! Bastard! Bastard!"

To steal the life of someone who had so much life, enjoyed it so! Never complained, never got down; Lyssa could never recall meeting Doreen when mere sight of her didn't pick her up. It was the effect Doreen had on everyone; without the least effort expended on her part, she stimulated others' happiness. If it was dormant, she woke it; if it needed elevating, she raised it to the level of her own. Lyssa recalled coming away from their dinner at Bassini's feeling marvelous. Credit a healthy injection of Doreen's personality. As for the new widower, did he pull the wings off flies when he was a small boy? Did he kick dogs, torment cats?

The matchbox was full. How she'd love to burn the place to the ground! What time was it getting to be?

"Don't look at your watch. . . ."

It would only aggravate her panic. She pulled open the doors to an Italian painted armoire. The drawers had been removed and two shelves installed; the upper one supported a TV. On the shelf on either side of the TV lay catalogs from Neiman Marcus, Bloomingdale's, other stores: dresses, sport clothes, shoes, accessories. There was the TV remote control, a little Chinese box, empty, a folded comforter, a sewing box. What was Doreen doing with that? She didn't sew, didn't cook; more recollections from Bassini's. Had it belonged to the first Mrs. Carlyle? In it were two pairs of scissors, pinking shears and large, all-purpose scissors. She worked the latter; they were new, very sharp. She turned slowly from the armoire, eyeing the bed hangings, the pleated wall coverings. The windows were draped with a brocatelle fabric, in olive and gold. The material was thick, sturdy. She stood on a chair and cut down the left drape then the right. She reckoned she would need all four.

She lay them on the floor side by side, full-length. Then tied the first two together. She tested the knot, it pulled apart easily.

"Damn . . ."

She thought a moment. She knew little about knots, only that a square knot differed from a granny knot, despite the resemblance between them. A granny knot was useless: witness. A square knot couldn't be pulled apart. She joined the ends in a square knot.

Then, setting one drape on the floor, she stepped on it, holding it down while attempting to pull the other upward and free it. She could not do so. Working furiously, fumbling, fighting her fear, sweating furiously as her nerves thrashed and jumped, she quickly joined all four drapes. And tied one free end around a leg of the bed under the headboard, close to the wall. At the window, looking out and down, she slowly let down her rope. To her relief, it proved longer than she would need.

She glanced about the room one last time. It struck her

that a diversion might help. Retrieving the matches, she lit the bed canopy. It flared up. Moving around the bed, she lit the corner diagonally opposite. Smoke rose in twin clouds, flattening against the ceiling, joining. She threw open the window opposite the birch tree and ran back to her escape window. She stood for a moment watching the now-blazing bed; the wall coverings would catch, the armoire, the entire room. In a few minutes it would be an inferno.

Raising the window as high as she could, she got a firm grip on the drape rope, got out over the sill, and twisting her legs around the rope beneath her, started slipping slowly down. Hand over hand, she lowered herself about ten feet before looking upward. Smoke billowed from both windows, she could hear flames crackling above.

In her haste to get away, she had overlooked one thing: she should have knotted the rope. Making it far easier to descend. Twisting her legs around it helped, but to have been able to rest her feet on the knot below would have greatly reduced the strain on her arms. Already they were beginning to hurt; pain filled her shoulders, shooting up her arms to her wrists and hands, rapidly increasing in intensity, threatening to weaken her grip. Her bag bobbed at her hip, the carrying strap slung at an angle across her front. Afraid to look down, she gauged her progress from the sill above. And estimated that she had descended nearly twenty feet, past the halfway point.

"You can do it, you can do it, you have to," she muttered through clenched teeth.

The pain in her upper arms was becoming excruciating. Would she dislocate her shoulders? Her hands felt like they were on fire; gripping, completely enclosing the soft material became harder and harder. Any moment now she could lose all control of the muscles in her fingers.

Down, down. Not far now, she'd make it. She'd make it!

"Thatta girl, keeping coming. . . ."

She glanced down for the first time. Corey stood leering up at her, his arms upstretched, fingers curling inward, beckoning her down.

"You can do it. . . ."

⸻ FORTY-NINE ⸻

Her heart seized; for an instant she thought she would black out; he was laughing.

"Come on, come on. . . . Boy, wait'll Mr. C sees what you did to his drapes. And the room! Come on, almost here. Or you think you might want to go back up?"

Corey laughed uproariously. Her shoulders and arms were killing her, it was all she could do to hang on. He was behind her; looking down, she could see his shadow stretching toward the house, his arms raised. With all her remaining strength, inhaling, dispatching the last of her energy upward into her exhausted limbs, she untwisted her legs, spun about, dropped four feet, burning her hands so she cried out, drew back her right leg, and kicked as hard as she could.

Squarely in the face. He cried out, his hands flying to his nose, blood spurting through his fingers. Back he staggered, falling, sitting. She had spun back around, facing the house. Dropping the last few feet, she drove her foot against his chest, flattening him. And rushing forward, kicked his head. His hands fell away from his face, he groaned and lay still.

She threw a glance upward; smoke piled from both windows, rising above the peak of the roof. One last look at Corey unconscious, the blood seeping from his nose down both cheeks, and she turned and ran, heading for the fence beyond the gazebo. Pushing through the rhododendrons concealing the fence, she came up to it only to find the palings set too closely together for her to squeeze between them. Panicking, she ran back onto the lawn toward the gate. Reaching it, she pushed through, leaving it ajar, and took off.

Up the block, diagonally across the street, and down the next block until, looking back, she could no longer see the house, only the smoke clearing the taller trees in the area, climbing toward a solitary rain cloud. And still she ran, until a steel band materialized, strapping across her chest and tightening, forcing her to fight to breathe. Cars passed, drivers eyed her curiously. She tripped, falling to one knee, rested a moment. Corey's face crossed the screen of her mind's eye; up again and running, running, putting block after block behind her, stretching the distance separating her from him, from Derrick, who must be arriving about now.

Again she fell, not tripping but collapsing from exhaustion. Brakes squealed behind her. She looked about, thinking she might have fallen in the street. She was on the sidewalk; she turned to look back. A woman about her age, her hair in curlers under a bandanna, was getting out of an ancient station wagon. Her round face was fretted with worry. The station wagon was filled with little girls. The woman approached.

"My dear, what's wrong? What happened?"

She helped her to her feet. Lyssa stood panting.

"Out . . . breath. Help me . . . get . . . to a phone."

"Of course, just relax, take a deep breath, and rest."

The woman released her, tentatively. Lyssa was able to stand upright. The woman guided her to her car.

"Amelia, Janice, get in back with Connie and the others. Make room back there, girls."

"There's no room," protested Amelia, flashing an outrageous-looking orthodontic retainer, her expression furious.

She gawked accusingly at Lyssa.

"Do it!" snapped the woman.

The two girls piled out muttering, one getting into the backseat, the other trying to, unable to, climbing over the back onto the floor, joining three others. Lyssa sat with both hands on the dash, bracing herself, her head lowered, catching her breath, conscious of little eyes staring at her from behind, from beside her. The woman got behind the wheel.

"Sit still, Eunice. You, too, Melissa." She started out. "There's a convenience store on Birch Avenue in the next block. I'll get you there in two shakes."

"You're a good . . . good Samaritan."

"Good deed for the day. What happened?"

"Long story. A man grabbed me." She glanced at the two girls remaining between them. They gaped expectantly. "I . . ."

"That's okay, you can spare me the details. Little pitchers, big ears, you know. I'm Hildegarde Conklin. Only two of these are mine. We're heading home to make cookies. We're a Brownie troop out of uniform."

"Lyssa Morgan. I don't know how to thank you. . . ."

"No need. What should I do, leave you back there kneeling on the sidewalk? Us girls got to stick together. It's not really a man's world, you know, they only think it is. I'm a paid-up member of NOW. You didn't see the sticker on my back bumper. I had another one alongside it." She laughed. " 'I brake for everything except male chauvinists.' Somebody tore it off, wouldn't you know? There's the store, Bigelow's, I know there's a pay phone."

She pulled to a stop.

"You going to be okay?" she asked.

"Fine, thanks to you. You saved my life."

"I doubt that. You don't look too bad, except for your PH—you've got a beautiful run down your right leg."

Lyssa checked. "Good Lord . . ."

Hildegarde Conklin laughed, waved, drove off. Lyssa got out a quarter and went into the store. The woman behind the counter bore a vague resemblance to the woman in charge of the out-of-town-newspaper stand in town. Same age, hair coloring, similar features, but this one was cleaner, tidier.

"The phone?" Lyssa asked.

The woman nodded toward the far end of the store. She had been checking lottery tickets; they were strewn all over the counter. Lyssa hurried to the phone. Two girls about twelve were using it; one was talking, the other was giggling and interrupting her.

"Billy French is a world-class nerd."

"Tell him you only went out with him on account he begged you," whispered her friend, and giggled.

"I only—"

Lyssa snatched the receiver from her. "Sorry, emergency."

"Hey!"

The girl scowled; she and her friend backed away and ran toward the counter. Lyssa killed their call, inserted her quarter, punched 911. A woman came on.

"Police emergency."

"Let me speak to Sergeant Hugh O'Fallon. Hurry!"

"His extension is four-eighty-three. Ringing . . ."

It rang and rang; someone finally picked up, not O'Fallon. Lyssa detected the faint trace of a Scottish brogue.

"He's away from his desk, can I give him a message?"

"Yes. No. Switch me over to Roarke."

"Captain Roarke?"

"Tell him it's Mrs. Derrick Morgan. And please hurry, this is an emergency."

"Okay, okay, keep your shirt on."

Another voice came on, confirmed her name, spoke to a third party.

"Hello, this is Captain Roarke."

"Lyssa Morgan, Captain, please listen."

She hurried through the sequence of events from the cab ride to her escape.

"You're a very lucky woman."

"Can you send somebody to pick me up?"

"Where are you?"

"Birch Avenue in Chase Ridge." She paused and called back to the woman. The two girls were still at the counter. "What's the address of this place?"

"Seven-fourteen Birch Avenue, corner of Gresham Road. Bigelow's."

She relayed the information.

"Stay where you are, somebody'll pick you up in about five minutes."

"Thank God."

She hung up and walked slowly back up to the counter.

"This little girl says you took the phone away from her," rasped the woman.

Plunged into thought, Lyssa didn't hear; the words were repeated, the tone even sterner. Lyssa got out a single, gave it to the taller of the two girls. Wrong girl; the other one snatched it from her friend.

"We go halvesy!" she shrilled.

They ran out. Fire sirens pierced the quiet of the late afternoon. A hook-and-ladder truck nearly a block long, a fireman perched on the rear driver's seat maneuvering the back wheels, roared by. Two men came in; they had on work shirts, denims, work shoes. Lyssa had started back toward the phone. She looked back at the firemen then rushed up to the phone.

"Hey, Angie, you should see the fire over on Crestview," said one man.

"I don't have to, I can hear it."

"That big house on the corner, the whole top floor's blazing."

"There must be seven trucks over there," said the other man. "Gimme two lottery tickets."

"Gimme five."

Preparing to insert a quarter in the slot, the other hand on the receiver, Lyssa stiffened. Had anyone died? Had Corey? The last she'd seen he was lying on the ground, out cold. Or had she killed him, kicking him in the head? She didn't hang around to check. And if anyone died in the fire, it would be manslaughter.

She called the store. Ellie came on.

"It's me, El, let me speak to Aggie."

"She's with a customer."

"Take her customer, put her on!"

"Okay, okay."

Aggie came on. "Where the devil are you?"

"Never mind, just listen."

She raced through the sequence of events.

"My God, you started the house on fire?"

"I had to, I had to do something."

"You're safe where you are now?"

"I guess. I won't feel really safe till the police show up."

"Listen to me, you can't go back to the apartment."

"I've got to, everything I own—"

"You can't! You're not thinking. You say Derrick was on his way to Doreen's house. You got out just in time, before he showed. He'll figure you'll head for home, to call the police from there. He's probably already there!"

"You may be right."

"I know I am. When you're finished with the police, get them to bring you straight to my place. You're staying with me. I'll get a damn gun! What time is it?"

"A little after five-thirty."

"I'll expect you about six-thirty. Don't disappoint me, dear heart, and don't, I repeat, don't go near your apartment."

"I must be thick as a wall, but I still can't believe he'd harm me. He loves me."

"Sure, but when Carlyle finishes filling his ear and it becomes a choice between you and the rest of his life behind bars . . . or worse . . ."

"I don't care, I have to talk to him."

"Are you crazy?"

"He's my husband. He won't take Reggie's word over mine."

"That's not the issue. You just got through saying Reggie told you everything about him. Enough to string him up ten times. Take it easy. You'll get your chance to talk to him, only not today. And not without wire mesh between you."

"I've been thinking. What it comes down to is I only have Reggie's word that he did all those horrible things."

"Lyssa, Lyssa, stop thinking with your heart! You're smarter than that."

The door opened behind her; a policeman came in.

"The police are here, I've got to go," said Lyssa.

"Talk to O'Fallon, talk to the captain, they'll tell you, don't go near your apartment!"

"Right."

"Six-thirty."

The policeman introduced himself and helped Lyssa into the cruiser. The radio in the front crackled, rendering the voice coming over it incoherent. As the door was closed for her a black Lincoln Continental passed, heading in the opposite direction. Its windows were tinted, but the front-seat passenger's window was down. She recognized Jack Corey, a Band-Aid strapped across the bridge of his nose. She ducked as he started to turn to look.

On the way into the city they stopped at a light. Glancing out, she could see into a laundromat. A woman was removing sheets from a dryer. Her wash basket was on a table in the front window. The sheet became an armful of money, the basket heaped and overflowing with it.

~~~~~ FIFTY ~~~~~

Captain William Rourke had to be nicknamed Big Bill. He looked at least six feet tall sitting in his posture chair. When he stood up to greet her, he looked ten feet tall. She felt like a five-year-old meeting an uncle for the first time when he shook her hand and it disappeared completely inside his. His office was three times the size of O'Fallon's and the furnishings up-to-date. The police department was like the business world; one could ascertain the level and importance of an employee's job by his immediate surroundings.

Roarke would have been handsome were it not for his nose. It dominated its surroundings: large, round, flabby looking, suggesting the cartilage had been surgically excised. When he sneezed, did it waggle from side to side? He had been on the phone when she was ushered in. Looking about her as she sat, she felt truly safe for the first time in hours. The house, the confrontation with Reggie, the room, the danger and escape seemed years ago. It was frightening, life threatening, but was the worst yet to come?

Roarke had hung up and was telling her how he'd been looking forward to meeting her and talking. Picking her brain, was what he was saying, only he hesitated to put it in such terms. O'Fallon came in.

"Lyssa . . ."

He looked very worried. For her, she knew. He had ample justification to be concerned; Aggie did, too. Not about Reggie; about the threat that Derrick posed. He had assumed the role of chief monster in the nightmare. Still, regardless of Aggie's warning, sooner or later he and Lyssa would come face-to-face and have it out. If he'd done everything Reggie claimed, even half the things, even just killing Elizabeth and Joseph Walsh, then she'd been living a lie, a lie beyond outrageous, beyond monstrous.

Their marriage. Their vows were a sham. He'd married her for the same reason Reggie married Doreen. And Carol, especially Carol. For appearances, for respectability.

The problem was that she, blind fool that she was, loved Derrick. Still. Reggie could have piled on six times the allegations and not affect that in the slightest. And Derrick loved her; everything about him confirmed it: the way he looked at her across the table, the way he kissed her, his gentleness, his warmth and kindliness. He was still, after four years, as affectionate, as considerate as the most devoted suitor.

"Mrs. Morgan?" asked Roarke.

She realized he was asking her attention for the second time. She hadn't heard a word either of them had said.

"I'm sorry."

"That's okay. Now, this tape machine will record your statement, after which it'll be typed up and you can go over it. Edit it, change anything you want, add, delete, before you sign it. It represents your formal complaint against Carlyle."

"Incidentally," said O'Fallon, "he's been calling himself Reggie Carlyle for nearly thirty-five years, but his real name is Carlo Reggiero."

"We have to start somewhere," said Roarke. "We'll start with what he tried to pull this afternoon. The defense attorney'll paint it in sixteen different muted colors, but it comes down to attempted murder. It's separate and distinct from the other charges against him, against all of them. Against Cambridge Medical and Surgical Equipment. The IRS is interested, as you already know, but the Justice Department is as well. Are you familiar with RICO?"

"I've heard of it," she said.

"It stands for Racketeer Influenced and Corrupt Organizations," said O'Fallon. "It's a statute passed by Congress some time ago aimed specifically at the Mafia, the businesses they steal or buy or create as fronts."

She nodded. "Cambridge."

"To nail them, two, what's called predicate offenses, have to be proven," said Roarke. "In this case, money laundering and complicity to deprive people of their lives. Murder. Your testimony can go a long way toward proving that the accountant—Cochrane was his name?— was murdered."

"And Doreen Carlyle."

O'Fallon nodded. "Cochrane is tied directly to Cambridge, she's not. Not that her murder, any and all murders, will be allowed to slide by."

"Your husband's an executive with Cambridge," said Roarke. "You may be asked to testify against him."

"I thought wives can't testify against their husbands, or husbands against wives."

O'Fallon smiled. "Can't be compelled to. You can if you want."

"Will that be a problem?" asked Roarke.

"No . . ."

"Are you sure?"

"I've already told Hugh, Sergeant O'Fallon, I don't know very much. What I do know is really secondhand."

"From the late Mrs. Carlyle," said O'Fallon.

"But if it'll help bring them down, I'll testify."

"Good girl," said Roarke. "And keep in mind, it's generally very difficult to gauge the value of your testimony. Two or three words could provide the glue to hold together a couple important points. One other thing before we start.

What do you know about Anthony Minervino?"

"Doreen, Mrs. Carlyle, recognized him when he came to dinner with his wife. He was pointed out to her by a friend some years ago in Las Vegas. He's with one of the Mafia families."

"The Licata family in L.A.," said Roarke. "Minervino is the don's right hand. The way it works is the don gives the order or renders the decision, conveys it to Tony Boots, and he passes it on to the underlings."

"Reggie," she said. They nodded. "The Mafia set Cambridge up. He runs it and launders their drug money, or whatever they get their money from. That's it, isn't it?"

"That's it, that's the universal formula."

"But Derrick told me that Carol, Reggie's first wife, set him up in business."

The two men exchanged knowing glances.

"It does sound better than the Mob set him up," said O'Fallon.

"Would you happen to know how your husband and Reggiero first hooked up?" Roarke asked.

"Derrick needed a job, Reggie hired him."

"Your husband wasn't recommended, he walked in cold."

"I really can't say."

Roarke swiveled left and addressed the wall.

"Mrs. Morgan, how long have you been married?"

"A little over four years."

"And when your husband proposed and you accepted and you were married, did you have any inkling, the slightest suspicion of what he was really involved in?"

"Hardly. You think I would have married him if I thought he killed people?"

"Mrs. Morgan has, you might say, come to certain incriminating conclusions only recently," said O'Fallon.

Roarke frowned and shook his head. "You do realize that getting away from that house is only the start. You're still in a very dangerous situation. You said over the phone that Reggiero threatened to tell your husband everything you know about him."

She wanted to say, "But Derrick won't believe him." She couldn't say it, couldn't say that she didn't believe.

"You're going to need round-the-clock protection. As a material witness before the grand jury you're entitled to it."

"I'm moving in with my business partner until all this is sorted out."

"I don't know," said Roarke. "That could be the first place he'd look when you don't come home. By the way, I have men out looking for him as we speak. I assigned them thirty seconds after you hung up when you called from that store. We'll find him, I'm sure, but until we do . . ."

"I'll stick to you like glue," said O'Fallon.

"That's good news. I can go back to the apartment. I need clothes, makeup. . . ."

"We can do that."

"I'm still leery about you moving in with your partner," said Roarke. "It'd be better if you took a hotel room. And register under a phony name."

"I guess. She's waiting for me at the store."

Roarke proferred his phone.

"That's okay, I'll call her from the apartment."

"Whatever you say," he said. "Okay, why don't we turn this thing on and you start from the beginning. You okay? Would you like a drink of water before you start?"

O'Fallon got her a paper cup of water from the bottle in the corner. She downed it, thinking, This is it. The moment she opened her mouth she would be putting in motion the beginning of the end. For Reggie, for Cambridge, for Derrick.

And like a breeze passing, a guilty feeling touched her heart in spite of herself.

~~~~~ FIFTY-ONE ~~~~~

They were in O'Fallon's car heading toward Huron Street and L'Image; it was getting on to 6:25.

"You setting fire to the house shook the captain up a little. Did you see his eyes?"

"I needed a diversion, I told you."

"Pretty risky. What if it got out of hand real fast? Blazed up before you could get out?"

"My 'rope' was hanging out the window, no problem."

" 'No problem,' she says." He laughed. "And you even remembered to take your handbag."

"I had it slung around my shoulder, on the opposite hip, like I always carry it. No big deal."

"You're good under pressure."

"I was petrified. And when Corey called up to me, I nearly had a heart attack. I nearly let go."

"He's lucky you didn't kick him to death. Boy, I'm glad you're on our side."

"Mmmmm."

"Don't get down, it'll all work out. This, too, shall pass, right? And an hour from now you'll be stashed away in a suite at the Hampton House as safe as if you were in your mother's arms."

They passed a fire truck coming the other way; the fire must have been extinguished by now. The same thought crossed O'Fallon's mind.

"I wonder if they were able to contain it?" he mused aloud.

"I take back what I said. I didn't start it as a diversion, I did it for her, Doreen. She couldn't get even, I couldn't either; but that was better than nothing. And you know something? Seeing the smoke climbing into the sky felt gooood."

They rode in silence; she could feel his eyes on her again and again.

"One thing I'm curious about," she said at last. "A few things, but . . . his first wife, Carol. They were married for nearly thirty-five years. He evidently didn't have any 'problem' with her."

"Maybe she had a stronger sense of self-preservation than Doreen."

"Doreen worried about him, how many times do I have to tell you? There's a big difference between being nosy and being concerned."

"Apparently not to Reggie. Carol must have been out of the same mold as the two at the dinner party—Minervino's and the other guy's wives."

"Arnold Carlson." She nodded agreement with this.

"I'm sure that's his real name. I remember you telling me they behaved like mannequins—the three monkeys, right? Speak, see, hear no evil. No nothing. Carol recognized her role and filled it. Doreen, on the other hand . . ."

"I know. Huron Street's around the next corner. You should be able to park in front."

"About Derrick. Nobody asked me, but my opinion is he's long gone."

"No," she said flatly.

"Really. Put yourself in his shoes. He gets to Carlyle's house, Carlyle fills him in on what's happened, his version. You, meanwhile, have fled the premises. Derrick's no fool, he can put two and two together. And you can't beat that type for resourcefulness. I bet he left there and headed straight for the airport. One stop only on the way, to close out his bank account. Don't go back to the apartment, don't take the chance. Climb on a plane, fly to one coast or the other, leave the country."

"I still say no."

He pulled up in front of the store. Aggie was waiting inside the glass door. She pantomimed kowtowing.

"Your ego says no. He wouldn't leave town without kissing you good-bye, right?"

"That's not it. I think he honestly believes I wouldn't speak up against him, wouldn't say anything to incriminate him. He loves me, Hugh. I'm not just saying that, it's the gospel truth. We love each other. I can't believe he'd willingly hurt me, and he believes the same about me."

"Devotion above and beyond."

She flared. "This is all very funny to you, isn't it? This week's soap opera."

"Take it easy. I'm sorry, I apologize. The last thing it is is funny. The fact of the matter is I'm jealous. Nobody loves me that much, with that deep a commitment. Except maybe my mother."

"That's what hurts about all this. If I didn't care for him so, I wouldn't give a damn what happens to him."

"Hold it right there. You can't afford to think like that, not at this stage. You've got to concentrate on number one."

Aggie came out. "You're two minutes late, dear heart. Sergeant, do you mind driving us to my place? It's the south side of Park Square."

"She can't stay with you," said O'Fallon. "Not till he's under wraps."

"I'm going to a hotel," said Lyssa.

"You are not!"

"She'll be safer," he added.

"Than with me? That's ridiculous!"

"She'll have police protection."

"It's better," said Lyssa. "If I stayed with you, I'd be putting you in danger. It won't be for long, Aggie, just till Derrick turns up."

"Till he's arrested."

The word caused Lyssa to inhale sharply between her teeth. But "arrested" was it. And time she faced up to it. He was on "their" side; they'd all be brought to account, including him. Unless O'Fallon was right: he was on a plane, on his way out of the country.

O'Fallon eyed the store. "She won't be in to work for the next few days."

"I hate this," said Lyssa, "hiding like an animal."

"Let's go over to your apartment, pick up what you'll need, and get you set up someplace. Out of town might be a good idea."

"Hiding from my own husband, who's never raised a hand to me. Never threatened me in any way . . ."

"His kind don't threaten," said O'Fallon, "they just—"

"Let's go. I'll be in touch, Aggie. The bug's out of the phone, so nobody can listen in."

They hugged.

"Take care of yourself, dear heart. When you get settled, let me know and I'll come visit."

"I . . . wouldn't do that," said O'Fallon. "Anyone looking for her might take it into his head to follow you around, hoping you'll lead him to her."

"He's right," said Lyssa.

She kissed Aggie on the cheek good-bye. They both had tears in their eyes.

~~~ FIFTY-TWO ~~~

He parked across the street from the apartment building. Otto was nowhere to be seen. She started to get out.

"Wait," O'Fallon said, "there's something I want to say. Off the record, just between the two of us, I want you to know I think you're doing great."

"Doing what?"

"This. I mean you're married to the guy, you love him. The strain has to be horrendous, but you don't blink an eye. You can take it, lady, I admire the hell out of you."

She laughed hollowly. "Under this case-hardened steel exterior I'm solid Jell-O. This has to be the rudest of rude awakenings on record. It makes me wonder about myself, if I'm all my ego tells me I am. We met, we fell in love, we married, we've stayed in love. It's improved with age. Now I suddenly find myself questioning my intelligence, my judgment. My ability to read others. What ability?"

"He was very good at covering up."

"Nobody can be perfect at that. I should have seen something ages ago. Other people can tell when somebody's lying or holding back. There's always signs. I didn't see a one."

"You didn't look."

"Blinded by love, I know."

"I didn't mean that. How can you fault your judgment? You can't. You're not some starry-eyed schoolgirl who fell in love with love."

"I don't know about that, I did once."

"Not you."

"Howard Clemmings. In my sophomore year in high school. He was a senior and a Greek god. All the girls used to stare at him. All he did was smile and say hello when we passed in the hall between classes. I fell head over teakettle. For three glorious days my feet didn't touch ground and all my girlfriends were oohing and aahing and jealous as sin. Then he asked if he could buy me a soda. It was the same as if he proposed.

"Little did I realize that he was setting me up. He wanted to pick my brain. I was a whiz in geometry, he didn't know a right angle from an axiom of order. He wanted me to tutor him. For free, of course. A couple hours a week. I went into shock. I walked out halfway through my chocolate milkshake."

"He didn't love you, he loved your axiom of order."

"It wasn't funny at the time, it was disasterville. Don't let me get into the aftermath, you'll get tears in your eyes. My point is, I got carried away by his smile. I didn't exercise judgment because I didn't want to."

"How old were you when you married Derrick?"

"Twenty-nine."

"A mature woman, not a sophomore in high school."

"Not two different people, Hugh, just one—grown up and hanging on to the same flaws."

"Balderdash. And what's an axiom of order?"

"I'd need to draw it. Never mind, let's go up." His hand instinctively went to his shoulder holster, patting it once. "Do you think he's up there?"

They got out.

"He's smarter than that," he said. "He knows you got away from the house. He has to assume you'd go straight to the police. Figure as well that you'd realize he wouldn't hang around here with you gone. He knows you'll come home eventually—you have to pack your stuff. You'll come or somebody'll come for you. He knows we wouldn't let you come by yourself. In short—"

"He's not up there."

"He'd be stupid to come and he doesn't strike me as stupid."

Otto was still absent from his post when they crossed the street and walked into the lobby to the elevators. She was shaking her head.

"What?" he asked.

"The Mob, the Mafia. They really aren't an equal opportunity employer, are they?"

"I think that's a bumper sticker."

"Seriously. No blacks, no minorities. Definitely no women. One thing they're very successful at—exemplifying the difference between men and women. They symbolize it."

"And here I thought the differences were anatomical, silly me."

"Seriously, you can't even imagine a criminal organization composed of women."

"There are female gangs."

"Come on, you know what I'm talking about. Female gangs are just . . . male-gang auxiliaries. Like the American Legion Ladies Auxiliary. There must be one. I'm saying there could never be a female Mafia."

The elevator came; a pretty blonde with a poodle got off. The poodle went for O'Fallon's leg, the woman pulled it back.

"Mitzi, Mitzi!"

The doors closed. O'Fallon shrugged.

"If you say so."

"Not 'if I say so.' Such a thing doesn't exist because it can't. Women aren't macho like men, aren't freighted with such low self-esteem that they have to prove their manhood by killing each other, corrupting, stealing. If you stop and think about it, all the evil in the world is man-made."

"Here we go. . . ."

"Isn't it?"

"There are no evil women."

"A few, but I'm talking about organized."

"The Mafia Ladies Auxiliary, it has a nice ring to it."

The elevator stopped at eleven; the doors opened; she hesitated. He set a hand lightly against the small of her back; they got out. She led the way diagonally to her door. She tried it; it was locked.

"Let me."

He took her key, unlocked the door, pulled his gun.

"What *are* you doing?"

"Shhh."

Inside they checked both bedrooms, both bathrooms. When they came back out to the living room, O'Fallon holstered his gun.

"I thought you said he wouldn't come back?" she whispered.

"I never take chances. One reason I'm a good cop. Nor should you. Why are you whispering?"

"I'm not."

She looked about as if seeing the place for the first time. He watched her shoulders sag, her doleful expression. Her eyes glistened. She snuffled.

"Take it easy," he murmured. And set a consoling arm around her shoulders.

"I suddenly hate the sight of this place. Our love nest, our retreat, where happiness reigned. Four years of playacting, of calculated deceit. What a rousing success he was at it, what a rousing idiot I. A lesson learned, right? Never put all your love, all your faith and trust in one urn. When it breaks and spills, you can never recover it. Yes, I hate this place. I feel like the walls are laughing at me."

"You'll get over it."

"Sure."

"You will. Oh, when it's over and the dust settles, you can move out. But you'll take all this with you." He tapped his temple. "How about calling a hotel? Maybe, as I said, out of town? The Wessex Manor in Scarborough's nice. I've eaten there."

"I guess. What difference where I stay? Only not out of town, on second thought. I'll call the Sonesta on Broad Street. Wait . . . you call."

"If you want."

"Not a hotel, not yet." She dug out the phone directory, riffling the pages. "Call Reggie's house."

"Carlyle?"

"Here's the number. Call and ask for Derrick Morgan. See if he's still there."

"You know he's not."

"Then ask where he's gone."

"They'll ask who wants to know. I'll tell them I'm . . . Phil Minicucci."

"Who?"

"He's old-time muscle from Detroit. Everybody in the rackets knows Dandy Phil. He spends ten thousand dollars to dress himself. I once collared him on suspicion of dealing herion."

He punched the number; they shared the earpiece.

"Hello?" said a voice.

"Let me speak to Derrick Morgan."

"Who?"

"Derrick Morgan. This is Philip Minicucci, Esquire."

"Just a second."

There was a long pause. O'Fallon covered the mouthpiece.

"Somebody else is coming to the—"

"Hello, Reggie Carlyle speaking, can I help you?"

"This is Phil Minicucci, I'm trying to get hold of Derrick Morgan."

"He's not here at the moment."

"Do you expect him?"

"No."

"He was there, right? Do you know where he went?"

"He left about an hour ago, he didn't say where. Look, can we cut this short? We've got a problem here. Goodbye, okay? Good-bye."

Click.

She phoned the Sonesta Hotel, telling the reservations clerk that she'd be dropping by in half an hour.

Lyssa stood in silence for a long moment. O'Fallon hesitated to interrupt her train of thought. She finally spoke.

"Would you like a cold drink?"

"I'd love a Coke. I can get it, you start packing."

"Okay. The glasses are in the cabinet to the left of the sink."

In the bedroom she got her overnight bag down from the closet shelf. She drew open her lingerie drawer. As she moved her lingerie about, her hand touched something: the sheaf of newspaper clippings from the *Atlanta Constitution.* She'd completely forgotten about them. She looked through them and the past came swirling back. That day at the zoo when he admitted he'd gone to Atlanta, not Seattle. Again she could see his eyes as he told her he arrived at Walsh's apartment house on Hunnicutt just before the murder. He sounded so sincere; he was able to look straight into her eyes, not a hint of deceit in his manner, his face, his voice.

"A professional."

She studied the police artist's drawing of the stranger the witness Conolly had met at the front door. The sketch looked like Derrick, behind the flourishing mustache, his hat brim pulled down, raincoat collar up. The suspect's height, according to Conolly, matched Derrick's. "About a hundred and seventy pounds" was right. She dropped the clippings into the wastebasket. Then changed her mind, retrieved them, put them in the sleeve in the top of her overnight bag, not knowing why she wanted to hang on to them, only that she should. She packed three changes of clothing, a couple of skirts and blouses. Nothing for evening. Then changed her mind about that, adding to the pile a silk cardigan with allover sequins and beading and black polyester palazzo pants. O'Fallon hadn't mentioned he was married, or even a steady girlfriend; he might ask her to dinner tonight or tomorrow. If he didn't, she'd ask him. She had no designs on him, she just dreaded being alone. Especially after dark. And talking to him was so easy.

She stood staring down at the bed. From tonight on she'd sleep alone. Never again with him. In a way it was far worse than divorce. Like losing one's partner in a car accident, coming home to an empty house, empty bed. Cold and lonely bed.

How, she wondered, had he felt, coming home to his "empty house" the night Elizabeth was murdered?

Relieved that it was over?

She packed a couple bags of shoes, panty hose, a few accessories. In the bathroom she studied herself in the mirror. For some reason she didn't look quite as poorly as she felt. She could not recall ever feeling so totally drained. It was an effort to keep her eyes open. She freshened her makeup, fussed briefly with her hair, and went back out, bringing with her the overnight bag. O'Fallon was out on the terrace sipping his drink, looking out at the city, at twilight coming on. He turned when he heard her.

"All set?"

"Mmmmm."

"You okay?"

"I guess. Maybe I should have changed, maybe take a shower."

"You still can, there's no rush."

"I'll wait till I get to the hotel."

"You sure you got everything you want?"

She had come up alongside him at the railing. "For the rest of the week."

Down below she could see that Otto's replacement had come on.

"In there packing, I got to thinking about Brian," she said. "Reggie's son. He got out, packed up, left town.

Do you suppose he found out something about his father, about Cambridge?"

"If he did, I hope he's gone a long way away. Would you like a cold drink?"

"I'd like a double Scotch," she said. "Wouldn't you? I mean you're not on duty, not really."

"I really am and I'd love a Scotch."

There was a sickening thump. She turned, his knees gave way, he sank to the floor. Behind him stood Derrick, his hand upraised, holding a gun by the barrel.

~~~ FIFTY-THREE ~~~

"Nooooo!"

"Shhh . . ."

He restored the gun to his shoulder holster. Dropping to one knee, she examined O'Fallon.

"You killed him!"

"He's okay, a love tap. Let him snooze."

"Where did you come from?"

"Reggie's, where else? I heard you two coming in here, I ducked into the closet in the guest room. Hid behind that big square plastic thing that's full of winter clothes. You came in, looked around, you weren't very thorough. I was about to start packing myself when you came in. This works out beautifully. Let's both start packing."

He paused, snuffled, got out his inhaler, and drew on it. Frowned at it, tossed it onto the sofa.

"Empty. I swear, they put about six drops of epinephrine in the damned things. What a rip-off. I think there's one in the medicine cabinet in our bath. Would you mind getting it for me? It's been a rough day for us asthmatics. Breathing's getting to be hard labor. Get it, okay. I'll just sit a little, try and catch my breath."

The inhaler wasn't in the medicine cabinet. She found one still in its box in his sock drawer. She picked it up, thought a moment, put it back, shoving it under some socks out of sight. He needed it, would need it badly in a half hour or so. And before then send her downstairs across the street to the druggist's to pick up some. She would come back with ten policemen.

She started back, stopped, freezing at a strange sound: like two champagne corks popping in quick succession. She started, ran into the living room. He stood straddling O'Fallon, the gun hanging from his hand, thin blue smoke issuing from the muzzle.

"No!" she shrilled.

She ran to him, pounding him with her fists. He holstered the gun, held her away from him. She swung wildly.

"Hey, hey, stop it. Stop!" He shook her. "Listen to me, we're in a tight corner, we've got to get out. Over his dead body, okay? There'll be a limo downstairs in about fifteen minutes, we're going to Detroit."

"Murderer!"

"From there we fly to Manzanilla on the west coast of Mexico. From there to Fanning Island in the mid-Pacific. Then to Bora-Bora. It was all set up months ago, every detail. We've got nearly eight hundred thousand out of the country. Safe, nobody knows where it is, nobody can touch it."

She had plunged into shock. For a time she stood rigid, staring down at O'Fallon's body. Then she edged toward the sofa, feeling for it, dropping onto it. Holding her hands to her head, shaking it slowly.

"Snap out of it!" he rasped.

"How could you?" she murmured. "So easily, casually. Like . . . like switching on a light."

He snickered. "Switching his off." He sobered. "I had to, he's in our way, he's all that is. Don't you understand?"

"Like Doreen, like that poor woman in the hospital—Elizabeth, Walsh, Cochrane . . ."

She raised her eyes to meet his. And he was no longer Derrick, he was a killing machine masquerading as a human being, as her husband, her love.

"You've killed seven people," she whispered.

"A few more than that. I'm sorry, I apologize, okay? But snap out of it. Take a deep breath or something, get hold of yourself. We don't have time for this. Where's that inhaler?"

"In cold blood . . ."

He leaned over her, shouting. "The inhaler!"

"There aren't any more."

"There's got to be."

"No."

"Shit! Listen to me, are you listening? Go pack! Everything you want, anything, just as long as we can carry it. All we can take is what we can carry, understand? I'll go dig out our passports. When we get to Manzanilla, we'll take on new identities. It's all arranged. Would you believe the bastards get five hundred U.S. apiece for phony passports? Highway robbery. Listen to me. When we get to Bora-Bora, there'll be a schooner waiting. Our private yacht—captain, crew, all arranged.

"Reggie thinks we'll be meeting him in Manila. Will he be surprised. When we leave Manzanilla, we leave our lives behind us. Cambridge, him, Bellingham, everything. Mr. and Mrs. Derrick Morgan will vanish from the face of the earth. Magic, right? All it takes is money. Get up; go and pack."

In a daze she rose and started for the bedroom. At the door she looked back at O'Fallon's body. She could feel tears starting.

"Don't worry about him, I'll shove him under our bed.

They won't find him for a couple days at least. By then we'll be halfway across the Pacific. Go pack, let's get out of here."

She came back to him. He frowned threateningly.

"Lyssa . . ."

"I have a question. You and Reggie talked."

"He told me he talked to you. He really badmouthed you. Made you sound like the most treacherous bitch in creation. He just doesn't understand about us, how committed we are to each other. He doesn't understand that our love is all that counts. And look at me. Walsh, Cochrane, the rest—that's all in the past. I swear, I'll never pull another trigger as long as I live. And I plan to live a good long time.

"There's no way we'll join him in Manila. He's poison. He's had it in for you ever since Doreen. He actually blames you for her getting it. And you can't stand him. I don't blame you. You can relax. We'll never see the son of a bitch again."

It was all coming out dripping with sincerity; no deceit in his eyes, none in his tone. Not the slightest evidence of conscience. Had it been removed with his tonsils when he was a child? Let him rave on; all his persuading, all his professed loyalty and love were empty words. Meaningless prattling. The only reason he wanted her along was to keep her away from Roarke, from any police. And to use her as a shield, if necessary. Once they got to Manzanilla, he'd have no further use for her. He'd kill her as easily as he'd killed the others. As effortlessly. As enjoyably.

His brow furrowed. "What are you looking at me like that for?"

"I'm not. . . ."

"Don't you trust me? *Me?* Your husband, the man you love, who worships you. Hey, if I wanted to hurt you, you'd be lying on the floor alongside him. I couldn't do that and you know it. You and me are for life!" He seized her hand, holding her wedding ring against his own. "Forever. Adam and Eve in paradise, that's what it'll be once we're out there and settled on that ship. We'll go anywhere we want, do anything we want. No more dress shop, no more nine to five, no more problems, no more separations, nothing but golden sunsets in faraway places.

"And we'll be free! Kiss me!"

He grabbed her, kissed her; she yielded. He held her at arm's length and snuffled.

"Goddamn, I wish I had some Bronchodane. On the way to Detroit we'll stop off and pick up a load. But I bet I won't need it out there. That pure air, glorious weather. The plane takes off a little after eight." He patted his pocket. "I've got our tickets."

She searched his eyes. "Do you really love me?"

He laughed. "You have to ask? Doesn't what happened at Reggie's today prove it? He ripped you up and down, trying to turn me against you. He wanted me to ice you."

"What did you say?"

"I didn't have to *say* anything. By the time I got there, you were gone. By the way, congratulations, you took Jack Corey out like a pro. Like karate. He admitted he never knew what hit him. Sweetheart, forget about Reggie. Pretend he doesn't exist and this afternoon never happened. Now go pack."

"You'd better come, too, tell me what you'll want to take."

"Okay, if it'll hurry things up."

They were in the bedroom, he was getting the suitcases down from the closet shelf. The phone rang. She moved to pick it up.

"Don't," he cautioned.

"It's for me, I'm sure. Aggie. She knows I'm here. If I don't pick up, she'll wonder."

He thought a moment. The phone rang and rang. He nodded; she picked up.

"Lyssa? What's going on?"

"Nothing, Aggie, just packing."

"You're taking your sweet time about it. I called, I didn't think you'd still be there. But now I've got you, tell me where you'll be staying? I know O'Fallon said not to tell me, but I won't tell anybody. And I won't go there, so somebody could follow me. I promise. I just . . . wanted to talk. I'm as worried as you are."

"Aggie . . ."

"So which hotel?"

"I . . . haven't decided."

"What's wrong? You sound weird . . ."

"I have to go now."

"Wait, wait."

Lyssa hung up; Derrick had been listening along with her.

"Why did you hang up?"

"What should I do, keep talking, tell her what's going on, that you murdered Hugh?"

" 'Hugh'? Pretty friendly, aren't you? I didn't 'murder' him. Murder's a nasty word. It's the desperate amateur's tool of retribution against people he knows." His eyes glittered. "You never introduced us, remember?" He smirked and took her in his arms. "Darling, darling, why so stubborn? Why so blind to what we're up against? He was in our way. Now we can catch our plane, fly off, start a whole new life. . . ."

She said nothing. She could only marvel at him: he hadn't killed a man, he'd swatted an annoying fly. And, from all appearances, everything Reggie had told him about her, all her "crimes" made no impression on him whatsoever. Or did they? Was he playing games with her? Either way why fight it? How could she, as long as he had the upper hand? And a gun to back it. Genuine or pretended, his loyalty, his faith in her guaranteed her survival, at least for now. She still couldn't believe he'd let her leave Manzanilla alive.

He went back to the living room to retrieve his used-up inhaler; he came back trying to suck the last bit of epinephrine from it, but there was none left. They began packing; she transferred the contents of her overnight bag to her suitcase, taking care to leave the clippings from the *Atlanta Constitution* in the lid sleeve. He pulled open his sock drawer.

"I'll get your socks," she said, gently pushing him aside.

"Okay, but let's get a move on."

"I'll pack, it'll only take me five minutes. You go find our passports."

He went out; she waited till she heard him rummaging through the desk in the study then sprinted for the living room, the terrace, and O'Fallon's prostrate body.

"Lyssa?" he called from the study. "They're not here. Check the drawers in both the nightstands. I dimly remember . . . Lyssa? Where are you?"

"Out here."

"I know they're around here someplace, I've seen them recently." He appeared. "Did . . ."

He stiffened. She stood by O'Fallon, two-handing his pistol, aiming it at Derrick. He narrow-eyed her, he relaxed, he chuckled.

"What are you doing?"

"Don't make me shoot."

"Hardly." He held his hands up defensively. "I wouldn't dream of it. Can you make yourself? I doubt it, you've never pulled a trigger in your life. You despise guns, remember? What makes you think you can shoot me?"

"I don't want to."

"That's a relief. Put it down."

"No."

"Heavier than it looks, isn't it? Look at your hands, they're getting white from the strain, they're starting to tremble. Look. Give it here, darling."

He started toward her, his hand out.

"Stop!"

He stopped.

"Look at you," he said, pointing, "you're getting tears in your eyes. It's really a struggle, isn't it? Not really. Face it, you love me so you can't possibly shoot. Any more than I could you."

"Oh, you could, for you it's easy."

"Never."

"You'd kill anybody in your way, even me."

"Why in God's name would I? What would it gain me? This is crazy. The limo'll be here in a few minutes and we've hardly started packing. Sweetheart, we have to catch a plane, remember?"

"No."

"Okay, have it your way. But either shoot me or put it down. One or the other. Lyssa, Lyssa, I'm not that insensitive, I understand your problem—discovering after so long what I do for a living is throwing you for a loop. But ask yourself this. Does it change anything? How we feel about each other, what we mean to each other? Don't we still have the best marriage in the world? You know we do."

"Stop talking."

"What is it, have you suddenly flipped?"

"I fought this so hard, my heart against my head. Ever since Walsh came to town. I didn't want to believe any of it. I didn't, for the longest time. I kept telling myself it was all coincidence, all stupid suspicion without a grain of truth to any of it. But I was wrong. God, was I wrong . . . Blind. Stupid."

"Look at your hands shaking. Funny how the longer you hold it, the heavier it gets. It's getting like an anvil. Look at the way the muzzle's starting to dip. Give it to me."

"No!"

"I said give it to me!"

Tears rolled down her cheeks, she trembled, he took a step forward, she fired. The bullet winged over his right moulder. He ducked instinctively.

"You crazy bitch!"

He crouched slightly, pivoted, swinging about, present-
ing his left side, jerking his gun out, facing her. Barely
able to see his face through her tears, she fired again.
The bullet struck him squarely in the forehead, tunneling
into his brain. He stood stunned, his jaw sagging, eyes
rounding in disbelief. A single drop of blood oozed from
the hole and started down his forehead.

She screamed; he pitched forward on his face.

She fainted.

~~~~ FIFTY-FOUR ~~~~

The black blanket snugged around her turned gray then
dissolved into light. Her head pounded in unison with her
heart. She started up from the bed. Agnes pushed her
gently back down.

"Lie still. Drink this, it's just water."

"Aggie . . ."

"Shhh, drink."

She sipped a little, it spilled down the sides of her
mouth; Agnes wiped it with a tissue.

Derrick . . ."

"He's dead, you . . ."

"No!"

"You shot him in self-defense. Listen to me, don't
interrupt. When you hung up on me, I headed for here.
I stopped a police car out front, brought two cops up
with me. We found your neighbors pounding on your

door. They'd heard the shots. One of the cops kicked in the door. They found O'Fallon dead. Derrick, too—with a gun in his hand. He was going to shoot you."

"I killed him! I killed him!"

"You had to. Take it easy."

"Where is he? What have they done with him?"

"They're taking both bodies out. What the hell happened when you got here with O'Fallon?"

She told her haltingly, repeating herself, prey to confusion. Her head threatened to split from the incessant pounding. A uniformed policeman appeared in the doorway, his rugged horse face masked with concern.

"They're both out of here," he said to Agnes. "How you doing?" he asked Lyssa.

"Super, doesn't she look it?" snapped Agnes.

"Anything I can do?"

Agnes went on. "She just told me what happened. She shot him in self-defense."

"We figured, ballistics'll confirm it when they remove the slugs from both bodies. Ma'am, should I call a doctor?"

"No thanks. I just want to sleep . . . so exhausted."

He started to leave.

"Wait, call Captain Roarke, tell him Reggie Carlyle is on his way to Manila, the Philippines."

"It's after seven, the captain's off duty."

"Call him at home. It's important."

"If you don't want to, get somebody who will," snapped Agnes.

"I'll call," said the cop, "the kitchen phone. Reggie Carlyle, Manila, the Philippines."

He left.

"I'll get them all out of here in a minute," said Agnes. "Give you some peace and quiet. I'm staying with you tonight."

"You don't have to."

"Shhh, can I get you anything? Want some aspirin?"

"Please."

She had difficulty getting both tablets down, finally managed to. Agnes undressed her, readied her for bed. Lyssa fell asleep before Aggie left the room.

~~~~ FIFTY-FIVE ~~~~

Three days passed. Sergeant Hugh O'Fallon was buried, Derrick Morgan was buried. In plots in cemeteries at opposite ends of the city. Lyssa, Agnes, and Maggie Donovan were the only attendees at Derrick's funeral. The night before, Lyssa went to the funeral parlor and, before the casket was closed, removed her wedding ring, setting it on Derrick's chest. Thinking as she did that some would have thought it a tasteless gesture, even, perhaps, one of disloyalty, of rejection of their four years as man and wife. But it made sense to her: let him take their marriage with him to the grave.

Standing by the gravesite listening to the minister drone on, she could hear Maggie Donovan softly crying. Where were the other Cambridge employees? No doubt all out looking for jobs, what with the roof fallen in on them. Still, it was sad to see him laid to rest and everyone he knew except Maggie turning their backs on him.

Reggie Carlyle flew to Manila, as Derrick told her he would, for all intents and purposes taking Cambridge Medical and Surgical Equipment with him. It vanished from Bellingham. Two FBI agents in the company of Manila detectives were at Manila International Airport to greet Reggie when his plane landed. He was descending the stairs with his fellow passengers and the agents were preparing to step forward and arrest him when a shot was fired from an upstairs window in the main terminal. Reggie collapsed and died before the authorities could reach him. Airport security pursued his assailant, catching up with him about two miles away on the road north into the city. And, in a running gun battle, shot him dead. He was identified as John Walter Corey, a U.S. citizen of no known permanent address.

Reggie's luggage was retrieved. His four bags contained clothing and other personal effects. But in the carry-on bag slung over his shoulder, the police found nearly 1.3 million in thousand-dollar bills and negotiable securities. And in the breast pocket of his suit coat was a first-class ticket to Hong Kong.

Anthony Minervino and Arnold Carlson seemed to disappear into the woodwork.

Late Saturday afternoon Lyssa, having returned to work, made a long-distance call to Gail Horvath in Atlanta. Gail came on dripping warmth and friendless. Lyssa filled her in on the "accident" involving her sister on the Belvedere Road years before.

Gail clucked and sniffed. "It may sound petty, even a little cruel, but Lizzie could have been a little choosier."

"Me, too, Gail."

"Oh dear, I didn't mean . . ."

"I know you didn't. The irony of it is he was a good husband. In all the ways that count. And I really, honestly believe he loved me. Just as he loved her."

"I suppose. . . ."

"He did, no 'supposing' about it."

"What I don't understand is how could he behave like a paragon and make it believable when all the while he was sneaking around murdering people? Dr. Jekyll and Mr. Hyde. Was he sick in the head, do you think?"

"That's easy to assume, who knows? Myself, I don't think so."

"How are you doing?"

"Okay, I came back to work today. I'll keep busy. Like they say, this, too, shall pass. I do think I'll be getting rid of the apartment. Every time I walk in, close the door behind me, the walls start closing in. I'll move, maybe I'll take a vacation. Get somebody to move me, I can come back to whole new digs."

"Good idea, come back down to Atlanta, we'll have a ball."

"Maybe. Well, I just wanted to call and fill you in. I'll say good-bye."

"Good-bye, Lyssa, take care of yourself. What a story. Maybe we should write it up, peddle it to the supermarket tabloids. I'm sorry, excuse my bad taste. You did love the guy."

"Yes."

Lyssa asked Agnes to drive her to All Saints Episcopal Church in Chase Ridge after the store closed.

"What for?"

"Unfinished business."

"In a church?"

"In the cemetery. Doreen."

There was no one about when Agnes drew the Peugeot up in front of the church.

"I get the feeling you'd prefer to do this alone," she said.

"If you don't mind, I won't be long."

"Take your time."

Lyssa climbed the steps, circling the church and ascending to the little cemetery. The oaks, ashes, and birches were all coming into leaf, it was a warm day, the sky azure and cloudless. A rabbit hopped across her path as she entered the gate. The flowers set near the newly installed headstone were already beginning to wilt. The mound surmounting the grave had not yet begun to settle. She stood at the foot of it, then looked about, to make certain she was alone. The rabbit had vanished, birds chirped overhead, the breeze picked up, rattling the new leaves and briefly tugging her skirt.

Looking down, she saw again Doreen's smile, heard her cheery laugh. She was cheering up the angels now, amusing them, filling their hearts with fondness for her. She was by far the best thing to have come out of the whole black nightmare. Lyssa vowed she would come and see her at least once a week from now on.

When tears came, she wiped her eyes, turned about, and left.

In the car heading back to the city in silence, she reached into her bag and brought out the telephone bug.

"What are you hanging on to that for?" asked Agnes.

"I don't know. I guess it encapsulates the whole sorry business. Every time I look at it, it all comes rushing back."

"Is that what you want? Throw it away. Give it here, let me."

"No."

Agnes snatched it from her, threw it out the window. Lyssa looked back, saw it bounce once, gleaming like silver in the sunlight, then come to rest.

One-handing the wheel, Agnes slipped her arm around her.

"What do you say we eat out tonight? Talk nothing but business for four hours. You may not have noticed, but it's good, booming. We should think about expanding. Maybe open another store. L'Image Two, you like that?"

Lyssa reached up and patted her partner's hand. "I like it, let's talk about it."

467